The Victor

To Rachel
Enjoy the adventure!
God bless
Mewayne Guion
Psalm 37:4
3-27-10

The Victor

A Tale of Betrayal, Love, and Sacrifice

MARLAYNE GIRON

TATE PUBLISHING & *Enterprises*

Published by Tate Publishing & Enterprises, LLC
127 E. Trade Center Terrace | Mustang, Oklahoma 73064 USA
1.888.361.9473 | www.tatepublishing.com

Tate Publishing is committed to excellence in the publishing industry. The company reflects the philosophy established by the founders, based on Psalm 68:11,
"The Lord gave the word and great was the company of those who published it."

Published in the United States of America

ISBN: 978-1-60799-184-7
1. Fiction
2. Christian/Fantasy
09.02.05

Acknowledgement

To Cindy Jordan, my sister in Christ and "*Victor's*" illustrator.
    Thank you for "listening to the Lord's still small voice" and contributing your wonderful drawings for His use. May we both glorify the Lord through this mutual endeavor!

Contents

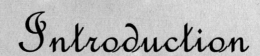

Introduction

Almost thirty years ago, a "light bulb" went on over my head while listening to the song "Fairytale" by famed Christian vocalist, Amy Grant (written by Brown Bannister and Amy Grant).

I saw the epic battle between good and evil as described in the pages of the Bible in the form of a medieval fantasy-fiction story with a knight in "shining armor" and a black knight crossing swords over the "bride."

I began this story in my early 20's on an IBM Selectric typewriter and now, almost thirty years later and after many, many rewrites (thank the Lord for the invention of personal computers!) it comes to you in its present form as *The Victor*.

It is the fulfillment of a life-long wish to see this in print. Enjoy.

Marlayne Giron

"My heart overflows with a good theme; I address my verses to the King;
My tongue is the pen of a ready writer."

Psalm 45:1 (NASB)

Prologue

An icy wind streamed over the hilltop from the nearby sea, chilling the sentries who stood watch from high atop the castle's battlements. Below them in the dark courtyard a solitary figure in hood and cloak ducked under a stone archway, shouldering open the door to the gatehouse. *"Greetings on this frigid morn!"* he nodded to the frowning guard, throwing back his hood. He withdrew a small leather wineskin, uncorking the stopper with his teeth.

"Segrid, what are you doing here at this ungodly hour?" Thaddeus scowled, pushing away the skin. "You know drink is forbidden upon the watch!"

Segrid's hand flashed out and caught hold and with a violent yank, he pulled the guard forward into his dagger, impaling him. Blood spewed from the wound as he twisted the blade out, gutting him. Thaddeus's eyes stared at him in horrified surprise then he slumped lifelessly onto the floor. Segrid straightened, watching dispassionately as the pool of blood slowly blossomed outwards from the body, convinced that Thaddeus would not rise again. He grasped hold of the drawbridge's winch and began working it downwards to lower it for his Master's waiting army. Thus preoccupied, the assassin failed to notice the small page cowering within the shadows of a nearby alcove, awakened by his foul deed. Hardly daring to breathe, the trembling lad inched along the wall toward the rope that held the portcullis aloft, hoping he could escape the murderer's notice before he was slaughtered alike. With slow, quiet movements, he took out a small knife and quietly began to saw upon the taut rope.

Baron Lucius of North Umberland waited anxiously under the nearby boughs of surrounding trees staring intently at the slowly lowering drawbridge in anticipation. The wind was bitterly cold, but its incessant howling masked the rattle and chink of his men's mailcoats and the snort of their impatient horses as they waited to commence their surprise attack. Suddenly, he froze in his saddle. With pounding heart, he watched the portcullis suddenly drop. The page had done his work before Segrid could kill him. The sound of his anguished scream instantly alerted all the guards upon the wall but it was too late!

Lucius had lost his advantage, but there was no turning back now… *"Fire the arrow!"* he snapped to the archer on his right. The archer stared at him in disbelief. *"Mi'lord!"* he protested. "We're outnumbered three to one! *'Tis madness…!"*

"I've yet one chance at victory!" Lucius growled in the archer's face. *"Fire the blasted arrow!"*

With a grim frown of disapproval, the archer ignited his pitch-dipped arrow in the concealed campfire and shot high, giving the signal for Lucius' army to storm the walls. Trumpets blared forth from the trees, mingling with the screams of his men. *"Attack! Attack! Attack! Breach the walls! Bring Ellioth to its knees!"*

Armed with swords, crossbows, and arrows, Eloth's knights poured from their quarters in various stages of undress, fitting arrows to the string even as they ran. In short order their long bows and crossbows were returning fire, filling the air with a deadly hail of projectiles that slowly and systematically decimated their enemy outside the walls. Alarm bells pealed loudly, adding their clamor to the growing concert of war, clanging loudly for reinforcements to join the fray.

Out thundered Lucius' men on horseback, shooting a thicket of flaming and poisoned arrows over the walls. Many found their mark, felling whom they pierced instantly or igniting fires which divided the castle's attention between its' defenses and putting the flames out before they could spread. It was a clever but desperate ploy for Lucius had no real hope of victory through conventional battle; all he could do was diminish Eloth's forces until the King's sword of power had been safely secreted away.

Ephlal.[1,2]

Just the thought of possessing it sent powerlust coursing through Lucius' veins. Though he knew little of its lore, like all in the kingdom, he had a healthy respect for the blade's awesome capability to lay waste to entire villages and slay with but a mere point of its blade tip. Were it not for his hope of possessing this mightiest of weapons, he never would have openly dared challenge the King he had once faithfully served. His men did not know that they were merely sacrificial pawns in a ruse to divert attention from his actual goal of stealing the sword! Once Ephlal was in his grasp, he could capture all of Ellioth and not even the King himself could stop him! Lucius closed his eyes, not for the first time relishing in the idea of Eloth being dragged before him bloody and beaten, forced to witness the slaying of his household and especially that of his only son, the young Prince, Joshua. Only after the whelp died an agonizing death would Eloth meet his own when Lucius plunged Ephlal's blade into his breast!

"*Go!*" he shouted, shaking his fist in the air as the first wave of his army raised their ladders against the wall. "*Slaughter them all! Show no mercy!*"

Upon observing the attacking hordes successfully scaling the outer bailey, Eloth's men took up positions upon the top to shove away the ladders and hew down the ropes before the encroachers could enter the city. Squires pelted them with rocks and poured boiling oil upon those below to slow their progress. Lucius' men fell back, screaming with pain and rage.

"Penloth!" shouted Finrod, Captain of the Guard, as he ran to the stables. "Post thy archers every fifteen paces upon the wall; shoot the traitors down!"

"I never thought I'd see the day when I'd have to spill the blood of our own kinsmen!" Penloth shouted back.

Lucius continued to watch with growing anxiety as the ranks of his men swiftly dwindled under the fierce retaliation of Eloth's men. *What is taking him so long? Where is Servern's signal he has taken Eloth's sword?* Lucius knew he should make his escape but still he hesitated, torn between his lust for Eloth's throne and self-preservation. As long as there remained the slightest chance Ephlal had been successfully taken, he would wait until the last possible moment. A sudden blast of trumpets issuing from the castle ramparts froze his heart in terror. Before Lucius' horrified eyes, the portcullis rose high and out of the castle gates rode a sortie of knights *led by the King himself on his white charger.* All blood drained from Lucius' face when he saw the weapon raised aloft in Eloth's hand.

Ephlal had entered the battle! Blind terror seized him. Flashes of fierce light lanced out in all directions from the shimmering blade, cutting down all in its path. Lucius dug his spurs deep into his horse's flanks and wheeled about, desperate to escape before he was spitted. The black gelding whinnied in protest as he applied the crop, then with an angry snort, sprang away through the trees and down the hill, throwing up dirt clods as it carried him away at full gallop. A cry instantly went up from those upon the wall.

"*'Tis Lucius! He's fleeing!*"
"*Stop him! Drag him from the saddle!*"

Eloth twisted around, shocked and angered to see his former steward flee unhindered down the hill, riding down all who attempted to block his escape.

"Rot his bloody, black soul!" cursed a knight, drawing abreast on foot. "My Lord, lend me thy mount that I may give chase and overtake the blackguard!"

"Nay, Captain," responded Eloth. "He has too great a lead. Gather thy men and ride to Lucius' keep. He and the whole of his household are to be taken alive. Dispatch knights to watch the crossroads and ports!"

Sir Finrod could not believe his ears. "You would have him returned to you *alive* after today's deviltry?" he sputtered. He had been expecting orders for Lucius' Keep to be fired and his body left for the carrion foul to feast on.

The King looked the Captain of the Guard deeply in the eyes and Finrod was amazed to see his face filled with genuine anguish. "Lucius *shall* meet his end," he responded quietly, "but not until he has drained the cup of his wickedness to the bitter dregs." He turned away, back toward the battlefield, sorrowfully observing the bloody wreckage. As Finrod galloped away, Eloth dismounted to give personal aid to those who had survived. He could do little more than offer words of encouragement and praise for their bravery and bind their wounds with naught but his torn shirt, their medical attention would have to wait upon the court physicians.

As he passed from one brave man to another, over and over in his mind he replayed Lucius' last years of service, trying to recall if he had noticed any change in his steward's behavior that might have been an early indicator of this treachery. Once they had enjoyed a great camaraderie, but it had seemed to slowly disappear over time, unmarked by any particular incident. Lucius' demeanor had become sullen and would brook no inquiry as to the reason. He had continued to govern Eloth's household, possessions, land holdings, and servants as expertly as before, but he did so in an increasingly perfunctory and irritable manner. As the months and years went by, Eloth began discovering subtle discrepancies in his accounting of the kingdom's output in food, timber, service, and taxes. On more than one occasion, his personal belongings had somehow found their way into Lucius' chambers *quite by accident* and returned to him without not so much as an apology nor explanation. Not only had Lucius' behavior changed toward him, but so had a number of those who worked directly under him. As time went on, Eloth sensed growing unrest within Lucius' sphere of influence and decided that enough was enough. With sincere regret, Eloth released Lucius from his duties, gifted him with a baronet and a castle on a parcel of land in token of his past years of faithful service. He had even allowed him to take those whom he chose with him as his personal servants. Lucius had accepted the endowment in stony silence without a word of gratitude. The following week he packed his possessions, removed his men and took occupancy within Ravenhurst Keep with all the sulkiness of a spoiled child denied the singular toy he most desires. He answered none of the missives Eloth sent to him and received no visitors. Years passed without any word of his doings until a fortnight ago when his messenger and personal valet had arrived bearing a letter requesting that Eloth house them in Lucius' old chambers so they could prepare it for his imminent visit. Eloth had greeted the news with great joy and given them every courtesy, even down to the particular linens and soap he knew Lucius favored. Yet their behavior had been peculiar from the first for they refused to join his household at meat and had kept to themselves until early this morning when the valet had slipped into his bedchamber intent on stealing his sword. Fortunately the assassin had made the mistake of trying to withdraw Ephlal from its scabbard first. The resulting scream had awakened all within the household. All that remained of the valet was a blackened, smoking corpse and next to it, Ephlal glowing white-hot upon the floor.

Eloth looked down and fingered the wondrous hilt with respect. He never withdrew it except in moments of greatest need or peril to his realm for its power was not to be used wantonly.

Ephlal surpassed blades of later legend in power and beauty even as they ranked superior to the wooden ones used by squires in practice. The time and manner of its forging were unknown and unlike conventional swords, its double edged blade required neither whetting nor oiling to keep it sharp and bright though he had borne it beyond count of years. Ancient runes of a long-extinct language were traced like fine filigree into the flat of the blade and the hilt was crafted of gold inset with diamonds and opals. The scabbard also was of ancient make, crafted in white leather, and hand tooled throughout with golden thread and studded with emeralds. Woven upon it was the device of a Dragon coiled about the base of a flowering tree and a Lamb standing upon its' head. His bard, Gillian, had presented it to him in his youth, saying that it had been passed down through the centuries through a long line of royal bards. When Gillian had knelt before him to gird the scabbard about his waist, he interpreted the solemn warning etched into the blade:

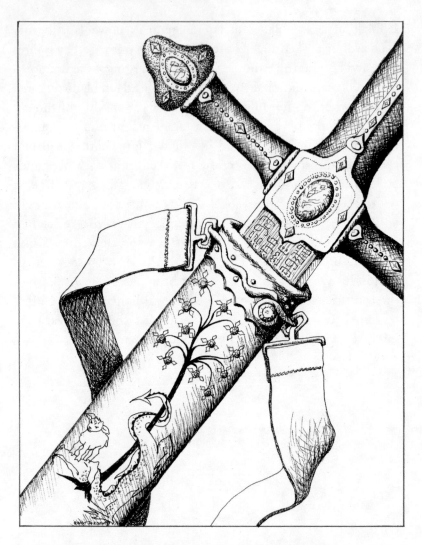

"Beware! I am Ephlal, Sword of Kings! Unsheathe me only in dire need! I serve not the self-seeking ambition of men, nor suffer the stain of innocent blood upon my blade. None save He to whom I am bestowed and His appointed heirs may handle me lest I smite them with death!"

Eloth came back to himself, sorrowful at the grisly sight of the green meadow scored and soaked with the blood of his people. With a heavy heart, he continued to pick his way among the wounded, kneeling at times upon the bloodied grass to lend comfort until the physicians could arrive to bear away the survivors on litters to the halls of healing.

Finrod strode into the castle armory, muttering curses under his breath.

"Finrod, have I heard the rumors aright?" bellowed Penloth the moment he appeared, frightening his squire who was fastening his armor on. "Is it of a truth that Eloth wants Lucius delivered to him *'alive and unharmed'*?"

"You heard correctly," Finrod growled, lifting his arms high so his squire could suit him up. This was greeted with exclamations of disbelief followed by a volley of questions. *"Leave me in peace! Plague me not with questions!"* he bellowed, sorely displeased with his orders. The seraphim exchanged glances amongst themselves then fell silent. Better to leave him alone than to push the issue, unless one was spoiling for a fight.

"Mount up!" he commanded, cinching in his sword belt. He swung up into the saddle of his Destrier, waiting impatiently for the others to follow, then spurred his horse, thundering out of the gates.

Lucius tore through the countryside as though the very hounds of hell were on his heels for so he considered the King's guard. His steed was covered in foaming lather, but he refused the poor beast even the slightest rest. He needed distance between himself and Eloth's knights or there would be no escape for him. If he could get enough of a head start, he might evade capture by fleeing into the wilderness or taking ship out of a distant seaport before word got out. But first he needed provisions and the gold he had been carefully hoarding. By late morning, his horse was stumbling with exhaustion, but it managed to reach the outer wall of his Keep before refusing to go any further. Lucius leapt from the saddle summoning all within earshot to attend him swiftly! Servants came running and were instantly alarmed at the look of naked panic in his face.

"You!" Lucius barked, pointing at his steward. "Fetch me wayfarer's food and water skins enough for a fortnight! You!" he pointed to the ulster. "I want a fresh horse immediately! Have him saddled and ready to ride in ten minutes! The rest of you, prepare for battle! Gather thy arms and go forth! The seraphim are coming!"

Exclamations of alarm issued from the ranks of his young squires. The seraphim were Eloth's fighting elite and the model to which Lucius had constantly held them up to in sorry comparison. *Did he really expect squires-in-training capable of defeating a company of battle-hardened knights?*

"What became of those who sallied forth this morning?" asked a young squire. "Were you not victorious?"

"Is his terror not answer enough for you?" answered the ulster angrily. "Our Master returned alone." He turned to Lucius. "Do you truly expect us to triumph where thy warriors could not? Are we not merely fool's bait to buy thee time for thy escape?"

Lucius stared at him, filled with indignant wrath at the shrewd guess. He raised his riding crop and whipped the man across the face with a curse. "Speak not so to me when the seraphim are already riding here with their swords drawn!" he hissed. "Think ye they will stop to ascertain the particular guilt of thee in these matters before disemboweling the lot of you?" He rounded on his squires. "All of you! Borgreth, Golbreth, Ranulf! Go! If you've not the stomach to save thine own skins then by all means linger here and await certain doom!"

This veiled threat had the desired effect. With dark looks of resentment in his direction, they gathered up what few weapons they could find and ran out on foot, hoping the advantage of a surprise ambush would turn the tide in their favor. Little more than a half hour's walk from the Keep, where the foliage was thick and path twisted, they took up offensive positions, concealing themselves in the forks of trees, behind rocks, and upon overhanging hillocks. With shaking hands they hurriedly strung and drew their crossbows and longbows taut, nocking poisoned arrows into place and fully expecting to see the scarlet plumes of the seraphim appearing over the rise at any moment. With nervous sweat flowing down their bodies they waited, faces twitching and muscles straining. Five minutes passed then ten. Their aching muscles quivering with pain and exhaustion, they began to lower their weapons in bewilderment.

Fifteen minutes passed ... *surely Eloth's knights would have sped after their master as soon as they could?* Twenty minutes. There wasn't even so much as a dust cloud upon the horizon to mark their coming.

Forty-five minutes ... and still they waited. After a full two hours their grumbles filled the air. Lucius had made out as if the seraphim were already in hot pursuit of him yet here they sat twiddling their thumbs! Maintaining vigilance was impossible! The noon sun was beating down upon them and there was no breeze to dry their nervous sweat. Another excruciating hour passed without event. *Where on earth were they?* A number of them had fallen asleep and were snoring loudly. Those who remained awake found their limbs growing stiffer and their wits duller by the moment with nothing to do but to sit perfectly still in absolute silence. To add to their discomfort, they had left without provisions. There was but one skin of water to share between fifty and no food! Borgreth squinted his eyes against the brilliant afternoon sun wondering if Lucius had even told him the truth ... perhaps things really had gone well in Ellioth and this was his deranged idea of a joke. When the distant thudding of approaching hoofbeats was first perceived, it barely registered on their conscience, so lethargic had they become. When the ground began to tremble beneath them, it was with stiff limbs that they struggled to arise.

"Up ye lousy sluggards and look lively!" Golbreth yelled, struggling to find his weapons. Upon the horizon, silhouetted against the sun, the outriders of Ellioth crested the hill, their standards snapping smartly in their wake.

"*Bows at the ready! Bows at the ready!*" he hissed in panic, struggling to nock his crossbow. Fear coursed through their veins while their stiffened fingers endeavored to reload their bows in time to take aim. Seconds later, the knights thundered under the very trees in which they were hidden...

"Now!" Sir Finrod cried aloud, wheeling his horse about and jumping the tall hedge that bordered the road. Lucius' squires gaped in astonishment, stupidly watching the seraphim split off into a dozen different directions, wheeling and checking with such speed that it was impossible to target them. The knights eluded the poorly shot arrows as if they were bodiless phantoms! The shots went wide, fell harmlessly to the ground or stuck fast into the boles of trees. In contrast, the seraphim's arrows answered with deadly accuracy, picking off each assailant as though he were a stationary target in a tourney match. Sir Finrod laughed aloud at their foolishness for he had anticipated just such an ambush and planned accordingly. Four of his knights had ridden forth to block the escape routes from Lucius' keep, then the rest of them had ridden hard to just where he expected Lucius to lay an ambush then had made his men to dismount and take a rest. They took their ease, and ate and watered their steeds while Sir Eric went forth to spy out the road ahead. He returned later with the report that a trap was indeed waiting for them. With a wicked grin, Finrod gave orders for two of their number to remain on guard in turns while the others rested, guaranteeing a long, boring wait for Lucius' underlings! He would wait just long enough for their wits to dull with boredom and then attack after a satisfying rest. Next Sir Penloth was sent forth, returning later to report that their would-be assailants were snoring loud enough to wake the dead. They had immediately mounted up and ridden hard, allowing the thunder of their approach to serve as a merciful notice to the sleepers of their imminent peril.

"Up there!" shouted Sir Penloth, pointing to a young squire in the fork of a spruce tree. Sir Eric, whose double crossbow was already loaded, sent a black hafted arrow whizzing into his unprotected breast with a curse, furious at having to shoot mere children. The lad fell with a cry of anguish to the grass, clutching at the arrow protruding from his breast in a welter of pain. Lucius' squires sent an answering volley of arrows back at them.

Sir Penloth heard the whine of one as it sped past his head, narrowly taking off his right ear. He wheeled about, cursing at himself to keep moving. An inch closer and he would have been dead; armor or no for crossbows could pierce even the heaviest steel plating. Fortunately, only a small number were armed with such weapons and they had little skill. The poor lads were so panicked most of their shots were wasted. It wasn't long before they ran out of arrows and unable to replenish their supply, were forced to drop to the ground and engage the seraphim in hand-to-hand combat. Finrod didn't know whether to laugh in derision or weep with anger at their folly. They were barely out of puberty and thus no match against the expertise, strength, and skill of his men!

"Lay down thy arms!" he shouted, beating a young boy before him onto his knees. "Lay down thy arms! For pity's sake, lad, don't make me slay you!" But the boy fought as if he had gone mad; tears of pain and fear running down his youthful cheeks. Finally it was over; his body lay motionless, beaten to the ground. Overcome with revulsion, Finrod paused to dash angry tears and sweat from his stinging eyes, realizing his fatal error too late. He heard the faint twang of a bowstring and felt an impact against his chest that sent him stumbling backwards. He looked down in wide-eyed disbelief at the feathered haft protruding from his breastplate and opened his mouth to cry out.

"Finrod!" bellowed Penloth, galloping to him. Finrod looked toward him, dazed, then fell forward, dead before his body even hit the ground. The arrow was poisoned.

Penloth leapt from the saddle and went to his captain, turning him over and searching in vain for a pulse. Finrod's eyes were open but fixed and unseeing. Penloth sagged in grief, heedless of his imminent danger at the hands of the same archer, who, encouraged by his recent success, had taken aim again, this time upon him. He drew back upon on the crossbow, aiming for Penloth' unprotected neck.

"Penloth! *Move!*" hollered Sir Matthew, leaning forward in his saddle and snatching him away just as the arrow pierced the ground where he had been only a moment before. Penloth hung on till he was out of harm's way then slid off, landing on his feet.

"Enough of this! Let us put an end to this miserable battle!" he grunted.

"Aye, I've no more stomach for it either!" Matthew agreed, swinging his bay about.

Penloth unsheathed his sword. *"Seraphim to me!"* he cried.

The seraphim roared in response and pressed the attack, their patience gone. They stood in their stirrups and physically hauled the squires down from the trees, hacking at them until they were too exhausted or wounded to oppose them any longer.

"Mercy!" cried Borgreth, throwing down his weapons. His companions gaped at him in shock then swiftly followed suit, throwing their bows and swords into a pile before Penloth's feet. With the last weapon flung upon the ground, they fell onto their knees, hands upon their heads in defeat.

"About bloody time!" Sir Eric snarled, smacking Ranulf upside the head in anger. "Five minutes more and you would all have been carrion fodder!"

Penloth wiped his sweaty brow, relieved they had given up before his men had been forced to slaughter them all. He raked his eyes over the "field of battle," in disgust. Flies were already gathering about the dead in sickening clouds. It was a virtual repeat of the morning's bloodbath! He felt like retching his guts out.

"Collect their weapons and truss them up," he wearily directed his men, returning to where Finrod's body lay. He knelt by the still form, touched his cheek in a silent gesture of farewell then shrouded him in his own cape to keep the insects off. Sir Bors stacked and tied the abandoned weaponry together while the others tied up the captives. They lay spent and docile as lambs on their sides, hands lashed behind their backs and drawn down to their ankles.

"No sense marching them back to Lucius' Keep since they will only slow us down," Sir Bors said, straightening from his task. "We can retrieve them on the return trip, but Finrod we must send back to Ellioth for an honorable burial."

Penloth nodded in agreement, noting how the vultures were already circling overhead, waiting for their grisly feast. "Sir Bors, bear our captain back to Ellioth," he said, lifting the body of his friend and gently laying him belly down over the knight's horse. "Falstaff, you shall keep watch over the rabble and keep the vultures away until we return."

"Yes, Captain," responded Bors and Falstaff, momentarily startling Penloth. With great heaviness of heart, he suddenly realized that he had been promoted into Finrod's position because of his death. It brought him no joy for Finrod had been like an elder brother to him. Dashing aside his tears, he grumbled to his men: "Refill thy quivers with Lucius' arrows and if he offers us further argument he shall have a taste of his own venom!"

"Lucius is long gone by now!" smirked Golbreth, lifting his head with difficulty to gloat at the knights. "He took off hours ago!"

Penloth turned back to stare at him as if the information were of little concern. "Off to the seaports in disguise is he?" he replied, eyebrow arching. Golbreth gaped in response. Penloth continued. "The King has dispatched knights to intercept him at all seaports and the roads there are under surveillance even now. Lucius will have to prove cleverer than a fox if he expects to elude Eloth's nets!"

After carefully collecting all the arrows they could find, the seraphim remounted and galloped the remaining distance to Lucius' Keep without further incident. For all intents and purposes, it looked as if it had been completely abandoned. Penloth had his crossbow at the ready and unsheathed his sword, wanting to be fully prepared should there be a second ambush waiting for them. They scanned every window and doorway for signs of life or hidden archers. If it took them a lifetime, he would hunt Lucius down and nail his foul hide to the nearest proclamation post with the word *TRAITOR* branded upon it! They rounded the hedge and found the gates gaping wide open and livestock wandering freely. Suddenly a cloaked figure on horseback shot past them at breakneck speed, making a beeline for the forest.

"Fire and tongs! *It's him!*" shouted Sir Eric, pointing. The figure on horseback gave a swift look behind him then spurred his horse faster.

"Don't allow him to reach those trees!" cried Penloth, unable to believe their good fortune. They galloped like the wind after Lucius' fleeing figure.

Lucius crouched low over his saddle in terror as the wind whistled through his streaming black hair. There having been no other horses available, he had been forced to wait around for hours to give his horse adequate rest, hoping the ambush would have made flight unnecessary. But when he had spied the seraphim approaching, he fled rested horse or no. Though they were only a furlong behind, they were swiftly overtaking him. His horse was already exhausted and refusing to go above a canter. He withdrew the crop and flogged its rear quarters harder, causing its flesh to run red with blood, but the stubborn animal only slowed its pace more.

"Faster, damn you, faster!" he screamed. But the seraphim were swifter and what was more, they had split off into two companies, approaching him from behind like the point of an inverted arrow, cutting off his escape. The thunder of their hooves pounded loudly in his ears, but he dared not look behind a second time to see how close. A large gray stallion suddenly reared before him and Lucius found himself flung bodily onto the ground. He landed hard with Penloth on top. The air was forcefully expelled from his lungs as the knight's heavy body and armor were brought fully to bear upon his chest.

"*The horse! Grab his horse!*" shouted Penloth as the frenzied animal neighed and danced about them in panic. Sir Eric jumped down and grabbed the halter of the spooked animal, bodily pushing it away as Penloth grappled with Lucius upon the ground. Penloth twisted about quick as a cat, dug his right knee firmly into the small of Lucius' back and yanked his head back by his hair, instantly terminating his struggles. Before

Lucius could blink an eye, Penloth had him hopelessly hog-tied. He was roughly hauled back onto his feet by the front of his tunic.

"Impudent knave!" he snarled at Penloth. "Thou shalt rue this mishandling of me!"

Penloth was furious. "Oh, shall I?" he glared in return, tossing the end of Lucius' lead to Sir Eric. "I think not!" He turned to the knight. "Lash him to my saddlehorn."

"Yes, Captain," replied Eric, yanking the scowling baron away. Penloth allowed himself the momentary luxury of a relieved exhale, glad to be rid of the baron's presence for at least a brief moment. He felt as though he had just gone a few rounds with a twisting, spitting serpent. Would that Eloth had not ordered him returned alive! Of all the blood let upon the sod that day, Lucius' should had been amongst it. No doubt the rogue probably considered this display of mercy a sign of weakness and would do everything in his power to ensure them a miserable return to Ellioth. Penloth glanced around to find his comrades already mounted and waiting patiently for him. Tethered to his saddlehorn stood the Baron, his black eyes glaring hot daggers of naked hatred at him. Averting his gaze, Penloth mounted, hackles rising on the back of his neck. They were soon off with the Baron and the remainder of his household in tow. Though Penloth refused to confirm his suspicions by turning around, he could feel Lucius' eyes upon him throughout the rest of the day. Despite his efforts to appear unconcerned, he grew more unnerved by the hour and flinched at every abrupt sound. At one point he almost fired off his crossbow at a swooping raven. The seraphim exchanged glances amongst themselves but pretended they didn't notice out of sheer respect. They wondered when Penloth would finally reach the end of his legendary short temper and take matters into his own hands.

A twig snapped under his horse, making him jump in surprise. Penloth balled his hands into fists of rage and swore under his breath for the hundredth time.

Night was nearly upon them when they finally reached the site of the failed ambush. The knights wearily dismounted and made a bivouac to rest for the night. After making sure Lucius' bonds and those of his men were secure, they kindled a small fire and ate a simple meal of fresh game, wayfarer's bread, cheese, and dried fruit. After a few moments' conversation, they wrapped themselves in their cloaks and bedded down with Sir Eric and Matthew taking the first watch. Night settled upon the earth, the stars came out, and the crickets began their serenade.

But Penloth could not sleep despite his fatigue. Lucius lay not more than fifteen arms length away, linked to him by the end of a rope. He didn't need to open his eyes to know that the Baron was still boring invisible holes into his skull with his beady, black eyes.

Damn him; does the viper never sleep?

With a muttered curse, Penloth turned his back on him, too obstinate and proud to get up and move out of Lucius' range of sight. The night dragged on while he continued to lie upon the cold, hard ground in mounting frustration, listening enviously to his comrades snore loudly in deep contentment. He watched the moon rise high into the night sky and was still awake when she began her slow descent, growing more desperate by the minute for the blissful forgetfulness of sleep.

"*Hooo Hoo Hoo Hoo!*" cried a great horned owl somewhere nearby. Penloth bolted upright to find Lucius smirking at him.

That was bloody it!

He flung off his blanket with a snarl, sprang to his feet and marched over to where the baron lay on the grass, his sword already out of its sheath. The sentries came running up to see what was going on, hoping their Captain was not going to disobey orders and dismember the baron (much as they would have enjoyed it personally). Penloth stood with his arms at his sides, his sword out but lowered, contemplating how much liberty he could take in dealing with the baron without violating his Lord's command. He racked his brain for a moment, chewing on his mustache in frustration when sudden inspiration struck him.

He pointed at the sullen baron with his sword.

"String him up!" he ordered watching for Lucius' reaction upon hearing the rest: " ... *by his ankles, upside down on yon tree limb!* We'll see if he'll be so bloody well inclined to stare with his innards in his throat!" Satisfied with his harmless but effective vengeance, Penloth marched back to his spot and lay back down, eventually falling asleep despite the baron's caterwauling. He awoke feeling very pleased with himself the next morning and ate his meal, totally unconcerned by Lucius' curses as his legs slowly and very painfully regained their circulation after he was lowered onto the ground.

The return to Ellioth the next day was much slower than he would have liked as they were now obliged to reduce their gait to accommodate that of their prisoners who were forced to walk. Penloth rode in the rear, growing more and more furious by the moment; his patience and good humor again dissipated by Lucius' unrelenting glare of renewed hatred. He glanced back just in time to catch him averting his eyes before he could be seen, fearful of what Penloth might do to him next, but it was too late. Penloth had reached his limit! He stood in his stirrups and called an immediate halt. The other knights watched in silent fascination as he dismounted, wondering what he would do next and quietly placing wagers amongst themselves.

Penloth glared at the baron in black frustration. The snake deserved death thrice over for his crimes and yet there he stood, arrogant as a peacock, insolently defying him to try something, knowing he couldn't harm him! Penloth was stymied; what could he possibly do that would teach the jackal a good lesson and yet not disobey? At that moment, his horse swished its tail right into the Baron's unappreciative face. Lucius stepped back with an oath, raising his bound hands to fend off a second swipe.

Penloth grinned, instantly struck with inspiration. "Since thou art so determined to stare at something, my good baron, then I suggest you feast your eyes on this!" With swift yanks, he promptly shortened the length of Lucius' leash until his face was mere inches from the rear end of his horse with orders that his hands be tied behind his back. Lucius glared at him, sputtering in outraged disbelief, instantly comprehending the humiliation Penloth planned for him. Every time the bloody animal relieved itself of gas and waste, he would be the first to know about it, even before the horse! Penloth grinned at him with supreme self-satisfaction and turned about, not giving the sputtering baron an opportunity to even think of a good response to his impending humiliation! Penloth's only regret was that he had not thought of it earlier. If their pace had been sluggish before it now slowed down to a snail's crawl for Penloth was determined to allow his horse to gorge itself and drink at will (which was practically every few paces) to insure that Lucius' return to Ellioth would be a memorable one.

When the seraphim finally reached the village outskirts two days later, Lucius was completely befouled and beside himself with rage. They were greeted by people who had lined up on either side of the road to watch their procession, and after taking one look (or whiff) of Lucius, burst into derisive laughter. Those who didn't laugh pelted him and his men with whatever was close at hand ... mostly rotted vegetables.

"*Bloody traitors!*"

"*Murderers!*"

"*Yer not fit to clean Eloth's boots!*"

They rode up the hill and finally through the portcullis, drawing abreast of the tourney field which quickly emptied of squires who ran forward to watch. One young lad plucked an extremely ripe tomato off the top of a nearby basket and bullseyed it smack into Lucius' face. It exploded upon impact, splattering into his black hair and beard, and running down his neck onto his front vesture. There was a burst of appreciative laughter from the other lads which died the instant Lucius directed his murderous glare upon them.

"Penlorian!" snapped Sir Penloth, glaring at his young

brother. "That tomato wasn't yours to throw! Reimburse that farmer at once for his loss!"

The squires erupted into gales of laughter, infuriating Lucius all the more.

Penlorian defensively pointed to the farmer. "He was the one who told me to throw it in the first place!" he protested.

"Oh, never mind, then!" replied Penloth with a snort of laughter.

Lucius ground his teeth and screamed in rage.

The prisoners finally arrived before the castle doors. Penloth and his men dismounted while above them curious courtiers peered over numerous balconies and out of windows to watch. Stable boys took charge of their horses while the castle guards removed the prisoners for judgment. When they came to take custody of the Baron, Penloth waved them off, wrapping Lucius' leash tightly about his fist. "Not this snake," he said, rubbing his reddened, watery eyes and runny nose. "I wouldn't wish this stench on my worst … uh … I'll just take him myself."

"Is something amiss, Sir Penloth?" inquired a young boy before the doors to the Great Hall. Penloth looked down to find Eloth's son, the crown Prince, Joshua, looking up at him.

"Aye, mi'lord," he replied with a meaningful wince. "I thought to teach the wretch a lesson but ended up riding downwind of him for the better part of a bloody hot day!"

"Oh," replied Joshua, observing the baron's filthy and extremely pungent clothing. Lucius lunged forward at him, snarling like a mad animal as if to rend him to pieces. Joshua fell back in astonishment, his eyes round with surprise at the force of his hatred. Their former steward had never behaved so to him before. Penloth choked back hard on his rope collar, forcing him to his knees with the point of his sword.

"*Down, knave!*" he snarled as though the Baron were an errant hound. "Before the sun sets on this day I'll see thee properly trounced, orders or no! Excuse me, mi'lord, but I must see this criminal to his trial!" He turned about, dragging the struggling baron forcibly behind him into the hall.

"I'll not forget this," Lucius choked out in a dangerous voice. "I'll make you live to regret this!"

Penloth rounded on him menacingly, all patience evaporated. "One more word from you, Lucius, and blast my orders, I'll deliver thee to Eloth *without* thy forked tongue! Is that clear?"

Lucius favored him with a venomous look, but gave no further argument; the rope had been pulled too tautly about his windpipe. Penloth turned again, hauling him up upon his feet and forcefully thrusting him through the double doors into the Hall of Judgment. The mob crowded in behind; pushing and shoving each other to find a place from which to view the trial. The moment they entered the chamber the court began tittering and making snide remarks about Lucius' rank "aroma." One by one he sought out each whisperer and glared at them with his baleful eyes until they shut up. While the hall continued to fill, the other prisoners were made to stand behind Lucius to await judgment with him. Some had to be carried out, others hobbled in leaning on canes, crutches or carried in upon litters. All had been wounded in some fashion or other but had been tended to mercifully.

The court heralds blew on their trumpets, signaling the arrival of the King. The room hushed and Eloth entered the hall accompanied by his son, Joshua, the bloodstains of those who had fallen in battle still on his vesture in silent indictment of Lucius' heinous deeds. He ascended his throne and seated himself, laying Ephlal across his lap. Lucius regarded the powerful sword fearfully, backing away from it until he stood flattened against Sir Eric and Penloth who held him fast. Eloth turned to stare at him, his gray eyes stern beyond endurance.

The Court Chamberlain stood forth amidst a brief fanfare and read the charges aloud from a scroll.

"Baron Lucius of Northumberland, thou art accused of attempted assassination, high treason, and rebellion against the Crown. For each of these crimes, death by fire is the penalty–"

A loud cheer erupted from the crowd in unanimous approval. The Chamberlain held up his hand for silence, scowling.

"Dost thou have anything to say in thy defense before thy judgment is pronounced by the King?"

Lucius' mouth twisted into an ugly sneer. "I recognize not the authority of this court!" he spat, straining against his bonds. All in the court gasped angrily at his sheer effrontery, hoping Eloth would condemn him to a slow, painful, and torturous death.

The Chamberlain glanced at the King for a brief moment, took a deep breath and with a frown of disapproval, continued.

"Despite the gravity of thy transgressions and unrepentant conduct, the King has waived the penalty of death in the hope you shall find repentance. Instead of death by fire, upon thee and thy fellow outlaws is laid eternal banishment from this Kingdom ... "

The roar of the astonished crowd in response immediately cut him off and the Chamberlain was forced to pound his staff again for silence.

Lucius was *livid*! Eloth's show of mercy was the final humiliation! Better to die cursing him in flames than to accept clemency like a whipped cur!

"I want none of thy stinking mercy!" he shouted, lunging forward. Sir Eric could barely hold onto him and required the aid of four other knights to keep the baron subdued. Lucius' face was beet red with fury, spit flying as he flailed about.

"I would prefer the dignity of the flames to thy mercy!" He screamed. He rounded on the agitated crowd, his black eyes blazing. *"What is Eloth but a benevolent dictator and the kingdom of Ellioth the dwelling of sheep?"*

"Twas I who governed this miserable kingdom for years without number! 'Twas I who labored like a lap dog in his service whilst he sat upon his golden throne!" Lucius whirled back, directing his invectives at Eloth's impassive face.

"Never more shall I bow my knee in mindless submission to Him I do not own as King! I shall be my own master! I will raise mine own throne upon the rubble of Ellioth and it shall be my throne which ascends above the heights of the clouds! Do you hear me, Eloth? Do you hear me?!" [3]To punctuate his utter contempt for his former

lord, Lucius twisted his mouth and spat upon the marble dais before Eloth's feet.

A deafening hush descended upon the Hall; all eyes fastened fearfully upon Eloth as he rose swiftly to his feet, certain he would now execute Lucius himself. Eloth marched toward him, lifting Ephlal high, its blade glittering white-hot so that all in the hall had to shield their eyes from its brilliance save the King. Lucius blanched, his knees buckling beneath him; his bravado and arrogance gone in the face of the sword's oncoming terror. Eloth stopped before him, the point of his glittering sword aimed at Lucius like an accusing finger of doom. Lucius' entire body shook with uncontrollable fear and his bowels were loosed.

"Lucius of Northumberland," Eloth thundered in a terrible voice, heat from Ephlal's humming blade scorching the hair of his face. "Thou art stripped of thy title, property, citizenship, and lands and art forever banished from Ellioth and My presence. Upon the morrow, thou shalt be put upon *The Dark Angel* towed out to sea and set adrift. Henceforth, thy name shall be remembered as a curse and byword and thy memory blotted out from the records of Ellioth!"

Lucius' hands balled into fists of helpless rage, seething with fearful hatred.

"What care I for thy judgments, O King? I swear to thee this oath: Thou shalt rue this day in great bitterness and mourn that Thou didst not destroy me when it lay within Thy power!"

Eloth regarded his former steward and once most trusted servant with an impassive face, but in his gray eyes was an unfathomable pain that only two in the entire court filled with people could behold: Lucius and Eloth's son, Joshua.

"I know," was Eloth's silent reply.

The following afternoon at high tide, *The Dark Angel* was towed out to sea by Eloth's flagship, *The Morning Star*. The prison ship had been stripped of its rudder, anchor, sails, and all other equipment which might have served as a means to navigate, leaving its doomed passengers no means by which to determine their own course. The captives watched diminishing Ellioth with numbed expressions as they were towed farther and farther out to sea, leaving many aboard *The Morning Star* to wonder how far they would travel before it was set adrift, left for the current to carry them where it willed. When the sun began to dip below the horizon, and after sight of land had long since vanished, Eloth leaned down to cut the tow line himself.

"No!" screamed Lucius, hurling himself upon the railing. *The Morning Star* swiftly tacked and came about, changing course back for Ellioth leaving them powerless to follow. He raised his arm over his head and shook his fist at the departing ship in rage.

"You'll not be rid of me so easily, Eloth!" he screamed, his voice carrying well across the water. *"Our paths shall cross again and when they do, thou shalt pay heavily in innocent blood!"*

Eloth turned his back upon *The Dark Angel,* his heart leaden. "Oh, Lucius, Lucius ..." he murmured, " *... how art thou fallen...*"[4]

Chapter One

Eloth stood upon a high balcony which overlooked the harbor far below, watching the shipwrights make alterations to his fleet of merchant ships. In the very near future, they would be carrying passengers, livestock, and supplies instead of cargo to trade. He glanced hopefully again out to sea, looking for the white glimmer of approaching sails which might have signaled the return of his foster son, Ardon. He had been gone for over six months and was long overdue to return. Though Elliott was fertile, it was, nevertheless, an island with limited space to support a growing population that was becoming greater every year. It was Eloth's hope to transplant one-tenth of Elliott's population to a second kingdom, which Joshua would rule when he came of age in another five years or so. Ardon had reluctantly agreed to govern in his place as Steward until Joshua reached manhood, shortly after earning his spurs as a knight.

"Hullo, papa," said a voice behind him. Eloth turned about to find his son standing behind him, holding the hand of a young girl whose mop of russet-colored locks were festooned with a wreath of flowers. Eloth smiled, noting how the daisy crown lay cocked crookedly over her right eye. "Is this another or is it the same one as yesterdays?" he inquired. Llyonesse gazed worshipfully up at her hero while Joshua righted it upon her head.

"It is new," he replied.

"Joshua made it for my birthday!" Llyonesse volunteered. "I'm eight today!"

"Practically a lady!" agreed Eloth, taking her little hand and kissing it affectionately.

Llyonesse's cheeks dimpled and blushed with delight, pleased at being thought of as a real "lady." They joined him at the balcony railing, looking far out to sea with hopeful eyes.

"It seems a lifetime since he left, Father. When do you think he shall return?" asked Joshua.

"I know not," Eloth replied. "But I hope soon."

Joshua continued. "Me too, but as much as I want him to return, I know it will only mean a longer separation is next in store for us. I feel very torn."

"Come with us!" piped up Llyonesse, hoping to comfort him.

Joshua smiled at her and shook his head. "Thou knowest well that I cannot, Llyonesse. I am to enter the academy this winter, remember?"

"To become a knight?"

"Yes."

"Can't you be knighted now so you may come with us?" she asked with childish naiveté.

"I'm afraid not," Joshua replied.

"Then can you not be steward instead of Papa and so come with us?" Llyonesse persisted, upset at the thought of being separated from her best friend.

Eloth and Joshua exchanged beleaguered smiles, wondering how they were going to explain. "No, Joshua is not of an age to rule and so thy father, Ardon, must do so as his Steward."

"Why?" Llyonesse persisted.

"Because thy father, Ardon, is my foster son and Joshua the son of my body. A foster son cannot rule as a Prince unless the King is childless and appoints him as his heir."

"Oh," responded Llyonesse. Her brow wrinkled. "What is a foster son?"

"Now you've done it," laughed Joshua. "She'll be asking questions until the sun goes down!"

"A foster son is the adopted son of the family who raises him," Eloth explained with great patience. "Thy father's true father was a local fisherman who drowned when he was but a boy. Thy father was orphaned, so I adopted him as my foster son. Though I love him well, 'twould not be fitting to make him Prince when it is Joshua who has both the legal and blood claim to the throne."

"Father," said Joshua, suddenly worried. "Do you think that Ardon might harbor any ill will toward me in this matter? Will he be reluctant to relinquish his stewardship when I am of age to take the throne?"

Eloth smiled, recalling Ardon's response months ago to the very same question. "Fear not," he replied, patting Joshua's shoulder. "I put the same question to him and he just laughed and replied: *'Tell that little brother of mine that I will be unbearably weary of sitting on his golden chair by the time his legs have grown long enough to reach the floor! I would rather swab the decks of the entire fleet than be continually besieged with the petty squabbles of court!'*"

Joshua chuckled. "Still, I wish I could journey to the new land with him! I will miss him."

"Me too?" Llyonesse asked, tugging on his tunic.

He smiled fondly down at her. "Yes, I shall miss you, too."

"Thy time shall come all too soon, my son," replied Eloth softly, looking again out to sea. "In the meantime, we shall send Ardon before thee, to prepare the way."[5]

Ardon returned the following week with news of a land a month's journey from Ellioth. It was sparsely inhabited by small clans of agricultural folk who had neither formal government nor commercial trade. As a matter of fact, the few people that Ardon had encountered responded that Eloth's people and the goods they would bring would be most welcome. The news spread like wildfire amongst the villagers. Proclamations were posted throughout the realm, seeking volunteers to journey across the sea. A great many villeins weary of cultivating a mere acre or two of tired loam, jumped at the opportunity and those who chose to remain were leased equal shares of the vacated properties. With the return of Ardon's ship, preparations began in earnest for the Midsummer's Faire and tournament to celebrate the great discovery and give their countrymen an elaborate send-off.

After spending his first week reacquainting himself with his wife and daughter, Ardon went off for a hunt with Joshua as he had promised to do before he left. They journeyed together with a small retinue into Roshauna Forest, accompanied by their favorite hawks and hounds. After a successful day of hunting in which they had bagged a stag, two boar, and several rabbits, they sat with full bellies within their tarpaulin, laughing and reminiscing by candlelight.

"I swear that you have grown by at least three hands since I saw you last!" Ardon exclaimed, pounding Joshua on the back. "Ouch! Still not enough meat on those bones though; you're as scrawny as a newborn colt!"

"I'll fill out soon enough," replied Joshua, wincing as Ardon pinched his upper arm. "And when I do, I'll throw you over my shoulder like a sack of wheat and dump you into the stream for your cheek!"

Ardon laughed. "I'd like to see you try! You know, I had the devil's own time trying to convince Zarabeth to let me come hunting with you. Wanted me all to herself before the faire, but I succeeded in convincing her otherwise."

"Oh and how was that?" Joshua asked biting into a savory haunch of venison.

Ardon grinned at him. "I pulled your rank on her! I just told her: *'Crown Prince's orders!'*"

Joshua rolled his eyes. "It isn't enough that *you* are in trouble with her? Did you have to put me into her bad graces as well?" he replied. "But she needn't be jealous; she'll have you all to herself for years to come whilst I am sweating in the tiltyard."

Ardon shook his head. "Amazing how time flies. ... it seems only yesterday that you lie cradled in my arms ... suckling your thumb and soiling your swaddling clothes—OW!" Ardon yelped as Joshua thumped him on the head with a large cushion.

"*Churlish brat!*"

"Ill-bred lout! You shouldst not speak of such base things concerning thy sovereign!" laughed Joshua.

Ardon smiled broadly. "By the rood it *is* good to be with you again! Though I love the sea and the life of a mariner, it is mighty lonely ... I've missed Ellioth much these past months."

"You mean thy *wife!*" interjected Joshua smirking with satisfaction as Ardon turned a furious shade of red. "It escaped none of our notice that the first acquaintance you made upon thy return was with thy wife instead of thy king!"

"Aye, you precocious child, I did though I daresay you'll understand soon enough once you are grown to manhood!" retorted Ardon, his ears flaming.

"I remember the day you first laid eyes on her ... they nearly fell from thy sockets!"

"Aye and my noggin from my shoulders," added Ardon with a snort, remembering the incident well. "I couldn't keep my eyes off her! Not even whilst fencing!"

"Indeed, had Penloth not alerted thee, old Sigfried would have knocked it right off with that rusty old rapier of his ... and father betting so heavily on you, too!"

"Aye," smirked Ardon. "Sir Estaban saved my scalp but not Father's purse! But ho now! Look to thine own self, my young Prince," Ardon said, chucking a cushion at him. "Soon it will be you warding off the attentions of Ellioth's maidens; if those twigs you refer to as limbs ever grow some muscles."

"I have no interest in *romance whatsoever!*" huffed Joshua, as though the word were distasteful.

Ardon snorted. "Oh come now, little brother, do not try to convince *me* that you do not yet possess an interest in the fairer sex! I am not blind; I saw you on several occasions just yesterday making sheep's eyes at two of the serving maids in the kitchens while I waited for you to get our provisions!"

"It was only to get some of those almond pastries to take with us!" protested Joshua, knowing Ardon wouldn't believe him. "As it was, they were still baking."

"Of course," nodded Ardon, "and pigs will fly on the morrow!"

Joshua pounced, knocked Ardon backwards, and straddled him about the chest, pinning his arms to his sides with his legs, armed with a very large cushion. "Recant thy hasty words or face the consequences!" he warned.

Ardon smirked up him, knowing Joshua was obviously looking for another excuse to wallop him. "Admit it!" he laughed, obliging him. "Admit that you're madly in love with Prunella!"

"'Tis not Prunella I love, but her *almond cakes*!" Joshua protested, realizing too late how it sounded. Ardon collapsed backwards into howls of laughter.

"*I'll bet*!" he chortled.

"Fair enough. I'll shall prove what I say is true!" Joshua replied, standing to his feet. "Get thee up, Sir Laggard, and saddle our horses! We are going hunting!"

"Hunting?" smirked Ardon, standing to his feet with a wicked wink, "for scullery maids?"

"No, *almond cakes*," Joshua sniggered, donning his cloak.

With the stealth of thieves, the brothers rode silently back to the castle, arriving half an hour later. They hitched their horses up and gave them oats to keep them quiet. Silent as stalking cats, they tip-toed into the darkened kitchens, choking down their laughter. Ardon followed Joshua, who (he had to admit), led the way with the practiced ease of familiarity that bespoke of many such nocturnal visits. It was utterly pitch black, but Joshua was adept as an old blind man and didn't so much as knock over a single piece of crockery. Ardon felt more than a trifle foolish. Skulking around the kitchens at his age was a far cry from "mature" behavior. He couldn't help but wonder what Penloth would say should they be caught red-handed. Suddenly Joshua stopped before a large wooden board that Ardon would not have seen without bumping into it. Joshua groped about until his fingers lit upon a tray covered with a pastry cloth. He lifted it up and sniffed appreciatively.

"Almond cakes!" he hissed.

Ardon felt about. The tray was filled with a multitude of fragrant buns left over from the morning's breakfast. *The cook is going to think he has an awfully large rat with a sweet tooth prowling about!* Ardon thought gleefully, stuffing as many as would fit into his pockets and haversack. Licking his fingers with relish, Joshua quickly led the way back out.

Once back in camp and safely within their tent, Joshua withdrew their sticky treasures and placed a thick, golden-brown one in Ardon's outstretched palm. Sprinkled over the top were slivers of sugared, thinly sliced almonds drizzled with honey. Ardon grinned at Joshua then stuffed it whole into his mouth, unable to help groaning aloud with pleasure. The inside was filled with nuts and finely ground almond paste. The taste was beyond description! Light and delicate but with a sweet nutty flavor that, with every bite, made him crave more. Where had these been all the days he had grown up at court? With his mouth full and eyes rolling in ecstasy, he stuffed another and another into his mouth until his cheeks bulged like a squirrel's, conceding his argument with gluttonous enthusiasm.

The morning of the Midsummer's Day Faire dawned fair and bright. The sky was a deep blue, broken only by brilliant, white puffy clouds. Dignitaries and noblemen had been arriving for the past week in large wains, bearing large clothes trunks and accompanied by their valets, butlers, squires, and pages. The fairgrounds had been set up just outside the castle walls on the greensward where Lucius' failed attack had taken place months before. Now the green grass was festooned with a riot of colors by the brilliant tarpaulins and banners which were erected about it. Colorful pennants lined the tourney field, signifying the house and lineage of each man who was to participate in the lists: a rampant unicorn of white sendel upon an azure field for the house of Estaban, (Penloth's coat of arms); a silver swan rising with outspread wings upon a golden pennant (for the Earl of Devonshire); a yellow boar upon a black field (for a visiting Duke), a brown hawk against a green background for Sir Eric's family, and many, many others which curled and snapped proudly upon their flagstaffs in the wind. But high above them all flew the golden Lion of Ellioth with the heraldic motto: *To Reign in Righteousness*[6] upon it.

Eloth's pennants flew before the pavilion and floated high overhead upon each of the castle turrets where they could be seen clearly from afar. But there was one pennant that remained a mystery to all for it had been furled within a black shroud before the gallery. This was the standard that Eloth had commissioned for Ardon's Stewardship that would be revealed at day's end.

Traveling performers (tumblers, strolling minstrels, actors, and poets) had been summoned from all over the kingdom and employed to entertain the fairgoers. They roamed amongst the crowds, performing feats of magic, juggling, somersaulting, and composing impromptu love ballads, poetry, limericks or insincere flattery for anyone willing to pay a copper. Village merchants and traveling peddlers had set up booths and were loudly hawking their wares such as ribbons, laces, skin unguents, bolts of fabric, perfumes, musical instruments, toys, jewelry, and numerous other dainties to the delight of both the womenfolk and children. There were stalls featuring prized livestock for the scrutiny of the menfolk and exhibitions of fine needlework, woven baskets, and jewelry for the women. To feed the vast multitude, a large, open air kitchen had been erected next to the tourney field where the palace cook oversaw his minions in the roasting of several wild boars, venison, sheep, and hart upon large spits and in enormous pits. Scullery maids bore trays amongst the revelers, serving mincemeat pies, almond cakes, custard tarts, mutton, sausages, compotes, and baked apples with freshly churned cream. There was ale, wine, and mead in abundance, brewed by the best in the kingdom for all the thirsty combatants (as well as the onlookers) as they came off the field of competition.

At Penloth's insistence (and Joshua's nonstop needling), Ardon reluctantly had agreed to participate in the Lists despite the loud protests of his wife (and his own private misgivings).

"You haven't worn your armor in over a week of years!" she had protested, *"You will be crippled for life, maimed, or even worse: killed … providing it hasn't rusted fast by now!"*

As his squires struggled to assist him into the heavy armor (which had been wrought for a much younger, more slender body), Ardon found himself regretting his hasty consent in response to Penloth's accusation that he had become as flaccid as a jellyfish.

"Can you pull thy stomach in any further, mi'lord?" panted one of his squires, whom he had been watching with great pity. "Tis a narrow squeak, but if you can hold thy breath for just a moment more, I think I'll have thee in!"

How could he possibly back out now after the poor lads had labored throughout the night to polish away the years of accumulated rust and work the joints free? They had even rousted the King's blacksmith out of bed at the last moment to adjust its fit to accommodate his broader frame. Now he stood with sinking heart, waiting dejectedly as they feverishly labored to fasten it upon him, secretly appalled at how unbelievably heavy and unwieldy it felt. He never remembered it weighing this much! Not even the first time he had worn one at the tender age of thirteen! Just standing in the cursed thing was making rivers of sweat pour down his body. Though he knew better, he would have bet serious coinage it had grown heavier in just the last three minutes! It had already taken them the better part of the morning to get him in but that wasn't the worst of it. As if to add insult to injury, his squires were compelled to steady him by the arms so he could practice walking around without falling flat on his face or backside.

One good gust of wind, he thought miserably to himself, *and I'll be toppled over like a freshly axed tree!* He peered around the corner of his tent, sullenly observing just how well the other contestants were getting on. Sir Penloth was easy enough to identify; the powerful knight was tramping about as if he had on nothing more than a loincloth, hefting lances and broadswords as though they were no heavier than reeds! Ardon stared enviously, watching Penloth move about with great ease, squatting low to check the cinches on his mount's saddle then windmilling his arms about to loosen his shoulder joints—*All* - he was certain - *just for his personal benefit.*

The sudden blast of a trumpet signaled that it was his turn at the joust. Of all people to be paired with first, he had gotten the unlucky lot to be chosen to fight Sir Penloth! Well, at least his suffering would be brief.

He watched with naked envy as Penloth swung himself up into the saddle of his black charger unaided, grimacing when the knight offered him a grin and shrug. Now it was his turn to mount. Swallowing his pride, Ardon bent forwards, suffering his squires to thread the hook of the *Dunce's Tower* into the back of his armor so it could lift him into the saddle of his charger; a mechanism usually employed for those who were unable to mount a horse without assistance, such as children, the infirm, and old maimed warriors. It was the sole aim of every squire-at-arms to graduate out of the Dunce's Tower in the least possible amount of time.

"Need any help?" Penloth shouted.

"*No!*" shot back Ardon, waving him off. His sudden movement caused the rope to twist which resulted in him swinging about like a pendulum, scattering his squires and spooking his mare. Ardon sighed with exasperation, hanging in mid-air while he waited for his horse to be recaptured and placed beneath him for another attempt.

Keelhauling would be preferable to this! he thought miserably. No sooner had they gotten him firmly in the saddle than did his squire (out of shear habit) smack the backside of his mare to send her on her way. Asfoleth instantly took off at a canter. Ardon almost fell over backwards, barely hanging on for dear life, only one foot in the stirrup, the horizon bouncing up and down crazily before him. *Bloody hell!* He had forgotten how bumpy riding on a horse was! Even worse than a pitching ship in a storm! He fought his way upright and succeeded in pinching both knees against her sides; struggling to match her rhythm as her hooves pounded upon the sod. Upon approaching the gallery, he pulled back as hard as he could, but Asfoleth refused to obey. He pulled harder, still she would not slow. Obviously the mare knew she was in the hands of an amateur and was taking full advantage. Cold sweat poured down him in uncomfortable rivers as he yanked harder and more urgently upon the reins, hoping desperately she would stop before colliding with some immovable object, like the grandstand. At the last possible second the stubborn nag stopped. She turned her neck and lifted her upper lip at him, baring her teeth as if she were laughing in derision. Ardon could feel the heat rising in his face as the crowd tittered at his dilemma.

"Perhaps I can still back out," he thought in quiet desperation, wishing he could wipe the sweat from his face. A squire thrust a heavy lance up into his armpit and gauntlet, effectively sealing his doom.

"Best of luck to you, mi'lord," said the squire with deep sincerity.

"Combatants, approach the Pavilion!" cried the field herald.

In direct response to the verbal summons (and without benefit of his direction) Asfoleth wheeled about and took off with him again, cantering briskly back toward the gallery. Ardon steamed. The nag understood English but ignored the basic instructions of spur and reins! Again he vainly tried to push his faceplate up, but it was stuck fast. "So help me, Asfoleth," he growled, his voice muffled by the plating. "If you do not obey me, I shall have you butchered and made into glue before sundown!" The mare immediately stiffened her legs and came to an abrupt halt. The sudden deceleration almost threw him, but Ardon hung on, reeling wildly about in the saddle while the crowd *ooowwwed* and *aaawwwed* with each wild sway. Again she turned her head back and curled her upper lip at him, whinnying loudly. This sent the crowd into hysterics. Joshua had to look away, hoping Ardon would not see him trying to choke down his laughter. Penloth drew abreast on Graymane, and nodded at Ardon with a mischievous grin. He had personally selected Ardon's horse and treated her to a rich diet of oats and bran that morning, ensuring that the headstrong mare would be spoiling for a good fight. Ardon glared at him, unaware of Penloth's trickery but knowing somehow that he was entirely responsible for this humiliation. He finally wrenched his faceplate open and drank deeply of the fresh air. Lords and Ladies sat before them gowned in an assortment of colored finery and jewels, fanning themselves to keep away the flies and to circulate the air. Maidens bore handkerchiefs in the color of the combatants whom they favored: blue for Penloth or green for Ardon; most, he noted, wore blue. Ardon spared a glance in his wife's direction, noting with some pride that she and Llyonesse were both gowned entirely in green brocade with emerald ribbons woven in their hair. Zarabeth eyed his mare angrily, secretly vowing to find out just who had given him the most pigheaded of all the steeds in Eloth's livery. *"If the joust doesn't kill him that miserable nag surely will!"* she fumed.

"In the first joust," cried the herald in a loud voice to the assembled crowd, "riding in the blue and silver, Sir Penloth Estaban, Captain of the Guard, Chief Seraphim, son of Sir Tristan and the Lady Melbourne, and *undisputed champion for the past six years!*"

The crowd erupted into appreciative applause and cheers.

"Undisputed champion?" echoed Ardon, staring at Penloth in horror. He *had* been *set up*. *"Last six years?"*

Penloth smiled at him then shrugged.

"Riding in the green and gold, Sir Ardon Tolham, Captain of his Majesty's flagship, the *Eden Mist*, foster son of Eloth the Just!" The crowd paused momentarily, expecting to hear additional words of commendation. When they weren't forthcoming, they erupted into cheers anyway, *just to be polite*, Ardon thought morosely.

"Jousters to thy places!" cried the herald.

Penloth snapped his visor shut with the flared edge of his lance and wheeled about. A feat, Ardon was sure, which would have caused him serious bodily harm should he attempt to imitate him. Before he could even flick the reins, Asfoleth turned around and cantered to the opposite end of the tourney field. The crowd doubled over at her antics. Ardon cursed under his breath. If the nag was so bloody damned eager to joust, let her thrust the lance between her bucked teeth and have a go without him!

"Hail there, you old jelly fish!" shouted Sir Penloth, standing in his stirrups. "I hope you have stuffed plenty of wool into the backside of thy mailcoat!"

"Oh, bridle thy tongue, you loud mouthed braggart!" shouted Ardon, thoroughly annoyed at him for talking him into the entire affair. "Tis brains and skill which will decide the match, not brawn!"

The crowd roared with laughter, anticipating a good competition for Sir Penloth and Ardon's rivalry was the stuff of legends.

"We'll see!" returned Sir Penloth with a hearty laugh.

The tension built as the combatants and gallery waited for the signal from the heralds. Ardon settled down and squeezed the lance tightly against him, trying to recall all his former skills. Too soon the trumpets blared forth. The anxious chargers reared with loud neighs as spurs dug into their flanks and sprang forward, throwing up dirt clods as they galloped full speed down the field. Sir Penloth lowered his lance and leaned forward, squeezing it tightly under his armpit. He could hear the wind whistling through the slits in his visor and the pounding of Graymane's hooves as he closed the distance. He gripped the pummel and braced for impact. *CRASH!* Penloth's lance caught Ardon squarely upon the breastplate. Ardon flew backwards off the end of his horse and landed heavily upon the sod. He eventually rolled to a stop where he lay prone, gasping for breath. His squires ran out onto the field and took hold of his arms to help him up. It required four additional squires and two additional attempts before they finally had him upright and back onto his wobbly feet but Ardon rose with new determination. This time he was going to walk and remount that cantankerous nag unaided! He had done so a long time ago; he would just have to force his body to remember how! The crowd cheered as the first round was awarded to Sir Penloth who had been afforded more than ample time to gather the roses thrown to him from the ladies in the crowd.

"You were saying about brawn?" he cracked, unable to resist twisting the knife. Ardon waved his comment off as the crowd howled with laughter. He stood before the horse with his hands on his hips, glaring at her sternly. It wasn't that she was such a bad horse. In fact, she was actually one of the best chargers

Sir Gregory had trained, but she knew when she was bearing an amateur and was taking liberties a more experienced master would not have tolerated.

"On thy knees, my lady!" he growled, pointing to the ground. Asfoleth stared at him, her upper lip quivering as if she were laughing at him. He scowled at her darkly.

"*Down!*" he repeated much louder. When she did not respond he grabbed her forelocks and forcibly pulled her down. Asfoleth gave a low whinny then slowly went down onto her knees so Ardon could remount. Once he was in the saddle she sprang back up, nickering softly with newfound respect.

"Well done!" called Penloth, genuinely impressed.

Despite his small triumph, Ardon still had difficulty catching his breath. His chest felt as though a team of oxen had stampeded across him and it hurt to fill his lungs. Nevertheless, he guided Asfoleth back to the end of the field for a fresh lance. It was thrown up to him and he caught it expertly in mid-air, his confidence soaring. The trumpets blared forth again and this time Asfoleth politely waited for his spurs. Ardon leaned in close to her neck, pointing the lance just over her head as once again he charged down the field, bracing for what he was sure would be a suicidal encounter. Seconds later, Penloth loomed up before him. Ardon squeezed his eyes tight, hoping fortune would be with him and lifted the tip of his lance slightly. There was an ear-splitting *crack* accompanied by a loud grunt. His lance caught Penloth upon the left shoulder, knocking him cleanly off his horse. Ardon opened his eyes and looked back, watching with a mixture of exhilaration and disgust as Sir Penloth fell then rolled with the momentum, coming expertly back up onto his feet with all the grace of an accomplished acrobat. Ardon's pride in his victory was instantly deflated as he heard the crowd roar in appreciation. *Even when the knight was bested they cheered him!* He reined in and turned round just as Penloth was offering another deep bow to those in the gallery, milking it for all he was worth. *The nerve of that braggart to bow when he hadn't even won the second round!*

He lifted his visor. "Are you done curtsying yet, Penloth? There *is* yet a *third* joust, you know!"

The crowd roared with laughter, this time at Penloth's expense.

"Yes, I'm coming!" he shouted good-naturedly, recapturing his horse and mounting without assistance. The two men squared off for the last time and waited for the signal to be given. Zarabeth wound and rewound her silken scarf about her hands in nervous anticipation, willing Ardon to win the third round with all her might. Now that he had triumphed once, her hopes were greatly renewed that he might not be taken off the field in a litter after all.

The trumpets blew and the horses were off, lances lowered for the final match. Green and blue plumes streamed in the wind, hooves thundering upon the ground like war drums. The crowd rose to its feet with a loud roar as they met in a mighty crash of steel. Shields went flying, lances splintered asunder and both men were catapulted from their saddles, landing with heavy thuds squarely upon their respective backsides. Asfoleth and Graymane collapsed with loud neighs then just as quickly got up and bolted from the field, squires running to catch them. The audience and Zarabeth remained on their feet in alarm. Ardon and Penloth alike were both writhing on the ground in apparent agony. She watched in fearful anxiety as squires and the court physician ran out to inspect what injuries they had incurred. Jousting was often a crippling, sometimes fatal enterprise and it was not uncommon to lose a good knight in a contest of skill. The crowd fell silent when the physician straightened and shook his head in dismay. Zarabeth's heart plummeted to the soles of her feet. Ardon could not possibly be that seriously hurt! He was still conscious! And he was moving! He was thrashing about and gripping his middle as if.....*as if he were in the throes of hysteria!* Instant relief swept over her, followed immediately by embarrassment and then rage. He and Penloth were not injured at all but *laughing!* She didn't know whether to cry with relief or scream.

"Come, Llyonesse!" she said, angrily snatching up her skirts.

"Let us see to thy father at once!" She had a good mind to smack Ardon upside the head for putting such a fright into her! And she would too, as soon as she made sure he was not injured!

Eloth judged the match a tie and sat back down, nodding to the herald to announce the next joust.

The matches continued for the rest of that morning until the field of competition had been narrowed down to Sir Penloth and a visiting duke. In the end, Sir Penloth bested him and achieved the unique status of being the first knight ever to achieve the notoriety of winning the tournament seven years in a row. Though Ardon had not fared nearly as well, he was very pleased with himself for he had not been eliminated until his fourth heat. Not only had he managed to knock down the formidable Sir Penloth Estaban twice, (a feat matched only by the Duke), but Sir Gregory and Sir Edwyn as well!

There were numerous other contests of skill which took place throughout the day: fencing competitions, sword battles, javelin throwing, wall-scaling, and wrestling, pugilism and archery. Joshua competed in both the long-bow and cross-bow events with boys of his own age, winning blue and red ribbons for first and second place. It had been very difficult for him during his events to maintain his concentration for he had to contend with the intense stares of numerous young maidens (and their plotting mothers) whenever he took aim. Especially discomfiting had been the behavior of the Earl of Devonshire and his daughter, Marguerite, for they became hushed in awe whenever he drew near, gawking and whispering asides to each other as they pointed at him. As soon as the contest had ended, he quickly ducked out of sight to search for Llyonesse. He found her across the field, dancing about a flower-bedecked maypole with other children as they wove the long ribbons in and out with squeals of laughter. She had changed into a pink smock over which she wore a heavily embroidered kirtle. On her head was a wreath of flowers from which multi-colored ribbons floated and fluttered in the breeze. When the dance came to an end, he hurried forward, anxious to show her the ribbons he had won in archery.

"Llyonesse!" he called out. "Lessie!"

Several children and their parents looked about, and when they recognized their Prince, immediately grew quiet, dropping into awkward bows and curtsies. He greeted them all then motioned Llyonesse over with a wave.

"Llyonesse! Over here!"

Llyonesse ran forward to meet him, catching his hands in hers. "They made me Queen of May!" she announced breathlessly.

"Did they?" he smiled, happy for her. "I won first and second place in archery!"

"Oh, Joshua, how wonderful! May I see?"

"Yes, but later. Now we must hurry to the tourney field; it is almost time." He tucked her arm in his as they walked. "These are just the first of many trophies I intend to win. Just wait until I become a knight! Then my trophies shall fill a room!"

"Joshua, when you become a knight will it mean that you will be too old to play with me anymore?" asked Llyonesse, her voice solemn.

"I am already too old to be playing with you, Llyonesse," he replied, bringing her fingers up to his face. "Behold!"

Llyonesse gently touched Joshua's silky-smooth skin, wondering what on earth he was talking about.

"Can't you feel them?" he asked, deadly serious.

Llyonesse nodded obediently, feeling nothing but knowing that feeling *something* was in some way very important to him.

"Whiskers!" he announced proudly, his chest puffing out. "I felt them for the first time this morning. I dare say that soon I shall have a set of whiskers that will even rival Sir Penloth's!"

"Truly?" replied Llyonesse, her eyes growing round. She could hardly imagine such a thing growing on Joshua's baby-smooth face, but it truly would be a feat worthy of boast for Sir Penloth had one of the droopiest, darkest, and thickest mustache's she had ever seen. She could not picture Joshua sporting such a growth of facial hair, not even in her wildest imagination, but the thought of such a thing was impressive nevertheless.

"Of course!" Joshua replied, taking her hand once again. "It's one of the first things a knight is supposed to do!" He started as the herald's trumpets rang forth, watching the massive crowd gather before the pavilion. "We must hurry!" he said, running across the springy grass. "The ceremony is about to begin! We are late!"

A small dais had been placed before the gallery in the tourney field, in the center of which stood the mysterious standard. Eloth, the seraphim, Ardon, and Zarabeth were waiting for them as Joshua marched forward with Llyonesse on his arm.

The herald addressed the assembly.

"*Hear ye, hear ye, all ye peoples of Eloth's kingdom,*" he cried, "let it be known this day, that a steward has been named from among thee to govern Shiloh. Let Sir Ardon Tolham stand forth as his banner is revealed!"

The crowd stirred as the trumpets again sounded, their blasts echoing upon the wind. Eloth pulled the cord which bound the shroud and out billowed an emerald standard edged in gold with the device of a golden, flowering tree. Ardon felt the sting of tears come into his eyes as he beheld the pennant and recognized Zarabeth's handiwork. It was truly beautiful and the first his bloodline had ever known, being from a long line of common fishermen. Would that his natural father and mother could have seen this day!

There was a great roar of praise from the crowd as they cheered, "Long live Ardon, Steward of the Shiloh! May he govern in peace all his days!"

Ardon's heart swelled with humility and awe. He squeezed Zarabeth's hand, overcome with emotion.

"Ardon Tolham, kneel before me and speak now thine oath," said Eloth laying his hands upon Ardon's shoulders. Ardon knelt upon the dais, Zarabeth just behind him, watching her husband with proud and glowing eyes as he repeated after his king.

"I, Ardon Tolham, do hereby accept the office of steward and vow to serve king and country with all fealty and honor until my Lord, the Prince Joshua, takes his rightful throne."

"And I, Eloth of Ellioth, with all joy and confidence do bestow upon thee, my foster son, the rulership of Joshua's Kingdom until the day he claims his rightful throne," responded the King, setting a chaplet of silver upon Ardon's brow. Then before the stunned eyes of all around them, Eloth knelt, unclasped the buckle of his scabbard, and girded Ephlal about Ardon's waist. Ardon gaped in astonishment. The crowd gasped aloud.

"My Lord?" Ardon whispered in bewilderment.

Eloth stood again, raising both arms over his head to quiet the murmuring crowd.

"Take heed and behold the trust I lay in this, my foster son!" he exclaimed loudly. "Ephlal is given into his keeping until the day he returns it to Joshua upon his Kingmaking in Shiloh. May he wield it as guardian and protector of my people so they may dwell in peace and safety, fearing no untoward evil."

Ardon listened...thunderstruck. Ephlal was the greatest token of trust that Eloth could have shown anyone! Eloth had borne the powerful sword for so many years that they had all come to think of it as part of him. There was never a time when he had been without it and the thought that the same weapon now hung about his own waist shook him to the marrow. He could feel its awesome power emanating from the blade and wondered if he too were glowing with supernatural light. "My Lord King," he said, rising. "You have honored me with a trust most undeserved."

Eloth smiled affectionately at him. "I do not bestow my trust easily, my son, as thou knowest well. Thou hast earned my confidence many times over."

Ardon looked down and beheld the eyes of his daughter as she smiled adoringly up at Joshua, reminding him of the next part of their ceremony. He drew her forward by the hand and stood her before the king. "And now, my king...as thou besought of me long ago. I do now espouse my daughter, Llyonesse to thy son, Joshua. She who is the most precious of all my possessions."[7]

"Thou speakest truly, Ardon Tolham! Llyonesse is indeed thy greatest treasure," agreed Eloth with a tender smile. Joshua looked upon Llyonesse's solemn little face and smiled for he had always known of the arrangement and was not displeased. They had grown up together and he was very fond and protective of her. In all truth, he could think of no other he would rather claim as his future bride, but that was a long time from now.

For Llyonesse's part, there had never been a doubt about whom she wanted to marry. She had idolized Joshua since the first day she had been old enough to speak his name. Eloth joined their hands together in his then straightened to address his people.

"Let it be witnessed among thee this day that the maiden, Llyonesse, is hereby espoused to Joshua, Prince of Shiloh to be trothplighted upon his Kingmaking in Shiloh these seven years hence. Rejoice with me and be exceedingly glad!"

The crowd broke into hearty cheers at the happy announcement as Eloth bent forward to kiss his son and Llyonesse. There were a few disappointed groans from those who had hoped to wed their own daughters to the Prince (most notably the Earl of Devonshire), but they were quickly hushed by those around them.

"Today thine destinies art forever joined, one to another," Eloth said, smiling upon them. "Joshua, Llyonesse belongs to thee and thou unto her. What I have joined this day let no man put asunder!"[8]

Eloth's chamberlain banged his staff to gain the attention of the cheering crowd.

"The day waxes late!" he cried. "Banquet guests to the great hall!" The ceremony thus concluded, the crowds followed Eloth's court into the palace for the celebration feast. Llyonesse walked mutely alongside Joshua, still clinging to his hand, preoccupied.

"Why art thou so quiet?" Joshua asked her, squeezing her hand. "Where is the chatterbox of earlier today? Art thou unhappy, Llyonesse?"

"No," replied Llyonesse thoughtfully. "I was just thinking about what kind of crown I would like to wear when I am queen. Do I have to wear a heavy one of gold and diamonds?"

"No crown of gold and jewels could possibly be more beautiful than the flower wreathes I have woven for thee!" Joshua laughed, bringing a happy smile to her face. "I shall have an entire garden devoted solely to thy headdress and shall weave such a crown for thy wedding day that all the bees shall desert the meadows and hover about thy head like ladies in waiting!"

"Oh Joshua!" giggled Llyonesse, thinking the image very funny. "How wonderful, but it would frighten all the guests away!"

Joshua paused and suddenly pointed. "Oh, Llyonesse ... *look!*" he gasped when they came to the castle doors, "speaking of wondrous!"

Llyonesse stared in hushed awe at the sight of the great hall which extended before them in resplendent glory. The room was ablaze with the golden light of thousands of flickering candles set amidst crystal, silver, and golden candle stands; their amber glow reflecting off the highly polished, white marble floor. Colorful tapestries, silken banners and cloth of gold hung upon the walls and were swagged in elaborate folds between the white marbled pillars, gleaming in the golden light. Long tables had been placed end to end, covered with snowy white damask cloths, set with precious crystal goblets, ornate gold chargers and laid with golden cutlery. Exotic centerpieces of fruits, nuts, confections, and flowers stretched from one end of each table to the other in a multitude of colors, shapes, and sizes.

"We best hurry," said Joshua, dragging her after him.

Two servants in scarlet and gold livery strode forward at the Steward's nod and opened the large double doors that led to the kitchens once all were seated. The musicians lifted their instruments and struck up a lively fanfare. The doors opened and in marched the kitchen servants bearing large platters of elaborately prepared food. Each heavy silver tray was a masterpiece of culinary art in its own right and required two full grown men to carry in; all piled high with a festive variety of food that smelled as wonderful as it looked. There was roast pheasant sitting amidst a nest of sugared flowers, tail feathers and all; following this came a platter which bore mutton arranged amidst a wreath of savory herbs and rosemary, mint jelly aspics dotting the flanks like the pantaloons of a harlequin; an entire roast boar with an apple in its mouth, surrounded by pears soaked in brandy and pomegranates; lamb basted in citrus juices and garnished with baby vegetables; partridges nestled in baskets of noodles and quail eggs; peacocks and swans, their gorgeous tail feathers arranged as extravagant fans over the delicately seasoned meats; and finally an enormous white stag stuffed with currants, nuts and dates, rosy red apples impaled upon each sharp tine. For those whose tastes favored seafood, there was turbot basted with verjuice and spices; oysters soaked in vinegar and served on a bed of parsley, haddock cooked with garlic butter, boiled mackerel with sorrel sauce, fresh herring, crawfish, mussels, lamprey, and fish tarts. There was a moment's pause as the doors closed then reopened again to emit more servants carrying baskets of freshly baked breads; urns of mead, wine, and ale; followed immediately by squires who bore trays loaded with a variety of comfits including spiced fruit compotes, pastries with fillings of fruit and nuts, Prunella's famous almond cakes and marzipan confections artfully crafted into various mythological animals, fruits, and flowers. All were borne into the hall and laid on several boards with great pride as the appreciative audience broke into thunderous applause.

Ardon examined his elaborate place setting with baffled dismay wondering which of the five gold plated forks was for beef and which of the four goblets was for mead. Despite his courtly upbringing, his seaman's habits had become thoroughly ingrained and he was totally at a loss as to how to eat without violating some rule of courtly etiquette. Filling a hungry belly at sea required nothing more than a quick hand and sharp blade, but it certainly wouldn't be seemly for him to spear a hunk of meat from a passing platter with his dirk! He glanced to his left and peered at Sir Penloth wondering if he felt as at great a loss as he did. Sir Penloth's only response was to cock a mischievous eyebrow at him while covertly withdrawing a short knife from his shirt sleeve. Ardon grinned. At least he wouldn't be the only one at the high table who displayed an appalling lack of table manners!

The meal was sumptuous in every detail and amidst the

clatter and clink of glasses, the court minstrels played softly upon harps, flutes, lyres, mandolins, recorders, and tambours. Llyonesse was not so interested in eating her food as in playing with it, finding the myriad of marzipan figurines too delightful to ignore. She was rebuked many times for "flying" her marzipan dragons in the air and for creating a horrendous din with her growls, yips, and barks as her menagerie galloped across the table, leaving Zarabeth little choice but to have her physically removed. With a jerk of her head she summoned Clotilde, her lady-in-waiting, to gather Llyonesse up and remove her forthwith. Llyonesse waved a cheery good-bye to Joshua, grinning foolishly as Clotilde scolded her. Joshua waved back, trying not to smile too much so the adults wouldn't assume he was indulging her misbehavior. But he was sorry to see her go and wondered if her playful antics would extend into adulthood, forcing all his court to either join in on her play as a courtesy or if he would have to make his queen eat alone in her room.

A month following the Midsummer's fair, the morning of the great departure finally dawned. Eloth and Joshua dressed quickly and rode down to the harbor clad in heavy woolen tunics and hooded cloaks to keep out the chill air. A light morning fog had settled upon the harbor, its mist battling the sun for dominion. The cry of seagulls keened softly overhead and even the sound of the lapping waves seemed muted as they slapped against the sides of the sailing vessels.

Joshua and Eloth boarded *The Eden Mist* and found Ardon snapping out last minute orders to the crew. Crowds of well-wishers were already gathered upon the docks to bid their countrymen and loved ones farewell. Family members exchanged tearful embraces with their departing relatives, promising to correspond as often as permitted by merchant vessel.

While his father engaged Ardon in last minute conversation, Joshua went in search of Llyonesse. After an unsuccessful search on deck, he entered the captain's quarters below where he found Zarabeth and Clotilde.

"Forgive me, mi'lord, but milady has taken sick," explained Clotilde wringing out a wipe cloth. "I sent Llyonesse up on deck so she could rest easier. I thought the lass would feel less forlorn if she could watch the activity for a while."

"I saw no sign of her," replied Joshua, worried. "With all the activity top-side, a little girl could easily be overlooked or injured. I will look for her and bring her back to you."

"Thank you, my lord!" exhaled a grateful Clotilde, setting the cloth upon Zarabeth's brow. "T'would be one less load off my mind!"

Joshua closed the door behind him and climbed back out on deck. He searched the forecastle, quarter deck, and every other nook and cranny above the hold with no success. He tried to question the busy seamen, but none remembered seeing her. Joshua returned below decks, hunting in the cargo hold with a lantern so he could see in the darkness. After a long and careful search he finally found her sitting amongst the storage barrels with her face in her hands, sobbing.

"Llyonesse, I've been looking all over for you!" Joshua exclaimed with half relief, half anger.

Llyonesse turned her tear-stained face into his shoulder. "I'm sorry, Joshua, but it's just that I do-do-don't want to leeeeave! I'm afraid to sail, an- an- and I wu-wu-won't see you for such a lu-lu-long tiiime!"

"Sssshhh now," whispered Joshua. "I envy you this wonderful adventure!"

"You do?" blinked Llyonesse in amazement, her eyebrows rising. Joshua had never envied her for anything ever before.

"Of course! Who wouldn't?" he nodded. "You are taking part in a very important event in Ellioth's history! You are going to live in a new land and help thy father build a kingdom for us to rule one day!"

"Bu-bu-but that will take *years!*" wailed Llyonesse, distressed. "I'll be gone so long you'll forget what I even look like!"

"I could never forget thee," soothed Joshua, dabbing her eyes with a kerchief. "Remember, we are troth-plighted and that means we shall always belong to one another. I will look upon thy portrait at least once a day whilst you are gone!"

"But I have nothing to remind me of you," Llyonesse gulped in a very small voice, wiping her sleeve across her runny nose, which, had her mother seen it, would have earned her a slap for sure. "How will I remember you?"

"I have already thought of that … *behold*!" whispered Joshua, withdrawing a golden chain from his tunic. "I had it made especially for thee." Dangling upon the end was a heart-shaped locket. Llyonesse took it carefully from his hand and examined it in the light with awe. It was very beautiful and finely etched. Joshua put his arm about her and showed her how to open the tiny clasp. "See?" he said, opening it wide to reveal a miniature portrait of himself. "Now you may gaze upon my lordly visage every day!"

"Oh, Joshua!" Llyonesse giggled, a big smile spreading over her face. "I will never, ever take it off!"

"Not even to bathe?" Joshua smiled, lifting her up by the hands. "Come, it's time to go topside." Hand-in-hand they maneuvered through the crowded hold then scaled the wooden ladder up to the deck where they found their fathers drinking from the stirrup cup in farewell. The air was thick with silent emotion when Ardon turned to greet Joshua and his daughter.

"Look, papa!" cried Llyonesse, scampering up to show him the locket. "Look at what Joshua gave me!"

"It's lovely, sweeting," he said, chucking her chin affectionately. He turned to Joshua and hugged him close. "'Twas very thoughtful of you to do this for her," he said. "She's been beside herself for the past two days. I don't suppose you brought any more of those wonderful almond cakes *for me*?"

"No," Eloth replied for him. "But I did you one better. Clotilde has learned the recipe from Prunella and so will keep you in good supply. But have a care; eat too many and that flat belly of yours will go to pot."

"I will be too busy for that," Ardon sighed, hugging them both close. "When I find myself missing the sea too much, I shall comfort myself in knowing that what I do, I do for your glory. I will build a kingdom that shall have no rival in grandeur nor magnificence, save Ellioth itself."

"I'll miss our hunting trips and midnight raids," smiled Joshua, his voice cracking with emotion, "but take this in remembrance of me; it was made especially by Allred as was Llyonesse's locket."

"*The* Allred?" whistled Ardon, deeply impressed. "As in *the* master jeweler, Allred?"

"The very same," nodded Joshua, withdrawing a small black pouch from his cloak. He loosened the drawstring and emptied the contents into Ardon's palm. A golden ring rolled right-side up, glimmering softly. Ardon examined it closely, noting that it bore his device of office: the Flowering Tree. It was indeed the work of Allred, for no other craftsman in all the kingdom could fashion precious metal like he. "I thought you would have need of a signet ring in thy role as steward," Joshua explained.

Ardon slipped the ring carefully onto his index finger and smiled. "I will treasure it always," he said, kissing Joshua upon his damp cheek. This close it was easy to see the tears shining in his eyes.

"I have a gift, too!" piped up Llyonesse, suddenly remembering. She reached into her pocket and withdrew a folded handkerchief which she pressed into Joshua's hand. He unfolded it, finding a silky lock of her hair.

"Llyonesse!" he exclaimed, smiling happily. "I couldn't have asked for a nicer gift!" Llyonesse beamed with pleasure, happy she had pleased him so much.

Ardon lifted the stirrup cup toward his King. "Well, it is time, father."

Eloth took the cup, drank from it, then drew Ardon close in a fatherly hug. "Go forth with my blessing, my son,"[9] he replied. "May the wind be at thy back and the stars light thy way!"

"Ephlal shall be our light by day and beacon by night!"[10] Ardon replied. "Until we meet again!"

They exchanged a long last embrace then disembarked from the ship. With heavy hearts they watched the mooring lines loosed and sails unfurl, billowing full with wind. Eloth, Joshua, and their people watched from the dock, waving good-bye as the *Eden Mist* slowly negotiated her way out to sea with the rest of the fleet following gracefully in her wake, waving farewell until the ship was no more than a speck upon the horizon.

Chapter Two

The week following Ardon's departure, Joshua reported to Sir Luther, the Captain of Eloth's royal academy, to commence his training as a squire-at-arms.[11] Sir Luther was the master seraphim, senior in years to all of Eloth's other knights, a battle-scarred old war-horse who had retired twenty years ago to train his lessers in the fine art of war. He was gruff and intimidating, yet even-handed and there was not a knight alive in all the kingdom who did not harbor hero-worship for him.

Joshua was so excited it was all he could do to sleep the night before. Well before the sun was up, he was dressed and packed. He laid aside his opulent clothes and instead donned the simple tunic and woolen hose characteristic of a squire's dress, carrying another change of like garments down to the dormitory where they were housed. Even at this early hour there was already a great deal of activity for the squires routinely rose with the sun and were busily occupied with their daily responsibilities of grooming horses, running errands, and assisting knights in their toilet. Even the legendary Sir Penloth, the youngest knight ever to attain the rank of captain, had once done so, serving as Sir Luther's personal squire for over three years. The seraphim were the highest order of knights in Eloth's service, earning their position only after many years of dedicated service and arduous training. Only the finest acolytes were selected from the academy for this particular honor and were trained harder than the ordinary rank and file. Many years would sometimes go by without suitable candidates even though it was the aspiration of all the young men to achieve this privilege. Even if those who qualified were unable to successfully complete the seraphidic training, the nomination alone was considered the greatest of honors, second only to actually becoming a seraphim. Like his older brother, Penloth, Penlorian Estaban was showing immense promise in this regard and there was already talk that he would follow in his brother's footsteps. Penloth could not have been prouder for he had almost single-handedly raised his younger brother alone since their parent's untimely death when they were young. Though the brothers were very close in appearance and manner, Penloth excelled at arms while Penlorian was more adept at intellectual pursuits. He currently served as squire to Sir Gilbert, Captain of the King's Horse, but could just as easily have been a scribe, bard, or court solicitor. For years the betting men of Ellioth wagered good sums of money on whether Penlorian would choose to apprentice either under Sir Luther or Gillian, the King's Bard, but earlier that week Penlorian, whose sense of duty to his brother outweighed his own personal preferences, had finally made his decision. He would seek the office of seraphim. The news had Penloth strutting about like a peacock, issuing loud boasts of how Penlorian had done their name proud, and basically making a general nuisance of himself with his gloating.

Sir Luther led Joshua into a large common room and pointed toward one empty pallet in a long hallway full of them. "This shall be thy bed for the next three years," he said as Joshua looked it over with a small measure of dismay. His new "bed" consisted of a straw mattress, one blanket and no pillow; a great contrast to his luxuriant featherbed and pillows of eiderdown and soft, woolen blankets.

Sir Luther cleared his throat brusquely. "The king did inform me ye wish to be treated like the other lads," he stated, cocking a bushy eyebrow at him as if taking measure of his mettle.

"Yes, Sir Luther, exactly the same," replied Joshua resolutely. He never wanted it said that he had been molly-coddled through his training or given a "pass" because of his privileged position.

"Good," Sir Luther grunted in approval. "You will rise with the sun, make thy bed and report to thy assigned knight each day before breakfast. Your duties are to assist him in his toilet, serve him all his meals, bear and maintain his arms, groom and feed his horse and follow all orders without question. As far as meals go, the seraphim are served first after the King, then courtiers, and yourselves last of all, after *all* the crockery is cleared. After that, he will learn you in the art of chivalry, weapons and battle tactics."

"Yes, Sir Luther."

"Now, I have assigned you to ... " Sir Luther paused looking over a short list, then drew a line through one name and wrote in another, a smile twisting at his mouth. "Sirrrrrrrrr ... *Penloth.* Yes—Sir Penloth." *A perfect match; the good captain had been entirely too obnoxious lately and wanted taking down a notch or two in his estimation and the prince was just the person to do it!* He only wished he could be in the chamber to see Penloth's face when he found out who his squire would be for the next three years! "Now, squire, do you understand all that I have told thee?"

"Yes, Sir Luther," replied Joshua, wondering why the old knight suddenly seemed so pleased with himself.

"That is well. Now put your things away in that trunk and report to Sir Penloth immediately."

"Yes, Sir Luther," Joshua replied, still puzzled.

"Good! Dismissed," nodded Sir Luther, marching off. There was a moment's pause and then with the feeling that he was being watched, Joshua glanced about and noticed a small knot of boys staring at him; one of whom he immediately recognized.

Joshua smiled at him. "Hullo, Penlorian!" he said, reaching out his hand in a friendly manner toward the older boy. "It's seems we shall be bunkmates for a while."

"Yes, mi'lord," Penlorian replied with a grin. "Has Sir Luther really assigned you to my brother? He assigned Morgan DuPree to him only last month, but I'm sure Morgan will be greatly relieved. He's had horrible stomach cramps since his first day with my brother."

"Really?" replied Joshua, eyebrows on the rise.

"Penloth has a heart of gold as you and I well know, but he can be a fearsome taskmaster," replied Penlorian.

"Aye!" agreed another boy, joining their conversation. "He's been through five squires in just the past year; more than all the other knights."

"I overheard Sir Luther say he was becoming very annoyed with him and that he was going to teach him a lesson!" added another boy.

"I've never been anyone's *'lesson'* before," grinned Joshua, now understanding why Sir Luther had behaved so strangely.

"Penloth isn't cruel," Penlorian said in his brother's defense. "It's just that he doesn't believe in mollycoddling. If the truth be told, he's just following in Sir Luther's footsteps whom I'm told was an absolute beast to him for two out of his three years. The two squires who managed to serve out their full three years with Penloth worship the ground he stomps on!"

"Who are you assigned to?" asked Joshua, wadding up his bundle of clothes into a large roll and stuffing them into his trunk.

"Sir Gilbert," replied Penlorian. "He—"

"*What is this, what is this?*" interrupted a gruff bellow as Sir Luther marched back into view, eyebrows bristling. "*All of you! Stop lollygagging about and attend to thy duties!*"

Joshua slammed the trunk shut and scampered off, casting a parting grin in Penlorian's direction. "See you later!" he called and disappeared round a corner. After a long, breathless climb, he arrived at Penloth's chambers above the gatehouse in the guard tower. In the center of the heavy oak door was his coat of arms fashioned in silver and azure, bearing two swords crossed over the head of a rampant unicorn. Joshua knocked twice per custom and waited. When he got no response, he quietly entered the room and found Sir Penloth standing bare chested before a copper mirror trimming his brown beard and famous mustache and grumbling under his breath. His bare feet were immersed in a shallow pool of soapy water which had evidently sloshed out of the basin before him.

"Morgan! What took you so bloody long?" Penloth roared, assuming it was his original squire when he heard the door open. "Here..." he gestured at the basin, "dump this water into the privy! *And have a care you don't spill any on the floor like yestermorn!*"

Joshua raised an eyebrow at this last but decided to say nothing about the flagstones which were already swimming. Sir Penloth finished his trimming and stepped away to put on his tunic, still unaware that it was Joshua who had come to serve him. Joshua carefully lifted the surging bowl in both arms, walked cautiously toward the privy, and dumped the water out. He then gathered up the dirty linen strewn about the chamber and mopped up the floor with them deciding he would take the sodden clothes down to the laundress later.

"*Morgan!*" roared Penloth again, his voice muffled. "Help me with this infernal jerkin! C'mon, lad, I can't breathe!"

Joshua hurried forward, trying not to laugh aloud at the sight of the Captain of the Guard with the crown of his head peeking out of the neck opening and his arms stuck halfway through the sleeves. The tunic was at least two sizes too small for him, but pointing it out would only have been rude. He took a firm grip about the waist and vigorously worked the tunic down until it was finally below Penloth's ears. Quite suddenly, they were eye to eye upon which Penloth instantly paled. Joshua grinned at him. Penloth's mouth dropped open, his eyes went as wide as saucers and he almost dropped onto one knee. "Er...uh...th-thank you... my lord," he stammered, thoroughly disconcerted.

What in bloody red blazes was the prince doing in his bed chamber?

"Sir Luther has assigned me to you as thy squire," Joshua volunteered, fascinated at how swiftly Penloth's complexion went from beet red to pasty white and then to slightly green all in a span of a few seconds.

"M-my squire?" he rasped, finally finding his voice. "Surely you je- … er … I mean … uh … well … I am certainly honored to have been chosen as thy instructor, mi'lord."

"As am I, *mi'lord*," responded Joshua, bowing low so Penloth couldn't see him smirking. He did, however, peek up through his lashes just in time to catch his mustache twitch. Joshua straightened. "But isn't it rather improper to address me as *"mi'lord."* Is not "squire or Joshua" more suitable whilst I remain in thy service?"

Sir Penloth winced. "Of course," he agreed, unable to actually say the words but taking it as an order. He stood in awkward silence for a moment, staring at Joshua as though awaiting orders himself. He tugged at the clasp about his throat uncomfortably. "Shall I finish dressing and go to meat?" he finally inquired.

Joshua managed to "straight-face" his response. "As you wish, *my lord*."

Penloth visibly cringed every time Joshua addressed him so and sheepishly allowed him to finish helping him on with his boots and spurs. Joshua worked quietly and found it very difficult to believe that Penloth was really the gruff bear the other squires described him as, but then—he didn't suppose the poor knight had ever had his boots put on by royalty before. When he was fully dressed, Joshua walked docilely behind him as they negotiated down the winding stair toward the great hall. They were joined in the main passageway by two of Penloth's comrades, Sir Gilbert (escorted by Penlorian), and Sir Balin, now escorted by Morgan DuPree whose face was wreathed in happy smiles. Sir Gilbert and Balin's eyebrows ascended high into their respective hairlines upon observing Joshua in the role of squire, but Penloth's warning glance instantly quelled any verbal observations they might have wanted to make on the subject. They entered the great hall in tense silence, seating themselves at the high table; their squires taking up positions behind them.

The great hall was of enormous proportions, with high vaulted ceilings supported by intricately carved columns of white marble several feet in diameter and standing sixty meters high. A great stone hearth, (large enough to accommodate five mounted horsemen standing end-to-end), was at one end of the hall and above it hung an enormous pennant of scarlet silk and cloth of gold emblazoned with Eloth's coat-of-arms. Ancient tapestries hung upon the other walls, depicting events out of Ellioth's past, all woven in rich colors of russet, burgundy, deep green, yellow, black, white, and brown wool. Opposite the hearth was a dais upon which stood a long table of polished chestnut richly inlaid with mother of pearl. Another scarlet and gold banner was draped across the front. It was here where Eloth and his seraphim were seated, six to his right: Sir Perceivel, Sir Eric, Sir Bors, Sir Matthew, Sir Richard, and Sir Penloth, (looking genuinely uncomfortable), and six to his left: Sir Gilbert, Sir Vincent, Sir Falstaff, Sir Morgan, Sir Thomas, and last of all, Sir Luther (who was looking obscenely pleased with himself). Sir Penloth leaned forward, hoping Sir Luther would glance in his direction so he could give him a filthy look, but the brigand was feigning innocence and refused to look his way. Only the slightest twitching of his mouth betrayed the fact that he knew that Penloth was on to his "little joke."

The hall quickly filled with other courtiers taking their seats, waiting for the squires to return from the kitchens with steaming bowls of porridge, fresh loaves, honeycomb, bacon, fruit, pitchers of cream, an assortment of cheeses and cool, white mead.

Sweat trickled down Joshua's face as he hurried back and forth carrying empty crockery back to the kitchens, returning again and again with refilled platters. One by one as he waited on each in turn, he began to notice a distinct improvement in the table manners of those he served personally the moment they recognized him. They began using their napkins, practically tripped over their tongues to say *please* and *thank you* and even covered their mouths to belch. After an hour, Joshua's hunger pangs and the smell of the food were making his stomach grumble loudly, surprising more than a few guilt-ridden looks from those around him. Joshua was grateful that Sir Penloth chose to ignore it, unaware that the good captain was too preoccupied with his own "internal" problems. The battle-hardened knight sat quietly, trying not to grimace as his stomach cramped and seized with pain, feeling as though he had just swallowed a hot glede. He glanced down at his plate in dismay for despite the rich fare of Eloth's board, he had taken only a chunk of plain bread and wine to sop it in, hoping it would soothe his protesting bowels. He peered cautiously to his left and caught Sir Luther staring at him, the very picture of engrossed innocence.

"Food not to your liking, eh, Penloth?" he queried, popping a spicy sausage whole into his mouth with exaggerated relish.

Penloth grimaced. *"A pox on you!"* he seethed, gritting his teeth in agony. He tore off a hunk of bread and turned away, making a concentrated effort to ignore Sir Luther's amused stares throughout the remainder of his dismal meal. When the last platter had been scraped clean and tables wiped down, the squires collapsed in exhaustion, almost too tired to eat the gruel and mutton placed before them.

"Eat hearty, my lads!" ordered Sir Luther, passing through their ranks. "You'll get little else till supper and it's going to be a long, hard day."

With this warning in their ears, they quickly downed their food and returned their empty trenchers to the kitchens before joining the senior knights in the tiltyard. Sir Penloth was waiting for Joshua in the armory, drinking deeply from a cup that contained buttermilk. Together they selected gear to fit Joshua's stature and passed the first part of the day on how to maneuver in the heavy plating. Joshua struggled to move about in the thirty pound steel shell, wondering silently if the sweat pouring down him could rust him shut. At mid-morning he was afforded a brief rest and allowed to remove the armor so he could lie upon his back in the fragrant grass and munch apples with the other squires. The remainder of the day was comprised of an education about the various forms of weaponry used in battle, the differences between sword, rapier, saber, and cutlass, the techniques used for each and a discussion of the various tactics used in armed conflict. Joshua's untried muscles strained to lift the heavy weapons one after another, knowing that he must ignore the pain and learn discipline. He found it easy enough to wield the rapier, saber and cutlass, but when it came time to lift the heavy broadsword, he could not manage it, not even when using both arms.

"Don't be discouraged, Joshua," said Penloth, making it whistle effortlessly through the air with one arm as though it were a wooden stick. "It took me many years before I could so much as lift the thing; time, growth, and hard training will take care of today's lack!"

"I hope so!" replied Joshua, watching him with genuine awe. They continued to practice for the remainder of that day until just before sundown.

"You've done a fine job today, Joshua," said Sir Penloth at day's end, regarding his student with fresh respect and a good degree of sympathy. Not once had Joshua complained or whined about any of his duties or training, despite how hard Penloth had been on him. And once he had forced himself to overlook the fact that he was the crown prince, he had been harder on him than any other boy he had ever trained; just infinitely more polite about it. "Go see Sir Luther about getting some liniment on your arms and massage them well or they'll be useless by tomorrow."

"Yes, Sir Penloth," replied Joshua, turning to go.

"Oh, and one more thing, Joshua," said Sir Penloth, placing a covered basket into his weary arms. "Give this to Sir Luther when you see him—he'll understand precisely what it's for."

"Yes, my lord," Joshua agreed, too tired to inquire as to the contents. He returned to the dormitory and found Sir Luther in his study, dictating a report to a scribe. Joshua waited silently to be noticed, shifting from one tired leg to the other, staring numbly at the feathered quill dipping in and out of the ink pot and then as it scribbled on the parchment.

Sir Luther paused in his dictation. "Yes, what is it, squire?"

"Sir, Sir Penloth sent me to you for liniment," Joshua explained, shifting the basket in his aching arms.

"Ahhh yes," sighed Sir Luther, reaching up to a shelf which held several clay vessels of ointment. "Here it is. Take it with you; you'll be needing it until your muscles harden." He handed it to Joshua.

"Your pardon, Sir Luther, but Sir Penloth also bade me give you this basket."

"Eh?" Sir Luther grunted, instantly suspicious.

Not wanting to risk exposing whatever surprise Penloth had in store for him, Joshua thrust it into his hands. "With thy permission!" he bowed hastily and slammed the door behind him. He backed off a safe distance and watched in breathless anticipation, wondering what would happen next. Penloth had been moody all day, but had actually seemed gleeful when handing him the basket. Knowing Penloth's wicked sense of humor, there had to be a deuce of a surprise in store for Sir Luther. He wasn't disappointed.

The quiet of the afternoon was suddenly disrupted by loud bellows immediately followed by a terrible yowling and hissing and the crash of furniture. The bedlam grew in intensity, drawing a knot of curious squires together to see what was going on. Suddenly, the door to Sir Luther's chamber opened with a bang and a large, orange tabby literally flew out, hissing and spitting as though she had been launched by a catapult. The squires jumped back in alarm, too amazed and terrified to dare laugh. Sir Luther charged out like an enraged bull. His face red as a pomegranate, his eyes puffy and almost swollen shut; his nose running; cheeks scored with claw marks and a large ink stain spreading throughout the lap area of his tunic. Pieces of parchment were stuck to the soles of his jackboots. It took every ounce of discipline Joshua possessed not to dissolve into laughter at first sight, but as Sir Luther stared daggers at him, trying to ascertain his degree of personal culpability, Joshua somehow managed to keep a straight face. It didn't work. Sir Luther marched forward and thrust his beet-red face into his.

"The next time Sir Penloth gives you anything to pass on to me, I suggest you first check the contents to make sure it isn't a cat!" he roared. Without waiting for a response, he whirled about, strode to his chamber, slammed the door shut and sneezed almost loud enough to knock it off its hinges.

"I didn't know Sir Luther hated cats," Joshua whispered in an aside to Penlorian.

"He doesn't. He's just deathly allergic to them," Penlorian replied. "He'll most likely be bedridden for days."

"Oh," Joshua grinned, sorry that Penloth had not been present to enjoy his revenge; Sir Luther had more than received his comeuppance.

The following day, Penloth was practically hemorrhaging with curiosity. Joshua could feel his eyes upon him throughout the day as he trained, wondering when the Captain would finally break down and ask him what had happened. In all good conscience he didn't feel at liberty to volunteer the information; that would have made him a willing accomplice ... besides that, he was discovering a perverse form of pleasure in not indulging Penloth's desire for information. As the day waxed and waned (with nary a word or look of encouragement forthcoming from him) what little patience Sir Penloth did possess swiftly evaporated. He became surly, brooding, and fell to muttering under his breath. Joshua was currying his stallion in the paddock when he heard Penloth approach from behind and clear his throat.

"My lord—you require something?" asked Joshua brightly, turning around and bowing low. He watched in absorbed fascination as Sir Penloth's newly acquired resolve visibly wilted before his eyes.

"Er ... no ... well ... yes, in fact, Joshua. ... uh, how did you sleep last night?" Penloth ventured.

"Very well, thank you," Joshua smiled.

Sir Penloth stared at Joshua in mounting frustration, unable to believe that he wasn't able to interpret his subtle hints. Perhaps a more direct line of questioning would untie his tongue ... "Anything unseemly occur yesterday?" he pressed.

Joshua stared at him poker-faced, the picture of ignorance. "No, Sir Penloth, should it have?"

Penloth drooped. "No ..." he finally responded, looking

thoroughly disappointed. He had been sure that he had selected the most ornery tom-cat in the castle; a nasty feline guaranteed to keep Sir Luther smarting for at least a week. "You did deliver the basket to Sir Luther yestereve, did you not?"

"Of course!" responded Joshua. He smiled apologetically. "If that's all, sir, I should like to finish here then return to the dormitory."

"Yes, yes, go on, off with you! I'll finish Graymane!" Sir Penloth growled, snatching away the currycomb in exasperation and waving him off.

"As you wish, *mi'lord*," Joshua replied, hardly noticing Penloth's now customary cringe at his use of the word. As he walked away he began to reconsider his silence. Perhaps he was being too hard on poor Penloth. What pleasure could he possibly take in his prank if he knew nothing of its success? None of the other squires would dare tell him for fear of Sir Luther, but he had no such worries. Royalty, after all, did have its privileges. Upon arriving in his quarters, Joshua knelt before his trunk and looked both ways before opening the lid. Nestled within his clean tunics lay the orange tabby. It gazed up at him with lazy yellow eyes and yowled in greeting.

"Hullo, puss," whispered Joshua, casting another wary glance about to make sure that Sir Luther was nowhere in sight. He scratched the tabby behind the ears to calm it, then laid the animal upon his lap. After scribbling a rather cryptic message, he secured it to a leather thong about its neck and tucked it within his jerkin against his chest, wincing as it meowed in protest. "*Sssh!*" he hissed. Still unobserved, he climbed up to Sir Penloth's chamber, opened the door just a crack and deposited the cat inside with a sigh of relief. Feeling better for having thus made restitution, Joshua returned to the dormitory, massaged his sore arms with liniment, and fell instantly asleep.

Sir Penloth retired to his chambers somewhat later, after making sure he got thoroughly inebriated at the local inn on the grounds that if he could not satisfy his curiosity, he'd have to drown it. With faltering steps, he managed the last few stairs up to his chamber and thrust open the door with a loud *bang!* He was greeted by a terrifying yowl then a blur of orange fur. He fell back with a crash and curse onto his backside.

"*Yeeeooowww!*" greeted the tabby, alighting on his chest and kneading its claws into his leather tunic with feline ecstasy. Something bumped against Penloth's nose but it took him quite a few moments before he could focus on the note. As he fumbled to untie it, the cat rubbed its face against his mustache, purring loudly with pleasure. He unfolded the small parchment and pushed the furry orange head out of the way so he could read.

> "*Hell hath no fury like a woman scorned…*
> *Sir Luther is nursing his pride as well as his wounds!*"

Sir Penloth grinned lopsidedly; the brief message conveying clearly what he had desperately longed to know. He could grill Joshua on the details tomorrow, but for now it was sufficient to know that his prank had been a success. He heaved a sigh of pleasure then fell at once into a drunken slumber upon the floor. The tabby stared for a moment, then curled upon his stomach and also fell asleep.

Days turned into weeks, then months and seasons. Joshua's muscles ceased to pain him. With much practice and hard work, he learned to master each new skill, his training becoming progressively harder and more difficult. His once lanky body continued to grow, but it also began to fill out with muscle, making the armor, which had once seemed so unbearably heavy, easier to bear. Despite his busy days and exhausted nights, Joshua thought often about Ardon and Llyonesse and wondered when word would come from Shiloh of their doings.

Chapter Three

It had been two years since Eloth's people had come to the land which they had named Shiloh. During that time they had planted crops, orchards, and vineyards, some of which were already ripening for the first harvest. The outer wall and foundation of the castle had been laid and the gatehouse, drawbridge, and docks were under construction.

The air was filled daily with the sound of hammering, sawing, and beating of anvils as numerous craftsmen plied their trade into creating a working village out of the wilderness. The blacksmiths were busy filling orders, repairing worn and broken tools and farm implements, fashioning horseshoes, harnesses, and taking dents out of cooking pots. Not only were the carpenters, stonewrights, and blacksmith's busy, the various tanners, bakers, midwives, coopers, butchers, candlemakers, and other craftsmen also found themselves occupied from dawn to dusk just to keep up with the demand for their skills and products. Having had little contact with anyone other than themselves since their arrival, it was not surprising that they would greet newcomers from out of the wild with great enthusiasm and curiosity.

It was late afternoon when the faint cloud of dust appeared upon the horizon, causing men and women alike to straighten from their labors to watch the group of bedraggled strangers approach their village either on foot or upon emaciated horses. Children stopped their play and stared while field hands and villagers alike left their tasks to offer them food and water with words of greeting. By the time the band had cleared the last field, their arms were laden with loaves of bread, apples, dried meat, and skins of new wine. Word of their arrival was quickly dispatched to Ardon as they paused in the village square to water their horses at the communal well.

"Hail and well met," Ardon greeted them, exiting out of a nearby cottage.

The travelers turned about and gazed at him. Despite the heat of the summer day, they kept their faces shrouded within their tattered hoods which made it difficult to see their features. One of them nodded in greeting.

"Hail," he replied, his voice hardly more than a raspy whisper.

Ardon motioned toward the inn with a gesture of welcome. "You are welcome here. From whence come thee?"

"From the desolate wilderness out yonder,"[12] came the answer, the man's finger pointing east, over the distant hills.

"Well, then, you must all be hungry and thirsty. If you will follow me, I will see that you are given food and drink and thy steeds tended to."

The strangers hesitated for a moment, but reluctantly allowed the villagers to take charge of their tired beasts, following Ardon into the cool interior of a large, waddle & daub structure which turned out to be the common room of an inn. A large round hearth was in the center surrounded by tables and chairs with a long wooden bar which stood at the opposite end. At the top of a flight of stairs was the loft where guest rooms were currently under construction. They accepted the stools offered them and sat down, obviously uncomfortable. Ardon began filling wooden cups with mead from a nearby pitcher and handing them out. "What brings you to our village?" he asked politely.

They gulped down the sweet liquid as only the very thirsty could and wiped their mouths on their sleeves, whispering amongst themselves as if trying to decide who would be their spokesman. Finally, one of them stood up and bowed his head in respect.

"We are wanderers, my lord, driven by drought and hunger into the wilderness. We have suffered much hardship for many years and have been seeking a kinder land in which to dwell."

"Where are thy womenfolk and children?" asked Ardon. "Are there none among you?"

"We lost most of our womenfolk and children to wolves while on a vain hunt for food," the man replied softly. "The rest were taken by famine or disease."

Ardon regarded them in silence, his heart moved with compassion. "I am sorry," he apologized, feeling suddenly very awkward. "You must all be very weary and heartsore; I will have lodgings prepared where you may rest and heal for a time."

"Thank you," replied the stranger. "Thou art kind and generous, lord, yet, if you will forgive my presumptuousness, I would beg a greater boon of thee than just a few days of your hospitality."

"What is it?" responded Ardon, a peculiar reluctance coming over him.

"My men are weary unto death of our long, fruitless travel and would very much like to dwell among such people as thine for the remainder of our days. If thou art willing, Lord, receive us into thy kingdom, as bondslaves if necessary. We will serve thee gladly!"

"I am not the king that I might grant this request," replied Ardon, "but I have been given authority over Shiloh by him and it is to Eloth that you shall have to present thy petition. In the meantime, however, I will grant thy people leave to dwell with us for as long as you observe our laws. But this favor shall be withdrawn if you respect them not. When the king comes, he will render final judgment on whether to revoke or renew thy citizenship in our kingdom. Fear not, if you prove faithful, there will be naught to fear. Our lord is generous and noble in heart and welcomes all who come in friendship. Are these terms agreeable?"

"They are," replied the traveler without consulting his comrades, which Ardon thought queer. "And whatsoever be our fate, my people and I shall forever remain in thy debt. Only, I pray you, good sir, what is thy name and that of thy king that we might lift our cups to him in thanksgiving?"

"My lord is Eloth, King of Ellioth and Joshua, his son, is ruler of this kingdom of Shiloh. I am Ardon Tolham, steward to the crown and foster brother of the prince. And thy name, sir? What shall I call thee since we are to be countrymen for a time?"

Baron Lucius of Northumberland, murderer and banished traitor to the crown lifted his face to Ardon and drew back his hood.

"Call me *Lucan*," he answered with a smile.

Had Ardon not been so removed from Ellioth's recent political affairs, he might have recognized the former Baron but since the age of eighteen, Ardon had mostly been out to sea and remembered little of the somber man who had once governed Eloth's household. Also Lucius had grown very different in appearance from his days in Ellioth. His once short-cropped black hair hung in matted tangles to his shoulders and where before his face had been pale and clean-shaven it was now sunburnt, gaunt, pitted from years of wandering and overgrown with very black, scraggly whiskers flecked with gray. Only his piercing black eyes were unchanged, glittering with the same hatred as before, but he was very careful to keep them averted.

Lucius closed the door to their private cottage after Ardon left and smiled triumphantly at his men. "Did I not tell you they were of Ellioth?" he hissed, careful not to be overheard. He closed his eyes, trembling with excitement. "After months of wasting away in this forsaken wilderness, fate has smiled upon us and brought me the means by which to take revenge against Eloth and his snot-nosed brat!" He hugged himself with ferocious ecstasy. "Only a fool like Ardon would trust a stranger so easily and open the door of the sheepfold wide to the ravening wolf," he said, removing his filthy cloak and flinging it with revulsion onto the floor.

"Aye!" agreed his men, laughing and rubbing their hands together. "This place is easy pickings! Did you see those country wenches along the road, handing us loaves and cheese as pretty as you please?"

"I wish that hadn't been all they'd given us!" snorted another.

"Aye! Tis a long time since I had a woman! Not since our last raid and boy did the old crone fight!" guffawed Aldwin. There was a general round of raucous laughter as they remembered with relish one of their recent raids upon the hapless inhabitants in the land.

"There will be no raiding nor pillaging until I give the word!" Lucius warned them sternly. "We shall all become respectable citizens and endear ourselves in every way possible; I will not have my revenge thwarted because we were ousted for ill behavior before the time!"

"Revenge! What kind of revenge has us hoeing Eloth's fields and tending his sheep?" spat Borgreth in disgust.

"Aye!" agreed Golbreth. "Better if we slit their throats while they sleep and plunder the village before they discover who we are!" he growled, voicing the sentiments of the others.

Lucius drew himself up, his voice thick with anger. "You dare challenge me after all I have brought us through? Banishment! Shipwreck! Endless wandering and *hunger*! Had I listened to thee, we would not be in this cottage drinking cool mead and freshly baked bread!" he snarled, shaking a hunk of it in his fist for emphasis. "Burn, rape, and pillage! Is that all you are capable of? The thrill of it would last but a day and then vanish with the smoke! That is paltry compared to the revenge I wish to visit upon Eloth! I have waited *years* for this very opportunity, never daring to hope it could ever come to pass. I want Him to suffer a thousand deaths before I allow him the blissful forgetfulness of death!"

"What *is* your plan then?" demanded Borgreth.

"I am still thinking on it!" Lucius hissed. "I cannot destroy Shiloh nor Eloth whilst Ardon bears that cursed sword but rest assured: In the end I will not rest until I have destroyed all that he loves!"

"And what, pray tell, could *you* possibly do to cause *him* such agony?" guffawed Golbreth, folding his arms across his chest incredulously. Had he not been one of Lucius' favorites, he surely would have been smitten for such insolence.

"It is not what I shall do to him, but rather what I will compel others to do," replied Lucius with a curl of his lip. "The cruelest cut is dealt by those whom thou lovest best. For Eloth there could be no greater agony than to be betrayed by those whom he loves most!"[13]

"That's a tall order, even for you," interjected Borgreth.

Scheldrake snorted at Lucius in disbelief. "Do you speak of Eloth's people? You know as well as I that should any rise against him, he would be forced by his own law to execute them!"

"Yes," hissed Lucius, his lips curling into a smile. "Is it not delicious? The maddening, absolute justice of Eloth is precisely the blade I shall use to drive my revenge deep into his heart!"[14]

Ardon entered the darkened bedchamber quietly and sat by his wife's bedside, taking her clammy hand into his own, kissing it. "How fares my love today? Any better?" he asked with deep concern.

"Mummy is very sick," Llyonesse explained, her blue eyes round with sympathy.

"Yes, I know, sweeting," he said, lifting his daughter into his arms, noticing the milking pail close to his wife's bed.

"I feel worse," Zarabeth managed with a weak smile in his

direction. "But I am happier for knowing the reason. Husband, I have good tidings."

"Say only that you will soon be up from your sickbed, wife, and I shall be content," said Ardon.

"Nay, I cannot for the midwife says I am to lie in for at least another seven moons."

"Seven moons! The midwife?" repeated Ardon, vacantly.

Zarabeth removed the handkerchief just long enough to give him another weak smile. "I am with child," she explained. "Perhaps we'll finally have that son!"

Ardon's mouth dropped open in mingled shock and joy. "A son?" He had long wanted a son to carry on his family name.

Zarabeth's smile widened further. "Clotilde says if all goes well, the babe will be born at springtide."

Ardon's smile was beatific and bursting with pride. "We must have a great celebration! A feast with Clotilde's famous roast mutton and some almond cakes—"

"Ardooooon!" moaned Zarabeth weakly. "Please, please ... don't mention another word about food!"

Ardon instantly went red with shame, watching his wife recover her mouth with the handkerchief.

"My apologies," he said, eyeing her nervously as she pulled the milking pail closer. "I shall summon Clotilde immediately." With Llyonesse in tow, he beat a hasty retreat through the door.

Ardon lifted his head and peered groggily about the darkened bedchamber, momentarily disoriented then cursed softly. He had fallen asleep again in the middle of his accounting. He rose wearily from the chair, stretching his arms over and backwards to ease his stiffened muscles. Judging from the profound silence, it must be very late. Zarabeth was going to be powerfully angry if she found out that he had again fallen asleep with a lit candle. But what could he do? He had spent the morning surveying the fields, then helping a desperate farmer to gather in his hay before a freak shower could ruin it, and then the afternoon had been used up setting a heavy capstone into place. The remainder of the day he was occupied in making decisions on the digging of several cisterns. It was a rare day when he worked less than eighteen hours and it was beginning to tell on him. Even long after the sun had set, he labored far into the night preparing for the following day's activities, reviewing the plans for the palace and recording the day's accomplishments in his journal so he would not have to write from memory when the next report was due. More than anything he despised the tedious paperwork and political negotiating to get people to do what was required. He missed the freedom of the sea, the absolute autonomy of being a sea captain, the ocean breeze on his face, billowing silken sails, play of dolphins, and the cry of gulls. He looked down at the table and shook his head at the wax splatters on the parchment. The candle had burned down to the quick and once again he had been fortunate that his hair had not caught on fire when it had dropped onto the table in exhaustion. One of these days, his luck was going to run out and Zarabeth would wake up to either find all his hair singed off or he burnt to a crisp!

He removed his clothes slowly, his muscles aching from the day's labor and fell onto the cot to pass the few remaining hours of night in greater comfort. "I must start delegating more of my responsibilities ... " he murmured wearily to himself, then fell asleep again before he could remember to remove his boots.

"Ardon! *Ardon!*"

"Yes ... wha ... I'm sorry, wife, did you say something to me?" Ardon blinked, snapping his head up in sudden alarm.

Zarabeth glared at him in complete exasperation from her bed.

"Ardon, this must stop! You are working thyself to death! If you don't find someone to lighten thy load, our children will be fatherless!"

"I'm sorry, Zarabeth. It's just that—"

"—*you have great difficulty trusting someone else's judgment!*" Zarabeth finished for him. "*Or shoving thy work off onto others!* I've heard all thy excuses! Cannot Ciril or Stephen take more on? Surely you trust them sufficiently!"

"They already have as much work as they can handle," Ardon responded wearily, plucking bread and cheese off a plate and stuffing them into his pockets. At this, his wife's eyes grew wide, her mouth falling open in anger. Ardon knew that look.

"You will not even sit to breakfast with us after laboring half the night away?" she accused.

"There is much to be done today and I wish to get an early start; I can eat whilst I work..."

"*Enough!*" Zarabeth cried, flinging a pitcher of mead onto the floor where it burst asunder. Liquid splattered in all directions. "I will not allow this to continue a moment longer! You are going to orphan our children if you refuse to change thy ways. You *must* find someone to help—"

She was interrupted by a knock upon the door. Glad for the diversion, Ardon leapt to open it and found Lucan standing on the other side, his fist still raised in mid-knock.

"I beg your pardon, my lord, I hope I am not interrupting—" he stammered, looking rather ill-at-ease. Little wonder with Zarabeth glaring at him the way she was.

"No, No, No! *Not in the least!* I was just on my way out; we can talk on the way!" exclaimed Ardon, hastily exiting and hauling Lucius with him. Zarabeth stared in dumbfounded anger as they disappeared through the threshold then flung her own platter against the door, screaming aloud in frustrated rage.

As he half ran, half marched down the winding path, Lucius felt Ardon's arm go about his shoulders in a friendly manner. "You have the most remarkable timing," he said. "Another minute and I fear my lovely wife would have boxed my ears!"

"I hope that I was not the cause of thy strife, my lord," said Lucius, practically running in order to keep up with him.

"No, no, not at all! In fact, you saved me from another lecture on how I am neglecting my health. Zarabeth is right of course and concerned as any good wife would be, but what is a man to do? All my men are working as hard as they can; how can I ask them to do more while I go home to sleep or dandle my daughter upon my knee?"

"Forgive me, lord, but am I to understand that the reason for this morning's … er … scene is because thou art laboring too greatly?"

"Aye," confirmed Ardon. "And it won't be the last incident either! One of these days she's going to make good on her threat to slip laudanum in my mead and force me into getting a proper night's rest."

It was the opportunity he had been waiting for. Lucius laid his hand upon Ardon's shoulder and pulled him to a halt. "I believe then, that I, or rather we, can be of assistance to you, my lord. My people and I are fully recovered and quite ready to labor in thy behalf in this great effort. Speaking for myself and my men, we have all been feeling the effects of too much energy and time on our hands and nothing to do. It was for this reason that I sought thee out this morn. Will you not allow us to work and in some small way repay this debt of kindness we owe thee?"

Ardon stared at Lucius in amazement, unable to believe his sudden good fortune. He wished now that he had allowed Lucan to speak his piece for the benefit of his wife; it would really have smoothed things over for him.

"Thy people have taken good care of us, my Lord. Our wounds and hurts have been fully healed, but we are able-bodied men and anxious for meaningful work. It would be a great honor to serve thee in any way thou deemest fit. I myself am quite well versed in managing large households and land holdings."

"By the king's beard," swore Ardon, a grin spreading across his face, "you will never know how happy you just made my wife! If you're up for it, we can begin today! I'll take you on all my rounds and familiarize you with what's going on. When you feel you know enough, I'll begin delegating some of my duties to you. Fair enough?"

Lucius smiled. "Indeed, my lord … Tis more than fair."

By the end of two months, Lucius felt as though a lifetime's worth of information and responsibility had been stuffed through his ears and into his head. It had been difficult to feign ignorance for he was already well-versed in all the duties of a steward. Despite Ardon's staggering responsibilities he somehow managed to remain civil and friendly to everyone. They worked side by side for days without number and Lucius played the part of an apt pupil, even making suggestions which Ardon always thought to be excellent ones. With great relief, Ardon began delegating his responsibilities to Lucius, little realizing how he was giving his enemy the very foothold he needed; yet his hours of labor never seemed to decrease. Ardon still returned home late from each day's work so utterly exhausted that it was all Zarabeth could do to see that he got some food into him before he collapsed upon his cot to catch a few hours sleep.

Often she would sit by his bedside, stroking his forehead and watching his face with deep sadness, longing to hear his voice and feel his arms about her, knowing she must sacrifice so he could take some rest. Were it not for their cheery daughter, Llyonesse, her days would have been even lonelier, but even Llyonesse could not fill the void that had been left by her husband. Zarabeth pined for his company and was nearly at her wit's end with boredom. Because of her pregnancy, custom dictated that she be made to lie-in for the duration with the cottage shutters closed at all times, keeping out both the light and fresh air. Her ankles were so swollen she was restricted to her bedchamber with naught to do but stitch, card wool, play whist, or gossip with her ladies.

A month later, they were talking and stitching when a knock sounded on the door. Clotilde rose, put down her hoop, and opened it to find a bouquet of wild flowers before her eyes. She looked up to see Ardon's servant, Lucan, smiling down at her.

"I have come to pay my respects to the lady, Zarabeth, and

bear her a gift from her husband," he said by way of explanation. Clotilde opened the door wider with a smile and stepped aside to let him in.

"My lady will be most pleased," she responded, staring at him curiously. Lucan the vagabond had changed much since he had first come to Shiloh. He had filled out quite a bit and his black whiskers were now trimmed and shiny. There was something strangely familiar about him but try as she might, she just couldn't figure out what it was. "My lady, you have a visitor," she announced, feeling sure the novelty would perk up Zarabeth's flagging spirits. Zarabeth leaned forward, anxiously wondering who it could be.

Lucius entered the dim chamber bearing the bouquet and a wrapped package. He bowed low in a gesture of respect. "My lady, please forgive the intrusion. Mi'lord Ardon asked if I might bear this bouquet of flowers he picked for thee with his apologies for not presenting them himself."

"Oh," sighed Zarabeth, greatly disappointed. She studied the package under Lucius' arm with sullen curiosity, wondering what was inside.

Noticing her gaze, Lucius placed it into her hands. "I did not wish to come empty-handed, knowing thou wouldst no doubt be disappointed so I brought thee a bolt of fine, white lawn and colored thread from the village merchants," he explained.

A chorus of "oooohhhhs and aaaahhhhs" arose as the ladies unwrapped the package and beheld the fine material, rubbing it between their fingers to feel the delicate weave. It was indeed excellent fabric and would make a fine cradle cap. Zarabeth turned and nodded to one of her ladies to bring forth a tray of refreshments from the sideboard. Eloise curtsied and presented a platter of pastries, spiced fruit, and pitcher of mead. With many a glance over her shoulder at their visitor, she began arranging the food on plates and passing them about.

"It was very kind of you to do this favor for my husband," Zarabeth said politely, her sadness unmistakable. "He is always so busy."

"But he speaks of nothing but thy beauty and graciousness the whole day long," returned Lucius, bringing a blush to Zarabeth's pale cheeks. "Were I so bold, I would counsel thy husband to spend more time with his wife and beautiful daughter and less under the blazing sun settling petty disputes," he said. Looking down, he found Llyonesse staring at him. He caught her chin in his fingers and tilted her head up to look her in the eyes. Llyonesse scowled at him. She did not like the look of the large dark man with the black whiskers and pale face which reminded her of a hawk. She glared at him then ran behind her mother's bed to put a greater distance between them.

Zarabeth was mortified at her rude behavior. "Llyonesse, is that any way to act? Apologize at once!" she snapped.

"No!" came the immediate response. Lucius's piercing black eyes bored into her with undisguised anger. "No!" she repeated louder, stubbornness changing to fear.

Zarabeth was at a complete loss. Llyonesse had never acted so rudely before; usually she was very sweet and friendly to everyone.

"It is of no mind, my lady. Please do not compel the child against her will," Lucius said, removing his malevolent gaze from Llyonesse. Though his voice was deceptively gentle, his eyes clearly showed his displeasure. "She will come to accept me in her own time." He sat down, accepting a tankard of mead with a smile, but as he drank, he continued casting dark glances at her over the rim. Llyonesse stood transfixed for some moments as if turned into stone then suddenly she began to tremble uncontrollably in terror.

"Clotilde?" groaned Zarabeth in exasperation, gesturing to her daughter.

"Come, poppet," grunted Clotilde in a scolding manner, reaching for Llyonesse. "You're much too old to behave like this!" Llyonesse hid her face in Clotilde's skirts, weeping louder and louder as if she had gone mad. Zarabeth felt like crawling under the bed. If lying in weren't bad enough, now her daughter was behaving like a crazed person! Clotilde scooped Llyonesse up into her arms and carried her bodily from the cottage. Even after the door closed behind them, they could still hear her shrieks.

"I can't apologize enough," Zarabeth said, shaking her head in distress. "I don't understand what came over the child; she is usually very friendly."

"Pray do not fret thyself over it, my lady," repeated Lucius, finishing off the pastry and downing the mead. "Now if thou wilt excuse me, I must return to my duties." He stood to his feet and bowed low.

Zarabeth wrung her hands, distressed that his visit had gone so badly and extended her hand in a conciliatory gesture. "Thank you very much for coming and for the gift," she said, meaning every word. "You will always be welcome here as far as I am concerned. I will have a very strong talk with our daughter this afternoon about her appalling lack of manners—"

"Until our next visit, then, milady," Lucius said, somewhat mollified, bowing low.

"Until then," Zarabeth responded, allowing him to brush her hand with his lips.

Lucius turned and left the cottage but the moment the door closed upon him, the sound of animated chattering erupted from within. He smiled at hearing the mention of his name. Things had gone very well; Ardon's wife was easy prey; the woman was aching for attention! There would be little difficulty in bending her to his will. As for her daughter, the brat had almost spoiled everything, but in the end her tantrum had actually worked in his favor for there was no mistaking Zarabeth's mortification at her daughter's poor behavior. Now she felt beholden to make up for it by extending her hand in friendship more than she might have done otherwise. But eventually he would still have to win Llyonesse's favor. Her behavior would inevitably erode any goodwill her mother might harbor and that he could ill afford. At all costs he needed to win over the little vixen and right quickly! Tomorrow he would bring her a very special present, one guaranteed to delight a child's fancy. *After all, wasn't the surest way to a mother's heart through her only child?*

Lucius stopped dead in his tracks as though struck by light-

ning. Llyonesse was Ardon's sole heir and of his bloodline! As his eldest child, she alone possessed the birthright to withdraw Ephlal from the scabbard, perhaps even to summon its awesome powers! There was yet a chance at Eloth's sword! The thought sent shockwaves of euphoria through him.

Lucius hurried back to his duties, his plan for conquest and revenge quickly taking shape.

❀

"Greetings, fair ladies," greeted Lucius, bowing courteously.

"Welcome, Lucan," they replied, setting down their sewing to greet him. Dutifully, he kissed each upraised hand in turn, secretly despising the now regular ritual of bowing and fawning he underwent each visit to curry their favor.

He smiled at Zarabeth, giving no indication of his personal hatred for her and her family. "Thy husband extends his affectionate greetings," he said, looking curiously about the room. "Where is the child? I have a gift for her."

"In the next room sorting wool. Do you think perhaps this time shall do the trick?" asked Zarabeth, a worried frown on her face. All of Lucan's previous gifts of dolls, dresses, and even a pearl caplet had failed miserably. Despite his efforts each visit ended with Llyonesse being unceremoniously shoved out of the room because of her behavior. Zarabeth was growing very weary of her attitude and beginning to wonder if something were seriously wrong with her daughter… *or perhaps Lucan…*

"If this gift will not soften her heart nothing will!" replied Lucius, his humorous tone disguising his anxiety.

Zarabeth turned to her ladies. "What wager you? Shall this day's gift change my daughter's heart or shall we hear more wailing?"

"Llyonesse is an obstinate, head-strong lass; I'll wager my favorite pearl earrings that she will depart shrieking!" giggled Regina.

Zarabeth glanced up at Lucius. "We shall see!" she said. "Clotilde, bring Llyonesse hither."

Clotilde disappeared and returned a short time later, literally almost dragging Llyonesse into the room who already knew why she was being brought in. The instant she laid eyes on Lucius she began to sob, the usual precursor to the ugly scene which would certainly follow if he did not succeed in winning her over. With the most beguiling of smiles, Lucius knelt before Llyonesse and offered her a small, furry, black kitten with white whiskers. It looked up at her curiously, a tiny meow greeting her ears as he laid it gently in her arms and sat back on his heels to watch. The room was heavy with expectant silence; every breath held in abeyance to see what would happen next.

Llyonesse balked at first, but was quickly captivated by the tiny creature which turned its perky little face up to hers and batted at her curls. She smiled, oblivious to the audible sighs of incredulous relief by those in the room (except for Regina who had lost her favorite earrings).

"He is thine, little one," whispered Lucius, patting the kitten's head. "You must give him a name befitting his character."

For the first time ever, Llyonesse looked him straight in the eyes. "I shall call him Joshua," she announced, staring at him as if to measure his reaction to her choice.

Lucius flinched, unable to conceal the hostility which filled him at the sound of the name. He forced a smile, but it did not succeed in convincing Llyonesse of his sincerity. She backed away scowling, still clutching the kitten.

"Say *thank you*, Llyonesse! Do not be rude!" snapped Zarabeth, cross with her daughter as never before.

"Thank you," Llyonesse responded darkly in a sullen voice, inching away from him.

Zarabeth turned apologetically to Lucius. "You are kinder than my daughter deserves," she said, hoping he had not been offended. "I do hope that Ardon shan't become jealous at all the gifts thou hast bestowed upon us!" She forced a small laugh.

"I desire naught but thy friendship, my lady," responded Lucius politely, avoiding Llyonesse's eyes, so she would not start screaming and crying again.

"Which you have earned in great measure," replied Zarabeth.

"Reports of thy many kindnesses have not escaped my ears and I can assure you in the strongest possible terms that my people have come to accept you and your men as our fellow kinsmen, and I have informed my husband of such."

"You pay us great honor," replied Lucius, bowing low.

"An honor that has been well earned," replied Zarabeth. "Now do sit and take some refreshment with us. Llyonesse, take thy kitten outside and play awhile."

"Yes, mama," said Llyonesse, greatly relieved. She set the kitten on the floor. "Come, Joshua!" she beckoned, delighted when it obediently followed her.

"I certainly hope she will not be ordering the real Joshua around once they are wed!" laughed Regina, pouring mead for all.

Zarabeth shook her head in disbelief. "After last week's spectacle, I had surely thought we'd seen the end of you! Clotilde had to give Llyonesse laudanum to calm her down."

"Nay, lady," said Lucius, accepting a pastry. "The child's fear has only made me that more determined to win her heart. T'would be an empty joy were all of Shiloh to laud my name whilst my Lord's daughter screams at the sight of my face! I have been most anxious on this account; more than even you can reckon." This was true enough but not for the reasons they assumed.

Zarabeth stared at him in concern, noting the melancholy in his manner. "Be not so troubled on my daughter's behalf, Lucan! She may come around eventually!"

"Nay, lady, tis not the child which troubles me," Lucius replied evasively, his face exceedingly sad. "I am merely ... weary."

His ambiguous tone piqued Zarabeth's curiosity. As he hoped it would.

"Is there ought which vexes thee, my lord? Pray do not keep thy thoughts hidden. Speak freely, you are amongst friends!" she urged, gesturing to her women who nodded in enthusiastic agreement, always ready for a new bit of gossip.

Lucius grew pensive and paused long ere he answered her. "Nay, my lady, t'would not be appropriate among such refined company," he answered. It was just the encouragement the women needed to prod him.

Zarabeth's mouth set in a firm line, her brow furrowing. "I adjure you, my lord, speak! We shall give you no cause to regret thy trust."

"Verily do I regard thy wish as my command, my lady, and but for that, I would not otherwise confess ... "

"Confess what?" breathed Constance, leaning forward so as not to miss a single word. Would he tell them that he was secretly besotted with her ladyship or with another among their number? That would be rich indeed!

Lucius hesitated, determined that they should wring the information from him. He opened his mouth, then paused and shook his head. "Nay, thou wilt think me petty and craven of heart. I pray you bid me not speak of it. I do not wish to belabor thy heart as well."

"If it is great enough to vex you thus, my lord, then how am I to be at ease until I know you are comforted? Pray, tell me, I beg you ... " pressed Zarabeth.

Lucius bowed his head. "Forgive me, my lady, I did not think of it that way. I will confess as you bid me, but it is against my better judgment. It is only a petty matter to be sure, but I was wondering ... is not Ardon the eldest of Eloth's sons?"

"Yes," replied Zarabeth quietly, a strange foreboding stealing over her. "Yes, he is the eldest and by a great many years."

"Then why is this kingdom given to the younger? Why does not Shiloh's throne belong to thy husband? If not for the fact that he is eldest, then at least in recognition of all his labor! I would think he has already earned the rulership many times over!" said Lucius.

The atmosphere in the room became charged with tension. There was no immediate response to his query, as innocent as he could make it seem. Those who did not stare at him in shock sat with their eyes fastened upon their shoes. Zarabeth's face was white as fuller's soap. An extremely long and uncomfortable silence ensued and Lucius cursed himself silently. He had gone too far and dared too much, too soon! Beads of cold sweat broke out on his forehead as he held his breath, waiting to be ordered from her presence forever. His hopes for revenge disintegrated like snow under the onslaught of a warm rain.

"It *would* belong to Ardon had not *Joshua* been born to Eloth," Zarabeth finally replied, her voice strained. "But my husband is not of Eloth's bloodline and therefore has no *ancestral* claim to the throne; he was fostered throughout his youth as Eloth's son, but the younger, I mean, *Joshua*, has both legal and blood claim to Shiloh's throne."[15]

Oh ho! Lucius thought to himself silently. *I have struck a nerve indeed!* His eyebrows climbed high into his hairline in mock astonishment. "In other words, Ardon has been given all the responsibility of the position, but none of the honor? The younger will sit on the throne his foster brother built with his own sweat and labor without any of his own personal investment of time or labor?"

"What mean you by this line of questioning?" snapped Zarabeth, her green eyes flickering with anger. "Do you mean to ensnare me with my own words?"

"I mean no offense, my lady, but tis strange customs indeed to which you and thy people hold. Where I come from, those who labor hardest are those who receive the reward. Does not Ardon demonstrate by his deeds and loyalty that he is the truer of the two? To refuse him the throne which he alone has built makes me wonder about the good judgment of such a ruler. I would find it very difficult to give blindly of my fidelity to one who rewards sloth and ignores the laborer."

Lucius stopped, suddenly noticing that every woman in the room was gaping at him in naked horror. He had gone way too far... his personal hatred had got the better of his tongue. Zarabeth would surely order him banished or put to the stake for his treasonous speech.

But what Lucius mistook for anger on her part was actually silent fear. Zarabeth was struck dumb with terror. *Was this man a mind-reader? Had someone whispered the very thoughts into his ears that had been tormenting her night after night with resentment and guilt? Had she somehow slipped and revealed her most inner thoughts to him somehow? Thoughts she dared not admit to having, not even to herself!*

"Joshua is but a boy and so could not do what my husband does in his place!" she said, visibly trembling. "Such talk is treasonous! I couldst have thee jailed for such speech. You will never speak so again in my presence! No, nor anyone else's! Is that clear?"

Lucius almost exhaled aloud in relief. It was a very sharp rebuke … but only a rebuke and for appearance's sake alone. A far cry from calling for men at arms to haul him away to prison. She had not even ordered him put out of her cottage. Despite his private elation, he would dare risk no more.

He bowed his head in meek acquiescence. "I humbly beg thy forgiveness," he said quietly, rising stiffly to his feet. "I thank thee for thy indulgence. I shall do as you bid me and speak never again of it!"

Lucius' apology greatly mollified Zarabeth's anger, making her feel badly for having spoken to him so harshly. How was he to know that his words were considered sedition? He was a stranger in their land! She nodded curtly, silently dismissing him, struggling to maintain her composure. Lucius left the silent room, closing the door behind him like a whipped cur.

So he had exposed her dirty little secret, had he? he gloated. It made him wonder if her response would have been any different had they been alone together.

From that day on, his visits were greatly abbreviated. Never again did he broach the subject himself or question Eloth's fairness, satisfied that the well of her soul had been sufficiently poisoned to set his schemes in motion.

He was more correct than he knew for, once validated by that of another, Zarabeth struggled with her feelings as never before. Lucan's subtle challenge[16] of Eloth's fairness echoed over and over in her head but each time she sought to approach Ardon on the matter, he either shrugged it off or fell asleep, leaving her to deal with her doubts on her own. As time passed and she grew more lonely and frustrated, she again began to tentatively seek out Lucan's company, finding in him the sympathetic ear which she craved. He spoke little, but his subtle encouragement was all that was needed to stoke the embers of bitterness in her heart into roaring flames of envy and pride.

Zarabeth closed her weary eyes as Clotilde wiped her sweaty face with the cool rag, adjusting her hips in the hopes of finding a more comfortable position in which to support her heavy pregnancy. She was now eight months gone and for the past two weeks she had been plagued with strange, smelly sweats and unending fever, giving her no small amount of anxiety over the condition of her baby. This morning she had awakened to find her limbs heavy as sodden wood and without the strength to so much as lift her head. Clotilde and her other handmaids tended her without rest, sponging her feverish skin and spoon feeding her the medicinal teas her physician prescribed until she thought she would vomit. Despite all their care, she continued to wax ill and lose weight at a frightening pace. What finally brought Ardon to her bedside was the news that the baby's movements were becoming increasingly feeble and infrequent.

Ardon was beside himself with worry as he watched his beloved Zarabeth drift in and out of consciousness, forcing him to abandon all his duties to sit by the hour at her bedside and hold her hand, cursing himself for all his months of neglect and short-sightedness; only too painfully aware of how she had often complained about his absence. Only now, when she was ill past the point of recognizing him, did he sit by her side when she could no longer appreciate it. He was racked with guilt. Except for the bulge about her middle, his wife was gaunt and pale as a wraith, oblivious to all that went on around her until the day her labor pains came upon her without warning.

Ardon's head snapped up in alarm, jolted instantly awake by a piercing scream. He turned frightened eyes to his wife's bed and felt his heart plummet to the soles of his feet in despair. Zarabeth's once lustrous, auburn hair, sparkling green eyes and fair skin were long gone. Her face had become a death-mask, gaunt and thin with cheek bones protruding through her grayish skin; eyes sunken and dull; her hair hanging in limp, oily ropes.

"Clotilde!" he shouted, rising to his feet in alarm as his wife convulsed almost double in pain.

Clotilde rushed into the room, bearing fresh linen. She shoved it into his arms, pushing him aside as she did so to feel Zarabeth's belly under the bedclothes. Her face creased with worry. "It's time," she whispered, darting an anxious glance in his direction, "and she is already so spent! This will be a very difficult birthing, mi'lord, very difficult!"

"Do what you can for her," Ardon mumbled, his throat constricted with pain.

Clotilde nodded and set to work with the midwife while he tried to keep out of their way, helplessly watching Zarabeth moan with agony. The torment went on for hours without let-up. Clotilde and the midwives labored in shifts, changing the bed linen, sponging her limbs, force-feeding her only to watch in frustration as she vomited everything back up. Ardon stood by in total helplessness, knowing there was nothing he could do but watch.

The day waxed and waned and he too began to grow weak and dizzy from exhaustion. But whenever the women suggested he leave and rest, he refused, knowing these might be the last moments he would have with his beloved wife. Day passed agonizingly into night, candles were lit and brought into the room, rushes were swept out and replaced with fresh ones that smelled sweet and clean. Some thoughtful person, he didn't know who, had placed a bouquet of flowers in an urn near her bed to cheer her, but Zarabeth was oblivious to everything except her private hell. The contractions grew stronger, causing her to scream with a vigor he would have thought impossible for one so weak.

There was no rest to be had for any of them the whole of that night nor even when morning came. Push as hard as she may, the babe seemed no closer to being born than when the contractions first began. Clotilde then summoned and enlisted the aid of every midwife in Shiloh, but all were at a loss as to what to do for her. They milled about, shaking their heads in despair or arguing loudly amongst themselves as to what their next course of action should be. Exhausted and in total despair, Ardon fled to the adjoining room, buried his face in his arms and wept. Some hours later, when he was back at her bedside, dozing fitfully in a chair with his chin upon his chest, a weak voice summoned him out of his stupor.

"Ardon ... "

Groggily he looked up and found Zarabeth staring at him with recognition for the first time in days, tears running down either side of her face and into her ears. She looked so fragile and helpless. He swallowed down his tears and fell onto his knees beside her bed, bringing her hand up to his lips. "Zarabeth!" he murmured, his eyes hungrily searching her face. "It does my heart good to hear you say my name again!"

"My heart is steeped in agony, husband," she whispered.

"Your heart? But why, dearest?" he asked, bewildered by her words.

"Because I am dying with the knowledge that neither you nor our son shall sit upon Shiloh's throne as you ought!" she said and began to weep.

Ardon stared at her in astonishment. Shiloh's throne was the last thing on his mind at the moment! "What?" he exclaimed. "What are you talking about? Why would I begrudge my brother the throne to which he was born? I rejoice that for a time he has allowed me to share it with him." He couldn't believe he was actually arguing with her on this issue at such a time as this!

"Share? Shouldering all the responsibility and performing all the labor isn't *'sharing,'* husband," she retorted with uncustomary venom. "It is you who have taken all the risks and labored without rest to build Shiloh out of nothing! Yet when all is done and ready, Joshua will strut into Shiloh and sit upon its gilded throne which should, by all that is decent, belong to you!"

Ardon gaped at her in horror, truly appalled by her words then instantly forgot all else as she suddenly arched backwards in pain, screaming as though she were being ripped asunder. The sound of it sent hot pains knifing through his innards. Clotilde and the other women ran in and stopped dead in their tracks, staring at her bedclothes and sheets in wordless horror as they grew dark with blood. Clotilde went pale at the sight but said nothing, hoping to spare him, but she need not have bothered. Ardon needed no explanation to realize that he was losing his wife. He had never seen so much blood flow from a person, not even on the field of battle.

He felt himself pushed out of the way as the women hastened to prepare for the imminent birth of their child, shouting orders to one another and rushing to and fro with clean linen, hot water, and twine. Sensing that her time was short, Zarabeth reached desperately for Ardon's hands.

"Ardon," she gasped, struggling for every word. "I will not live to see our son born. ... oh!" she clenched her teeth as another contraction silenced her. "I have thought long on the request I am about to make of you and beg with all my heart that you will fulfill my only dying wish."

"Speak beloved," Ardon whispered, standing at the head of the bed, looking down upon her and caressing her brow tenderly. "If it is in my power I will grant it!"

Zarabeth stared long at him then turned to Clotilde. "Leave us!" she whispered. "But my lady!" protested Clotilde. "The babe ... "

"Just for a moment," she begged them, her eyes imploring. Against their better judgment they left, closing the door behind them with wary expressions. Zarabeth struggled to sit up with Ardon's assistance, then grasping his hand, pressed it to her cheek. "I ask but one boon, Ardon, *one*. If you would ease the pain of my death then swear to me that *you* shall sit upon the throne of Shiloh and our son after you!"

"I cannot do that!" cried Ardon, aghast.

"But you swore!" shrieked Zarabeth, clutching his tunic. "You swore!"

"'Tis high treason!"

"Is it?" cried Zarabeth, her voice turning shrill. "You are Eloth's eldest son! How can it be treason to govern as prince that which he entrusted to you as steward? Would it not had fallen to thee had Joshua never been born? 'Treason' is but a word to me when I lie upon my deathbed bearing a son who will never know me!" Her voice ended on a wail of such despair it crushed his heart.

Ardon put his arms about her, trying desperately to reason with her. "Zarabeth, I beg you! You—you are not thinking clearly! How—*how* can you ask this of me?"

"I asked and you swore to do it!" she wept, her tears genuine.

"But I did not know that you would ask such a thing!"

"Ardon, if you have ever born any love for me, any love at all, or for our unborn son—the only son I shall ever give thee—you would grant my dying request!"

Ardon stared at her in numb horror, his heart torn asunder. *Why was she forcing him to choose between her and his king, his beloved father? Why now, when she knew his aching heart could deny her nothing? Could he truly live with himself knowing he had refused her dying wish? Could he live with himself after betraying his king? The answer to both was no. He was a man divided right down the middle, yet as he stared into her beseeching eyes, his resolve wilted. He was doomed either way. The least he could do was to keep her from dying with a broken heart.*

"Very well, my beloved," he whispered, slumping in defeat. "If it is the only comfort left me to offer you, then it shall be so ... "

"Swear it!" whispered Zarabeth, clutching at him. *"Swear it!"*

Ardon bowed his head, hardly able to get the words out. "I forswear my oath of fealty to Eloth. Our heirs and not his shall sit upon the throne of Shiloh." Even as he uttered the words, his child issued forth from her womb in a gush of blood. Zarabeth died with a triumphant smile, her eyes fixed and open. Ardon gazed down with swimming eyes and beheld his son. The child was utterly still and bluish-gray; its lifeless body resting limply in his blood-stained hands—still-born.

Clotilde burst into the room at his cry of anguish. When she saw her lady and the dead babe cradled in Ardon's hands, tears filled her eyes. "I'm so sorry, mi'lord," she whispered, taking the tiny body from his arms. Ardon watched silently while she cleaned his son of afterbirth then laid the tiny body beside its mother. Gently she drew the sheet over their still forms, unaware of all that had been lost in the space of a few moments.

Chapter Four

"**W**ell, well, well, Scheldrake," gloated Lucius, pouring himself a large goblet of red wine. "Thy talent in pharmacopoeia is indeed without comparison. Ardon's wife and heir are dead and our 'little' secret with them."

Scheldrake cackled, rubbing his knurled hands together. "Did I not tell thee there would be no suspicion if the midwife administered the tea? But there is still another heir to deal with, mi'lord. The girl-child?"

Golbreth entered the room, grinning from ear to ear. "Ardon weeps in his cottage like a forsaken maiden!" he announced, accepting a cup of wine.

"Yes, I know," replied Lucius with a grimace. "The moment has come for me to play the role of sympathetic friend and offer craven words of comfort." He downed the last of his wine, wiped his mouth with the back of his hand and left, walking briskly across the square to Ardon's cottage. He knocked softly, waited, and then knocked again. There was no response.

"My lord?" Lucius gave a slight push and entered the darkened dwelling. His nostrils were immediately assaulted by the smell of spoiled food and animal refuse. When his eyes adjusted he could see chickens roaming freely about, pecking at spoiled food. A nanny goat bleated at him in protest as he yanked away the discarded tunic it had been munching on. He picked his way farther in, stepping over heaps of soiled clothes that lay strewn upon the floor amongst broken crockery. Lucius squinted his eyes and looked about, wondering if Ardon was even there in the first place. He finally found him hunched before a small table with his face cradled in his hands, his shoulders heaving with sobs. A scroll of parchment, an ink bottle, and quill lay on the table before him.

Lucius softly cleared his throat to announce his presence. Despite the fact that he was personally responsible for orchestrating the death of Ardon's wife and child, it was nevertheless a shock to behold the broken man Ardon had become. He lifted his head and stared lifelessly at Lucius, looking like he had aged a thousand years in the space of a single day; his face was gray and haggard and his hair had gone completely white. He was emotionally and spiritually destroyed. The two men stared at one another in silence for a long moment then Ardon closed his eyes and sighed, raking trembling fingers through his matted hair. "There is something I need you to do for me, Lucan," he said, his voice barely more than a whisper. "I want this message dispatched immediately to Ellioth and given personally to the king." Ardon laid the parchment into his hands then turned away.

"As it pleases, my lord," replied Lucius softly. Not even for the sake of appearances would he now dare to offer argument. Greedy to know what the missive said, he turned away. "I will go at once."

Ardon nodded, silently dismissing him. Lucius left the cottage and gratefully shut the smells and door behind him, gulping down the fresh air with relief. When he returned to his own cottage, he unrolled the parchment and read Ardon's message, gloating in triumph. It was all he had hoped for and more and it even bore the seal of Ardon's signet ring in green wax; thereby effectively preventing any suspicion of a forgery. Lucius wasted no time in delivering the message to the Captain of the *Eden Mist* with instructions to sail at the next high tide.

Evening began to settle upon Shiloh as her inhabitants gathered in the castle courtyard to lay Zarabeth and her infant son to rest in a freshly dug grave. Ardon stood before the grave site holding an inconsolable Llyonesse with one hand and a torch in another, in dry-eyed silence as his people laid bouquets of flowers about her shrouded body. Gently his wife and babe were lowered together into the shallow grave, a sheet of fine linen laid over them. As was custom, a clump of fresh earth was laid in his hand to throw first. Ardon raised his fist of dirt but was unable to let fly. She had been alive only hours ago! How could he now be expected to throw dirt upon her beloved body? With all his heart he ached to lift her from the cold, shallow grave and cradle her cold dead face in his arms until, perchance, through sheer force of will and love, he might instill life again in her, but it could never be so! With trembling hand he closed his eyes and let it drop from his hand. A moment's pause and then a soft thud as the dirt landed upon her. Through a fog of pain, gentle arms reached out and led him aside in a vain attempt to comfort him as others stepped forward to finish the mournful task. Their mutual friends hugged him, praising Zarabeth's beauty and kindness, but their words fell upon deaf ears. Ardon watched, heart wrung with agony as the last shovel-full of earth was laid over her and patted down. She was gone forever and with her his very heart and soul. Eventually the mourners began to drift away to their warm homes and families, but still Ardon stood, rooted to the spot, holding his daughter as though he had turned to stone. He was caught between two worlds: the life he had left behind and the empty one which now yawned open before him like a dark void. He couldn't return to the first and he couldn't bear to face the latter.

Into his bleak reverie, his daughter, Llyonesse, yawned loudly through her tears and wavered sleepily on her feet, bringing him out of his stupor long enough to remember that he was not the only one who had lost someone dear.

Ardon lifted her up and planted a long, passionate kiss on her cheek. "Clotilde," he whispered after a long silence. "Take my daughter away now."

"No, daddy…" Llyonesse whined, her eyes widening with sudden alarm, clutching at him as though she sensed something desperately wrong. Clotilde reached for her but it only served to make the child hysterical. Llyonesse tightened her grip, burying her face in her father's shoulder. "No, daddy, *pleeeease!*"

It broke his heart to do so, but Ardon forced himself to unwind her little arms from about his neck. "Llyonesse, go with Clotilde!" he commanded.

"*Noooooooooooooo,*" wailed Llyonesse, her voice rising to a scream. "*No! No! NO!*"

"Go with Nana!"

"No, daaaadddeeeee, pleeeeeeeease!" she screamed, reaching out for him with grasping fingers over Clotilde's shoulders as she was carried away. Ardon waited until his daughter was completely out of sight before unbuckling the clasp upon Ephlal's scabbard. He grasped the hilt, wincing with agony as he slowly drew it out by the hilt.

"It is time," he said, closing his eyes and withdrawing the fiery blade.

His body was discovered the next morning. Though neither mark nor wound could be found upon him, Ardon lay as cold and dead as a marble statue, by what means none could tell save that Ephlal stood like a lone sentry near him, buried hilt-deep into a large cornerstone which had been awaiting emplacement.[17]

Fear and great mourning fell upon all of Shiloh and all work ceased as word spread throughout the village that Ardon, Steward of Shiloh was dead along with most of his family. A pall of somberness and fear hung over the land from that day forward, leaving many to wonder if the past few days' events represented a dire omen of greater calamities yet to come.

The following day, stonewrights and blacksmiths by order of "Lucan" thronged around the cornerstone, laboring feverishly to work the sword free while Lucius stood nearby, his hands mysteriously bandaged, watching their lack of progress with increasing frustration. The men labored unceasingly for two days and nights, until every last pickax, spike, chisel and hammer had become notched, dull or shattered from the effort. Not so much as a flake of stone could be chipped away. It was as though the cornerstone were held in the grip of a power greater than the strength or will of men. With an ugly scowl in its direction, Lucius gave orders for the cornerstone to be guarded in continuous watches around the clock with secret orders to kill on sight any who attempted to come near the sword.

If he, Lucius, could not possess the sword, he would make sure no one else did either, especially its rightful heir!

Only three weeks after Ardon's burial, messengers were dispatched from the castle, summoning the villagers to gather before the gates at noon. Golbreth stood atop the gatehouse as they gathered in the hot sun, unrolling a parchment when the square was completely filled.

"Hear ye, hear ye!" he shouted. "Let it be known to the inhabitants of Shiloh that Lucan, Ardon's second in command, will now govern as steward."

"Lucan! Who chose him?" Many in the crowd wanted to know with no small annoyance. Why had they not been consulted in this matter? Lucan was an outsider!

" … who has agreed to govern as he knew your late steward, Ardon, would have desired. You need have no fear; your daily lives will go on as before and the castle will be completed on schedule," continued the announcement.

"Well that at least is a small comfort," muttered others, glad to know that they would not be without a leader.

"Following his swearing in this afternoon," continued Golbreth, "the family names of all those who wish to enter sons of eligible age into a college of knights will be recorded and given coinage and titles for their pledge."

At this a stir of excitement passed through the crowd. This was news! Usually only the sons of nobles could enjoy such a privilege! It was a lofty new status indeed and one not to be lightly turned down, especially at the hint of receiving titles and/or additional lands proportionate to the number of children put into service. The crowds swarmed forward, eager to do just that, forgetful of the fact that when the first generation of craftsmen were gone, there would be no new apprentices to take their place in the family trade.

Lucius watched the milling crowd with satisfaction. Without the use of Ephlal, he had little hope of victory against Eloth's superior forces, but with patience, hard work, and sufficient time, he would have enough young men to challenge the king in fair battle. Getting the lads while they were still young and impressionable would make it simple enough to shift their loyalties. He would put Borgreth and Ranulf in charge. Being intimately familiar with their ruthless methods of training, he had little doubt that they would successfully weed out the meek and merciful and advance only those of fierce nature. None would dare complain of their child's expulsion, for peer pressure and public ridicule would ensure that it be considered the height of disgrace and familial failure for their sons to fail. Ultimately he would command an army of young men possessed of a single-minded, blind obedience to him alone. Memories of Ellioth would eventually grow dim in the day-to-day business of eating, working, and living and each day that came and went would work to reduce the anticipation of their coming king to little more than a distant, unreal event that might one day take place, far, far into the future.[18] His ultimate goal: to dull their love of king and country and to make their loyalty to him wax cold.[19] Given enough time, Joshua would be greeted with the sword and rebellion rather than cheers of welcome!

Lucius smiled. *In another's week's time the ship should make port into Ellioth and inflict the first of a thousand cuts to Eloth's heart as he learned the news of Ardon's betrayal and death. It was now only a matter of time before he would have his revenge!*

Chapter Five

A rmed with truncheons, swords, and shields, two mail clad warriors confronted one another in pitched battle before the gallery of begowned spectators. Down came sword upon shield and helm with ear-ringing clangs as each combatant hammered upon the other.

BANG....CRASH.....BANG.....CRASH...the battle had already lasted for the better part of half an hour but still no end was in sight. As tedious as it must have been for those in combat, it was even more so for the spectators. It was the last event of the day and all but these two had been eliminated from prior rounds. Now the red and blue warrior each battled for supremacy and the victor's cup. The gallery roared as an exceptionally heavy blow was struck by the blue knight to the red's shield. It would have toppled any other opponent, but the squire in red only stumbled back a pace or two then quickly recovered, bringing an answering blow against the blue knight's breastplate. Another roar of appreciation and additional points were awarded to the red warrior. The two were almost perfectly matched in every respect; meeting blow for blow, point for point with the only hope of a speedy outcome in ill-chance, a lucky hit, or the king calling a halt and declaring a draw.

The blue knight landed a blow to the breastplate of the red, knocking him sideways, certain he had knocked the breath out of him only to be caught by surprise as his opponent continued turning about to wallop him upon his helm. Stars and mind-numbing pain exploded into his brain, causing him to stagger backwards, lose his footing, and sprawl onto his backside with a loud grunt. Before he could recover his senses, he found the tip of the red's sword wedged between the joints of his helm and gorget. The crowd jumped to their feet with a roar of appreciation (and relief).

"Do you yield?" asked the red knight, his voice muffled by the heavy plating of his visor.

"Yes," panted the blue knight, stars still orbiting his face. "I yield. Victory is thine."

The red knight reached down and offered his hand to his fallen opponent, hauling him back up onto his feet. Another blinding flash of pain, only this time from his ankle.

Sir Penloth stumbled, clutching at his leg with a grunt. "Must have twisted it when I fell," he said, removing his helmet to drink deeply of the cool air. *Good, the stars were beginning to fade away now.* Sweat glistened on his face and his long, brown hair was plastered to his sweaty skull.

"Canst thou walk unaided, Penloth, or shall I carry thee off the field like a young maid?" asked Joshua, also removing his helmet.

Sir Penloth gave him a scowl. "Leave me some shred of dignity, will you!" he answered, wincing as he tried to put weight on the now swelling ankle. "After this day's pounding there won't be a man in the kingdom willing to take thee on in mock battle 'sides me, so you best watch yer P's and Q's, me laddie!"

"Indeed?" grinned Joshua pleased with the rather roundabout compliment.

"Yes. Now be a good fellow and escort me over to the victor's booth so I may fulfill my duty. Mayhap the victor's cup shall numb this pain in the process."

"…and thy brains.…..!" laughed Joshua, returning his grin.

"Even so!" agreed Penloth, slapping him on the back. "Thou knowest me too well. To our cups now!"

They shared a hearty laugh and vacated the tourney field,

allowing their squires to gather up their weaponry and see to their weary chargers. Joshua walked slowly to accommodate the injured Penloth who finally was forced to accept his offer of support. They arrived at a large booth where a great number of knights had already gathered and were greeted with loud, rowdy cheers. The elaborate, silver Victor's chalice was already filled to the brim with ruby red wine, waiting for them on its silver tray. Penloth took the first gulp then passed it to Joshua. With a sheepish grin, Joshua lifted it to his lips and downed it all in one long draught as tradition demanded.

"To the victor!" cried Penloth. "May all thy victories be as sweet as well-aged wine!"

Joshua could only nod in response, his head feeling quite light from the effects of the rich, dark wine.

"This time the stars are circling about thy head, no?" Penloth quipped, motioning to the ulster. "Ale," he said. "Two ... and keep them coming!" He handed back the chalice then turned back to Joshua. "I am sorry about Ardon and Llyonesse not having been here to see you," he said as the ulster handed them each a hogshead of ale.

"No more than I," replied Joshua, his disappointment clearly evident. "I had really hoped they could break away long enough to attend my knighting tomorrow, but Ardon's last letter was not encouraging. They all wanted very much to come, of course, especially Llyonesse, but Zarabeth was great with child and due almost any day. He did not feel it right to abandon her while he came here on holiday."

"Could not Llyonesse at least have returned with Clotilde alone?" asked Penloth.

"Clotilde is also Zarabeth's midwife," explained Joshua, sipping his ale. "She could not be spared at such a critical time and Llyonesse will have no other."

"There are none else who might have accompanied her?"

"None whom Llyonesse would abide; she is quite a handful!"

"Aye," agreed Penloth with a smirk, remembering one of Llyonesse's past "escapades" with a smile.

It had taken him years to finally see the humor in it and even he, the master prankster, had to admit that the little slip of a girl had outdone him. He had returned to his chambers late one night to discover his favorite mouser, a tomcat he had dubbed Sir John, dyed a disgraceful shade of purple. As he found out later, Llyonesse had thought it would be fun to see what color the tabby would become if dunked in a vat of royal blue dye and so had performed her little experiment by submerging the poor creature in a cooled vat. Fortunately, she had not tried to achieve a uniform coloration from head to tail, thereby sparing the poor creature from an early death by drowning. The end result was that Sir John ended up as two colors: bright orange from ear tip to ruff and deep purple from there to the end of his very bushy tail. The tabby had yowled inconsolably under his bed for the better part of a fortnight until the color had gradually grown out.

The other knights had found the situation infinitely amusing and had frequently heckled him as to when the tomcat was going to receive a crown and scepter to match his royal hue. Penloth's annoyance had only spurred them on to greater and more elaborate practical jokes and over the course of several nights, he returned to find Sir John sporting odd pieces of jewelry, curled upon velvet pillows, or enjoying a feast of kitchen scraps on silver chargers.

"What are you smirking about?" asked Joshua, interrupting his thoughts.

"Nothing, mi'lord," Penloth replied evasively, not wanting the pranks to be started all over again by Joshua. Then: "Do you still plan to depart immediately after the ceremony for the northern lands?"

"Yes, my people have not seen me for many a year and I am now obligated to learn more personally of their present needs and concerns. Moreover," he added, draining his horn of ale "Paracletis, my father's white stallion, has been spoiling for a lengthy journey for quite some time. I should not be gone more than a quarter of a year at the most; plenty of time for you to recover before our next engagement! Speaking of which, it's time we got thee to the physician; I like not the look of thy ankle; it has become exceedingly blue and swollen."

"All right then," said Penloth, draining his horn in one fell swig. "I'll race you!" and set off at a swift hop.

Joshua returned to his tarpaulin a short time later and wearily removed his heavy armor with the assistance of his squire. William hefted it over his shoulder with a grunt and carried it off to be cleaned and polished. It had to be gleaming like a mirror for that night's vigil and for the morning's knighting. Joshua smiled to himself, for true to Sir Penloth's word, it had indeed grown to feel like a second skin to him. When he took it off he felt almost too light; however, he did not miss the way it made him sweat. He removed his sodden underclothing, stripping down to his bare skin before submerging himself in a large wooden tub filled halfway with cool water. A short time later, William and two other squires returned bearing yokes upon which hung several steaming pails of hot water. Joshua closed his eyes in pleasure as they poured it over him, allowing it to sluice down his head and back in delicious streams of heat. Steam billowed up around his face.

A hot bath is truly a luxury worthy of kings... he thought to himself in appreciation as the heat began to permeate his tired limbs. He shut his eyes sleepily, submitting to William's strong fingers as they massaged the aches from his arms and back muscles with a cake of fragrant soap. When the water had finally grown quite cold, Joshua stood, picked up a pail of clean, warm water and poured the contents over himself to rinse away the soap then stepped out, wrapping himself in a course, heavy sheet to dry off.

William stepped back. "If that is all, mi'lord, I'll finish tending to thy armor."

"Yes, William, go thy way and take a sovereign for the good

service thou hast given me this day," replied Joshua with a warm smile. "I could not have triumphed half so well had you not oiled my armor so thoroughly. Thank you!"

"Thank you, my lord!" the lad replied with a happy smile, scampering off to finish his duties.

Joshua finished toweling himself off then changed into a fresh, white tunic and woolen hose. Over these he drew on a scarlet surcoat with the rampant lion of Ellioth emblazoned in fine golden embroidery across the front and back. Over these he girded a heavy leather belt studded with rubies and a scabbard ornately embroidered with golden thread and inset with fine gem stones. It was the eve of Midsummer's day, marking the third year that had passed since Ardon had sailed to Shiloh. He had matured much since then. No longer was he the skinny youth whose arms ached horribly after each day of training. Now he was a young man with a heavily muscled body hardened from days, months, and years of ceaseless training in which he had wielded weaponry that was oft times fully half his weight. Even his upper thighs bulged with muscles which had developed from learning to fight proficiently on horseback and his skin was bronzed from long exposure to the sun. He had undergone a complete transformation and wondered what little Llyonesse would think of him when she saw him again for the first time. She would not be so little any more either. She was no longer a child but in the first blush of womanhood. He was looking forward to beholding the changes which three years had wrought in her when they were finally reunited. If only she had been able to come to his knighting!

William returned a short time later bearing his newly polished arms. His armor, sword, and shield gleamed with a mirror finish that made them look as though they were plated of sterling rather than steel. With heartfelt thanks, Joshua gathered up his arms and strode to the chapel. Though it had grown dark, all within was basked in the golden glow from the light of dozens of white candles set in vessels of brass. He laid his sword and shield upon the altar, arranged his plumed helm, armor and spurs beneath it, then dropped onto his knees, bowing his head in silent prayer.

A moment later, Sir Penloth silently entered the chapel and peeked in to regard his star pupil with a great sense of pride. Joshua's face was serene in the golden light; his thick, shoulder-length brown hair tied back into a queue with a white riband to keep it out of his eyes. Their past three years together had been long and arduous ones, but Joshua had excelled as no other had before him and Penloth felt immensely proud. Despite his youth and gentle manner, Joshua had become a warrior to reckon with (to which Penloth's bruised muscles regularly testified). Already he stood head and shoulders above other lads his age and was half again broader in frame. And whereas most squires-at-arms grew over excited in the heat of battle, Joshua always kept his head, besting his opponents through his sharp wit, tireless, dogged patience and keenly honed skills. There were none left who were skillful enough to defeat him in matched battle, save for perhaps Penloth, but even he had taken a beating earlier that day he would not soon forget.

Sensing someone in the room, Joshua turned and looked behind him, smiling a silent "Hullo." Penloth returned the grin, nodded and left Joshua to his vigil.

Joshua remained on his knees throughout the night in quiet meditation, long after the candles had burned down to their quick and finally guttered out. Judging from the prolific bird-song outside and lessening darkness, dawn was just about to break. He looked out the stained-glass window to see a multitude of bobbing torchlights approach the chapel. The muffled tramping of shod feet grew closer. Joshua stood to his feet, nervous with anticipation. The door to the chapel opened soundlessly to reveal Sir Penloth standing before him in full battle regalia, backlit by the growing light of dawn.

"Rise and take up thy arms, young acolyte, for this day thou art summoned to stand before thy King to take thy knightly oath," he said solemnly.

Joshua gathered up his arms and tucked his plumed helm under his arm. "I am ready," he said. Sir Penloth turned, leading the seraphim back toward the castle. They marched in two columns comprised of six knights apiece with Joshua bringing up the rear. Each knight carried before him a scarlet standard upon a long golden pikestaff. The early morning mist was hovering over the greensward and the tiltyard was wet with dew. All was silent save for the singing of birds and the muffled crunch of dirt under their shod feet as they tread the footpath reserved specifically for ceremonial knightings. Down through the silent castle they marched toward the Hall of Judgment, striding in cadence to the beat of distant drums which grew louder with each step until they stood just before the doors. Guards stood on either side, holding the heavy, ornate golden doors wide open. Peering over the helmets and scarlet plumes of the seraphim, Joshua could see the entire hall before him, filled not only with pages, his fellow squires-at-arms, and knights, but dukes, barons and other courtiers who had come to witness his knighting. He was awed at the honor they paid him, but he would have traded all for but one glimpse of Ardon's familiar grin in the crowd and that of Llyonesse!

Those in the hall turned as Sir Penloth and Sir Eric, each leading a column, marched toward the marble dais, leading Joshua to his Father. Eloth stood before him, robed in scarlet, gold, and sable; a golden diadem upon his brow. He beamed upon his son in unabashed pride for not until this moment had he marked how tall and mature he had grown in three short years, nor how nobly he bore himself. The seraphim parted to the left and right before the dais, turned, then stood at attention. At that moment, dawn arrived and with it brilliant shafts of sunlight which streamed down through the tall windows of the hall, bathing the dais in pure, golden light just as Joshua knelt before his father as if in blessing.

Eloth lifted his arms. The murmuring crowd grew silent. "Behold the acolyte who kneels before thee, O people, and give ear. The squire-at-arms, Joshua, Son of Eloth, hath duly fulfilled all the requirements of knighthood and chivalry! Mastered are the crossbow, longbow and arrow; truncheon, broadsword, cutlass and rapier! Bear witness now as he makes his pledge of fealty!"

Sir Penloth stepped forward. "Joshua, Son of Eloth, dost thou swear to uphold truth, defend the weak, and serve thy lord as his knight of the realm with thy body, mind, and riches? If so, speak now thy oath of fealty!"

Joshua lifted his head high, meeting the eyes of his father. *"I, Joshua, son of Eloth, do hereby swear this day, to champion truth, defend the weak, and serve the cause of justice with fealty; sacrificing life, limb, and blood in the service of my Lord, shouldst need demand; treating with chivalry both commoner and nobleman alike. So swear I, Joshua, son of Eloth."*

"Having so sworn, Joshua," responded Eloth, "I bestow upon thee the order of knighthood." He lifted Joshua's sword from the altar and tapped the blade upon his left shoulder. "Upon thy brow be wisdom," then tapped the right, "and thy breast-plate righteousness." He then laid the flat of the blade upon his bowed head, "and in all thy doings honor and equity."

Sir Penloth knelt behind Joshua and girt upon him his spurs of knighthood.

Eloth turned the sword about, proffering the hilt to his son. "Bear this in token of Ephlal which shall be given thee upon thy kingmaking in Shiloh, my son," he smiled. "Gird now thy sword upon thy thigh and rise, Sir Knight!"[20]

Joshua received the sword with a kiss and faced the assembly as they stood to cheer him, his face beaming with pleasure. He raised his sword high. "Long live Eloth, the king!" he cried.

"Long live the king!" repeated the assembly. A loud fanfare sounded forth signaling that it was time to break their fast with the customary feast. There would be celebration all that day then early the following morn Joshua would depart as planned for the northern realm. No one, save his father, could tell how bitterly disappointed he was that neither Ardon nor Llyonesse had been there to witness his knighting.

Penloth yawned, pulling his cloak closer about him to block the early morning chill, and stamping his feet to keep warm. "Had I known he was going to get us up in the middle of the night, I wouldn't have agreed to send him off!" he complained to his brother.

"Oh yes you would," Penlorian snickered. "And you have no one to blame but yourself! Drinking ale until the wee hours of the morning! *Really!*"

At that moment, Joshua and his Father came out into the courtyard. Paracletis neighed in greeting, stamping impatiently and tossing his head, steam billowing from his nostrils.

"Morning, mi'lords," greeted Penloth and Penlorian, bowing to both Eloth and Joshua.

"Good morning!" Joshua smiled, the words becoming puffs of smoke in the chill air. Paracletis butted his head against Joshua's shoulder then nickered softly. "Anxious to leave, boy?" Joshua murmured, checking his cinches and adjusting the headstall to fit more comfortably.

"Do you still refuse my offer to attend you?" asked Penlorian, handing him the reins. "I would consider it a great honor."

"As would I, Penlorian," interrupted Joshua with an appreciative smile. "But thou art a senior knight and t'would not be fitting." He gestured to his haversack, "And as you can see, I have little need for a servant; I am traveling very light."

"What is thy first destination?" asked Penloth, handing him several saddlebags filled with wayfarers food of dried meat, fruit, and oat cakes.

"The village of Scarborough, two days journey north. After that, who knows? It is my desire to visit all the villages in the north, especially those which are the most remote."

"An adventure of which I am now most certainly envious!" grinned Penlorian. "I hear the maidens in Scarborough are surpassingly fair—"

"Ahaaa!" grinned Joshua, punching him in the shoulder. "So that is why you are so eager to come!"

Penlorian blushed a deep shade of red. Penloth grinned at his brother with undisguised pride. "Haven't you become the randy scoundrel!" he snorted. "Taking after yer older brother, eh?" Penlorian smiled sheepishly but made no reply. To do so would only have added fuel to the fire.

Joshua swung himself up in the saddle. "If it is any comfort to you, Penlorian," he said. "I will publish word of thy bachelorhood to the maidens of Scarborough. When they hear of thy knightly exploits, fair countenance, and unparalleled chivalry they will flock to Ellioth like locusts."

"Oh how you do go on!" groaned Penlorian, unsure whether to regard his words as promise or threat. "I take it back! Trouble not thyself on my behalf!"

"As you wish," grinned Joshua. He bent forward, offering his hand to his father. "Farewell, keep thee well until my return."

"Fare thee well, my son," returned Eloth, clasping his hand one last time. Joshua straightened, gave them all a last wave, then turned Paracletis about, cantering out of the courtyard and across the drawbridge. They followed him as far as the gatehouse then watched him disappear down the road.

Two weeks later, the sails of the *Eden Mist* were sighted upon the horizon. Even though there had been regular traffic between Ellioth and Shiloh over the years in which news, correspondence, and goods had been exchanged and countrymen returned to visit with friends and family; hitherto, the voyages had been made by the other vessels, not the *Eden Mist*, which was considered Ardon's flagship. When word reached the castle which ship it was, the entire village practically abandoned their duties to greet it.

"If only she had come sooner," griped Penloth to the king as they approached on horseback. "Joshua will be sorely grieved when he learns that they missed his knighting by a mere fortnight!"

"Perhaps we should send messengers to find him," suggested Penlorian.

"We know not of his whereabouts; it could take weeks," Penloth reminded him.

"All the more reason to begin at once," interjected Eloth, thinking it a capital idea. "It will take little persuasion on my part to convince Ardon to abide with us for as long as it takes to retrieve Joshua! Sir Penlorian, go thy way and see personally to this matter."

"Yes, mi'lord!" he saluted, wheeling his horse about and cantering back to the castle. It was disappointing not to greet his old friend, but he supposed they could more than make up for it later over a mug of ale. Penloth and the King watched him for a moment then turned about as the gangplank was lowered onto the dock. After handing the reins to their squires, they climbed aboard, ducking as several nets, filled with various cargo, swung past their heads into the waiting arms of the village merchants. A flurry of activity surrounded them as seamen continued furling the sheets and secured the mooring lines. Eloth looked about with a keen eye, searching everywhere for Ardon whom he had expected to find half-running toward him in his excitement. A strange feeling began to grow upon him as the minutes wore on and still there was no sign of him. He was getting the distinct impression that the crew was intentionally avoiding his gaze.

After several minute's vain search, Eloth turned to Penloth. "Perhaps he is still in his cabin."

"My Lord!" cried a voice behind them. Eloth turned to find not Ardon, but Joseph Fitzbaton coming toward him, his face haggard and woeful. A stab of fear shot through Eloth's heart upon looking into Joseph's eyes. *Something was seriously wrong.*

"Ardon dispatched me with orders to deliver this missive to you personally," Joseph said, handing him a rolled parchment of paper with his seal of green wax.

Penloth stared at him nonplussed. "Is not he and his family onboard?" he asked, paying little attention to Eloth as he unrolled the scroll.

Before Joseph could answer, Penloth felt the full force of Eloth's weight upon him as the King clutched his shoulder for support.

"*Ardon!*" he cried aloud in a voice that struck terror into the hearts of all who heard it. Before Penloth's horror stricken eyes, Eloth sunk onto his knees, his face pale as death.

"Joseph! Help me!" Penloth shouted, catching Eloth about the middle to support him. "My lord, what is wrong? What has happened?" But Eloth seemed not to hear him. His eyes closed in agony. The crew about them stared at him, frozen with horror as they watched Eloth grasp his tunic in both hands and rend it asunder, convulsed with sobs.

"Get the physician!" Penloth shouted at Joseph who stood rooted to the spot, dumbstruck. "Did you not hear me?" he yelled, struggling to keep Eloth on his feet. "Joseph! *Joseph!*"

"'Tis not a physician he needs," he replied, turning to Penloth with sorrowful eyes.

What the devil is he talking about? Penloth fumed in alarm. *Why is everyone standing around gawking?* The scroll! The king had been reading it at the moment he collapsed. Gently he lowered him onto a large keg which stood nearby then snatched up the parchment.

To Eloth:

Zarabeth and my infant son are dead. Soon I shall join them for with her last breath, she wrested from me an oath of betrayal. Only the lowest of rogues wouldst break faith with a beloved king and father and yet I have done so. I have forfeited my right to regard myself as thy loyal subject, let alone thy son.
A traitor's death awaits me at the edge of thy sword and at least in this last I shall prove myself more faithful though not even my own death can absolve me of the crime of loving my wife better than my king.

Farewell and grieve not ... Ardon

The writing blurred before Penloth's eyes. What had Ardon done? How could he, of all people, betray Eloth who had loved and trusted him as his own son? They three, he, Penlorian and Ardon, had been fostered together! Trained side-by-side throughout their youth. He himself had girt on Ardon's spurs at his knighting and stood by his side upon his marriage to Zarabeth. There would be no answers to this riddle for they had all died with him.

Alas, Alas! For Ardon whom he loved! "Come, my Lord" he said, lifting Eloth slowly back onto his feet. "There is much to discuss. Captain, join us in our lord's council chambers as soon as thy ship is secured."

"Aye, my lord," Joseph replied sadly.

Penloth mutely walked with Eloth, bent over with grief, threading their way through the melancholy crewmen and onto the dock where their horses stood waiting.

Upon returning to the castle they were met by Penlorian, breathless from his errand and completely ignorant of their grave tidings. He took one look at Eloth and stopped dead in his tracks having never before seen his king in such a state. "Squires are readying to depart within the hour!" he said, looking from his brother to Eloth then back to Penloth again, his brown eyes filled with questions and concern.

Penloth forced himself to meet his brother's eyes. "Penlorian—" he began, his emotions finally overwhelming him. He grasped his brother and drew him close in a fierce embrace, barely able to choke out the words for the lump in his throat. "Ardon, Ardon is ... dead."

Penlorian jerked back, staring at him as if he had gone mad. "That, that cannot be!" he said, refusing to believe it and looked to Eloth for denial. Never before had Penlorian beheld such naked pain in his Lord's eyes. The horrible truth hit him like a physical blow and with a strangled cry of sorrow, he flung his arms about his brother's neck and wept.

"Come," Penloth said after a few moments, gently pulling away. "A council must be called. We must decide what to do."

Penlorian nodded, dashing the tears from his eyes. "My lord," he choked, bowed and followed his brother from the chamber, leaving Eloth alone to grieve in private.

When the room was finally quite empty, Eloth dropped onto

the dais before his throne, cradling his head in his hands as he finally gave vent to the full measure of his grief.

"Oh, Ardon, my son, my son, Ardon! Would that I had died in thy place, Oh Ardon![21]

Penloth glanced around the Council Table with waning patience as Eloth's counselors and advisors slowly seated themselves. It had taken nearly an hour from the time the summons went forth until this moment to finally get them all together. He glanced across the table at his King, wondering what was going on behind his expressionless face as he silently waited for all to come to order. The chamber servants worked as unobtrusively as possible, lighting candles and dispensing refreshments with silent but nervous efficiency.

"Who is this Lucan?" Penloth demanded at the first opportunity. "And what has become of Ardon's daughter, Llyonesse?"

"Lucan became steward in Ardon's place, who, I believe, Ardon was grooming as second in command. As far as I know he is not of Ellioth but came out of the wild with his men some years earlier. As for Ardon's daughter, she yet abides in Shiloh," replied the captain.

Penloth brought his fist down upon the table. Cups and platters shuddered at the blow. "Then why in bloody blazes did you not bring the child with you?" he bellowed, frustration getting the better of him. "Did it not occur to you that she should be returned hither for fostering after the loss of both parents?"

"Peace, Sir Penloth!" chided Eloth gently. "I'm sure the good captain would have done so if he could." Penloth sat back down, muttering and chewing his mustache.

"I had intended to bring her, Sir Penloth," Joseph volunteered defensively. "But I was told she had taken sick and could not travel. I would have waited for her to recover, but Ardon's last orders were for the ship to return without delay with his message."

"And what of my sword?" Eloth asked him. "I gather it is not on the ship either?"

At this the captain shifted uncomfortably, avoiding his eyes. "No," he said, his voice barely audible. "I was unable to bring it to you, my lord."

"And why is that?" Penloth demanded to know.

"Because it is buried to its hilt in a cornerstone in Shiloh's courtyard."

"Buried in a cornerstone!" repeated Eloth, his eyes growing wide with alarm. "This bodes very ill. Ephlal has made itself unavailable for any to wield. Joseph, how soon could you put again out to sea?"

"Why as soon as she is resupplied and given minor repairs, my lord," he replied, his eyes widening. "Will you be journeying to Shiloh?"

"I have not that luxury," replied Eloth solemnly, standing to his feet. "Were Joshua here, I would send him. Messengers have already sallied forth to find him but there must be no further delay. If I do not receive word within a fortnight that he has been found, thou shalt sail without him." He turned to Sir Penloth. "Penloth, since thou art disabled, choose ye knights fit to voyage to Shiloh. Return Llyonesse with my sword in the cornerstone, and bring this Lucan with thee. I wish to speak face-to-face with him."

Penloth slumped, mightily aggrieved at not being able to go. "Yes, my lord."

"And Penloth," Eloth added, his face very grave, "they are to be armed for battle.....shouldst there be any trouble."

Leaning on an intricately carved staff before a throng of young knights, Sir Penloth read forth the names of those he had chosen for the voyage to Shiloh. *"Sir Morgan."* The young knight stepped forward, unable to hide his smile of pleasure. *"Sir Sigmund, Sir Guilford, Sir Baldor..."* One by one he ticked them off until a total of twelve stood forth from the rest. Penloth cast a wary glance toward his younger brother, Penlorian, noting with displeasure the red splotches of mounting anger spreading over his face. He glanced away, determined to ignore him. "The *Eden Mist* departs for Shiloh in a fortnight so make ready and bid farewell to thy families. Sir Baldor, you shall be leader. Stephen is to be appointed as steward of Shiloh and this Lucan returned to Ellioth with the Sword and Llyonesse. This is not a holiday, so you can wipe those self-satisfied smirks off yer faces!" he said sternly. He pointed to Sir Baldor. "Obey him as you would me, lads, that is an order!"

"Yes, captain!" they replied as one.

Penloth nodded grimly. "Good! Dismissed!"

The young knights hurried back to the tiltyard, excited about their adventure. Penlorian remained behind, still at attention.

"I said *dismissed*," Penloth repeated. He wanted no part in debating Penlorian who was obviously very displeased at not being chosen.

"Permission to speak, *captain*," Penlorian said, catching hold of his forearm as he made to walk past.

"You may speak to me about whatsoever you desire, Pen, save the fact that you were not assigned to this task," Penloth replied stonily, his face resolute. Two spots of bright color appeared in Penlorian's cheeks; a sure indicator of his rising ire.

"Nevertheless, I *will* bloody speak of it!" he shot back, tight-lipped. "This is not the first time I have been conveniently excluded from a task which involved any degree of risk! Sigmund was knighted less than a sennight ago and yet you chose him! *I have at least two years seniority over him!*"

"As captain and Chief Seraphim," interrupted Sir Penloth stiffly, "I am certainly not obligated to give an account of my decisions to you. *The subject is closed.*"

"I dare say it isn't!" retorted Penlorian heatedly, again stepping in his way. "You forget how well I know thee, Penloth! Thou art still playing the mother hen, forgetting that I am a man full grown. I have earned my spurs the same as you and wish to serve as a knight of the realm! How dare you hinder me from fulfilling my oath only to save thyself from anxiety! What is it? Art thou afraid something will happen to me or is it mere jealousy?"

Penloth bristled. He hated it when Penlorian was right and stared at him in silence, exchanging angry glares with his younger brother. The young whelp had tagged him good; he was behaving overly protective and jealous. His brother had already suffered a great deal of harassment from his comrades because of it, but how would Penlorian feel were their roles reversed? Despite his pride in his little brother, he was the only family he had left and found it difficult to order him into harm's way. He didn't dare reveal to him that he had a very bad feeling about the entire venture but had nothing to back up his dark premonitions with.

"Very well," he said reluctantly, a strange darkness settling over his heart. "You shall go as well though I can't help but feel that I will regret giving into this childish whim of yours!"

"Childish whim!" sputtered Penlorian, ready to give his brother an earful, then he grinned. It was just Penloth's way; he couldn't help it if his motherly instincts sometimes got the better of him! Beneath that gruff exterior was a heart of mush. Penlorian knew his older brother was secretly terrified of losing him and this more than anything served to swiftly dissipate his anger. With childlike abandon, Penlorian flung his arms about his older brother and gave him a bear hug. "Fear not!" he said happily. "Methinks this whole affair is naught but a chance to visit our kin in Shiloh and taste some of that incredible ale Dwayne has been bragging about in his letters."

When Penloth refused to return his smile, Penlorian aped his somber expression then put his hands on his hips in exasperation. "Good heavens, Penloth! It is only a brief voyage! There and back again with Llyonesse and the sword! I will return before Sir Luther has had her kittens! But should the worst befall me, or should old Joseph sail the ship onto the rocks, you must remember that just like you, I am willing to lay down my life for our king! Thou wouldst not shirk thy duty though you knew it to be dangerous! Then expect no less of me!"

"You missed your calling, brother of mine," Penloth growled, catching him about the head with his arm and pulling him close under his arm so he could not see his worried eyes. "A court solicitor thou shouldst have been, not a warrior."

"Perhaps," Penlorian replied, giving his brother a wink. "But for everything there is a season, a time to sing and a time to fight."

"Yes," agreed Penloth forcing a roguish grin. "But there are those like Sigmund and I who like to sing *as* we fight!"

"Aaaahhh," replied Penlorian, with a knowing nod. "So that is why thy opponents surrender so quickly! To silence thy voices!"

Penloth swung at him, but only thin air remained where Penlorian once stood, his laughter floating back to him from down the hall.

Chapter Six

It was nearly past noon when the sails of the approaching ship were sighted by the lookouts posted on Shiloh's seawall. A messenger was immediately dispatched on horseback, galloping up the hill at breakneck speed to the castle. He was ushered immediately into Lucius' private chambers.

"Is it the *Eden Mist*?" Lucius demanded the moment he entered.

"Yes, mi'lord, and she bears the colors of both Eloth *and* the seraphim."

"The seraphim!" Lucius repeated somewhat apprehensively. It was no surprise that they had come, but the thought of Sir Penloth in such close proximity made his flesh creep, despite the elaborate plans he had laid to capture him.

"Aye, mi'lord. Shall I have Dwayne, the Miller's son, take them to the chamber we've prepared?"

Lucius glanced at Scheldrake, his advisor, for confirmation who in turn gave him a comforting nod.

"Yes, and make sure none of our men are out where they can be seen," he instructed. "I don't want any suspicions aroused!"

"Yes, my lord," replied Golbreth turning to leave.

Scheldrake turned to him. "I will have the board laid out with food and drink."

"Make it rich fare," replied Lucius. "After all, it is going to be their last."

Penlorian and the other knights gazed about them, taking in their first sight of Shiloh in appreciative wonder. It was even more spectacular than they had expected and uncanny in its similarity to Ellioth. The castle looked down upon the mighty harbor from atop a tall, craggy hilltop just like Ellioth, accessible only by a singular road which snaked back and forth over the hilly terrain all the way down to the coastline. The harbor was greater in size and had twice again as many docks where they saw numerous fishermen repairing their nets. Unlike Ellioth, the village of Shiloh sprawled out in all directions, hugging the coastline as far as the eye could see.

Penlorian shielded his eyes, squinting to get a better look at the castle. The gatehouse and bailey were finished but what most impressed him was the Main house. It was enormous! Scaffolding rose high in the air about the structure where stonemasons labored to mortise and emplace blocks of cut limestone which lay piled everywhere. At least six towers were under simultaneous construction and half again that many arched bridges.

"Penloth! Is that you!" cried a familiar voice below him.

Penlorian looked down and broke into a wide grin of recognition. "Dwayne!" he cried, grasping his friend's hands in greeting.

"*Penlorian?*" Dwayne corrected himself upon closer examination. "You're the spitting image of your brother! Glad I am to see you again, lad, but where's Penloth? We were all expecting him to blow in with the first storm after Ardon's death!"

"Big brother is back in Ellioth nursing an injured leg and wounded pride," Penlorian answered, looking his old friend up and down. "You haven't changed much in three years! Except for the fact that there's less skin on those bones of yours!"

Dwayne grinned at him. "It's all the work! I hardly have time for a decent mug of ale anymore! But *you* have really changed! The last time I saw you, you were as high as my chest and playing with wooden swords! Now look at you! A knight of the realm and sporting a full set of whiskers to boot! Your brother owes me a drink, y'know!"

Penlorian laughed. "Then let me be the one to settle his debt! I've heard from a very reliable source that the ale here is surpassingly good!"

"Oh, it is! And this year's crop of barley is the best yet! One pint and yer head feels as light as a feather!"

"Penloth really will never forgive me for coming to Shiloh in his place now!" laughed Penlorian. "Unless, of course, I can manage to bring back a keg with me on the return trip?"

"No problem!" Dwayne said, scratching his beard. "But I'll lay odds to bodkins that if word gets out what's onboard, it'll be bone dry before it reaches Ellioth!"

The mention of Ellioth immediately sobered them both. Dwayne's face grew solemn and he squeezed Penlorian's shoulder. "I'm truly sorry about Ardon," he said. "It was a tragic loss for all of us but most especially for you and Penloth, I know."

"More so for the king," replied Penlorian. "He is a changed man, Dwayne, and it breaks my heart each time I see him. Eloth could not have loved Ardon more had he been his own son. But now to my errand: we are here to retrieve the sword and return Ardon's daughter for fostering in Ellioth. This Lucan is wanted for questioning! Stephen is to be appointed as steward for he thinks it very unseemly for this foreigner to have become steward without so much as a '*by your leave*'!"

"Lucan stepped in as a stop-gap, knowing it would be quite some time before Eloth could respond and only because he was the most qualified to do so," explained Dwayne in all fairness. "We have all been casting bets as to who would be coming back and had it been Joshua instead of you, I wouldn't now owe my favorite nanny goat to the blacksmith!"

"You almost won that bet!" said Sir Baldor, joining up with them as they walked up the road toward the castle. "We waited an entire fortnight for him to return, but he is upon errantry and could not be found in time. Who is this Lucan?"

Dwayne shrugged. "All I can tell you is that he and his men are of local origin and were nearly half-dead when they arrived over a year ago. They have done much to help us in building up Shiloh to what it is today."

"No small accomplishment, indeed!" commented Sir Morgan with sincere awe, gazing with the other knights at the enormous castle. The higher they climbed, the more apparent it became just how vast Shiloh had grown. When they reached the crest of the hill they could see that the fertile fields and orchards stretched off far into the distance, finally becoming lost in a haze of green.

"We have done much in the space of a few years, eh?" grinned Dwayne, leading them across the drawbridge and through the gate house.

"Indeed," agreed Penlorian, looking about him. "And where, pray tell, is our lord's sword?"

"In yonder courtyard," Dwayne replied, pointing. "How do you plan to get it out?"

"We don't," Penlorian replied. "You know as well as I that none may touch it save Eloth's heirs."

"Then how?"

"We shall take both blade and rock back with us," explained Sir Lawrence.

"It'll take four team of oxen to haul that hunk of rock all the way to the dock!" exclaimed Dwayne, eyeing the heavy stone.

"I'm sure you'll find us the very best!" replied Penlorian, slapping him on the back as they entered the massive court-yard. It was pentagon in shape and flanked by the main house, stables, mews, and towers with level after level of balconies that looked down upon it from all sides. Squarely in the center, laying on its side stood a large, hand-hewn cornerstone out of which brilliant beams of golden light shot out in every direc-tion. Eloth's sword hilt was blazing brighter than the noonday sun and none of them could look directly at it. A shiver passed through them as they drew near. Penlorian came as close as he dared to get a better look. He could feel invisible waves of power beating upon his brow.

"Do you feel it too?" whispered Dwayne, eyeing the sword with deep reverence.

Yes nodded Penlorian in agreement. "Ephlal is no blade to be trifled with." He gave it a quick look then drew back to a safe distance. It was even as old Joseph had said; the blade was fully embedded in the stone almost up to its pummel. There was no choice; they would have to bring the cornerstone back with them. How on earth had Ardon managed to put Eloth's sword through solid rock after mortally injuring himself?

"Come, I will you give a brief tour on the way to your chambers!" Dwayne said, leading them through a set of double doors. They followed him in pensive silence through a dizzying myriad of corridors and hallways and up several flights of stairs while he gave them detailed explanations of the various rooms, the materials used in their construction and the finishing touches yet to be applied. After the better part of an hour, they arrived at the chambers that had been prepared for them. Several wooden tables and chairs stood at hand as well as comfortable pallets on which to rest. The board was laid with platters of inviting fruit, various cheeses, meats, breads, and pitchers of cool mead and ale.

"This is as far as I come!" Dwayne said, squeezing Penlorian's shoulder with a smile. "No doubt Lucan will be by shortly to greet you, but I can't wait. I've got grain to mill and only a few more hours of light to do it!"

"Could have fooled me at the rate your tongue wags!" Penlorian chided him, ducking his swinging fist just in the nick of time.

"Cheeky brat!" Dwayne grinned good-naturedly. "In all sincerity, let us meet in a day or two and talk at leisure over a noggin of ale at the new inn!"

"Most assuredly," agreed Penlorian, waving him off with a smile. "Give my regards to your family. Tell them I will call upon them at least once before we depart."

"I will," replied Dwayne and shut the door behind him.

"Wonderful lad but his sails are certainly full of wind!" commented Sir Morgan, pouring himself a flagon full of mead. "Here now, this is quite a feast they laid out for us. Shall we set to, lads, while we await our benefactor?"

They needed no second invitation for they were exceedingly weary of stale water and hardtack. They quickly set to the food and drink with gusto, paying little heed to the slightly bitter aftertaste it left in their mouths until it was too late.

Lucius cracked open the door and peeked in. Satisfied that it was safe to enter, he quickly entered and shut it behind him, smiling with triumph. Eloth's knights lay sprawled where they had fallen, in mid-drink or mid-bite; broken vessels strewn across the floor amongst their prone bodies. Lucius picked his way amongst them, checking to make sure they were all fully drugged by kicking them roughly in the ribs. There were soft groans of pain but none could rise to deflect the blows; they were incapable of response. Golbreth entered the room moments later.

"Is all prepared?" Lucius asked him.

"Yes," he nodded. "Our men will board the ship at nightfall."

"Good," Lucius said, scrutinizing each face. He scowled for a moment as if displeased then smiled maliciously in satisfaction. He squatted next to a young man with dark brown hair and grabbed a fistful of it, roughly yanking his head up for a better look. The resemblance was unmistakable, but the face was far too youthful. No, it wasn't Penloth Estaban, as he had hoped, but his younger brother, Penlorian. A soft moan of pain escaped his lips. *So the brat had become a knight had he? Sent to do the dirty work of his older brother?* He abruptly let go, allowing Penlorian's head to fall hard upon the flagstone beneath him. Lucius stood. "Golbreth, after you have taken the ship, bring its captain to the dungeon."

"Aye," Golbreth replied. At that moment there came a knock upon the door. Golbreth waved several men in and one by one they lifted and slung the prostrate knights over their shoulders like sacks of meal, lining up before a tapestry which Scheldrake pulled to one side. Feeling with his fingers he found a small niche in the wall and pressed upon it. A large section of wall silently swung away, revealing the mouth of a very dark, secret passageway. One by one they carried the knights through until all had disappeared into the inky blackness.

Excruciating pain brought Penlorian back to consciousness. He opened his eyes slowly and looked upon what he at first took to be Hell. It was very, very dark all around him except for a faint red glow in the distance. The air was warm, oppressive, and fetid with a horrible stench. The faint wails and sobs of souls in torment rose immediately to his ears. Gulping down his fear, Penlorian looked down upon his own body to see what manner of demon was slashing at him with hot knives of pain to find himself hanging by his wrists, shackled by cruel iron rings that hung from the ceiling and bit unmercifully into his flesh. He was half-hanging, half-standing, with all of his body weight hanging upon his wrists which had swollen to nearly twice their normal size. What manner of nightmare was this? The last thing he remembered was drinking a cup of mead … then instant blackness … nothing … not even dreams … until he opened his eyes onto this pit. He heard the sound of approaching footsteps and looked upon a face he had thought never to see again in waking life, finally convinced beyond all doubt that he really was in Hell.

"Lucius!" he gasped in horror.

"I'm so pleased that you remember me!" Lucius fairly cooed. "How flattering! In all truth I had been hoping and expecting thy brother to come sailing into my harbor but you shall do just as well. I wonder if Penloth would have been as foolish as you to drink mead laced with belladonna?"

"Then I am not dead?" Penlorian wondered aloud.

Lucius threw back his head and laughed. "Not yet!" he answered, genuinely amused at Penlorian's confusion. "The last time I saw you, young Estaban, was when I had just been paraded through the village at the end of thy brother's leash." He watched with amusement as Penlorian's face went deathly white at the memory.

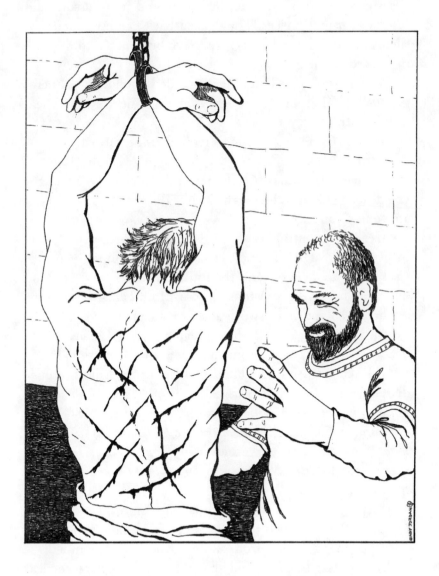

"I see you remember the incident well," he continued, referring to Penlorian's bull's-eye of a ripe tomato in his face. Lucius turned as several people entered the darkened chamber, a voice raised loud in anger. Joseph Fitzbaton was brought struggling to stand before them, his loud protests ceasing the instant he beheld the nightmarish scene around him. All of Eloth's young knights had been stripped naked, beaten mercilessly and were either shackled or bound in an assortment of cruel torture devices. They gazed back at him in terrified silence, trying desperately to be brave but unable to disguise the naked terror in their eyes.

"What is going on here?" he demanded, rounding on Lucius furiously. "What mean you by this abuse? The king shall hear of this outrage!"

"I certainly hope so," Lucius replied, unperturbed.

At that precise moment, Joseph recognized him. "Lucius!" he growled with undisguised hatred and disbelief. "We thought you dead! What mischief is this? How did you get here? What are you up to now?"

"Cease thy ranting, captain," Lucius snapped, in no mood to be interrogated. "I simply wish to impress upon you precisely who is in charge and the futility of thwarting me. I am not alone here. Many of those whom Eloth banished with me are here also and have sworn absolute allegiance to me." The captain stared at him in horror, realizing that Lucius was in deadly earnest as he continued. "Listen well, my good captain," Lucius continued. "Thou shalt return to Ellioth immediately and deliver this warning in Eloth's ears: *his sword of power, his ship's crew, knights, yea all who dwell in Shiloh are my hostages. Commerce between the two kingdoms has ceased as of now. If so much as one sail is sighted upon our horizon, the corpses of the dead will litter the streets before the first cannon ball can be lobbed over our walls!*"

Joseph glared at him, his hands balled into fists of impotent rage. "And what if the ship is not from Ellioth but some unsuspecting merchant from another land?" he demanded.

Lucius stared at him and shrugged, making it quite clear

that it mattered little to him either way; people would be murdered regardless.

"You're mad," Joseph whispered, shaking his head in disbelief. "Absolutely raving mad."

"Perhaps," smiled Lucius, the insult bothering him not. "I am now in power and not to be trifled with and think not, my good captain, that once you have sailed off that you can thwart me by turning about and firing back upon me. Even as we speak the cannons are being off-loaded and mounted onto the bluffs above the harbor for my defense."

Joseph shook with the effort to control his fury. "You'll not get away with this, the king will—"

"—The king will *what*?" Lucius demanded his lip curling into a sneer. "He is bereft of his precious sword and without it he is just another man with a crown on his head! I think we can both agree that I have very little to fear on that account!" He interrupted with a dangerous laugh.

"Will ye promise to do these lads no harm if I do all that you ask?" Joseph half-pleaded.

Lucius chuckled, shaking his head. "Thou art in no position to parley!" He turned to Arghast. "Take him back to the ship and lock him in the hold. Penloth's gift shall be delivered to you before daybreak tomorrow then set sail at the first opportunity for Ellioth. You know what to do ... "

"Yes, my lord," replied Arghast, casting a wicked smile in Penlorian's direction.

Before he could utter another protest, Joseph was knocked out cold, bagged and carried out like a sack of potatoes in a large burlap sack. Lucius turned back to Penlorian, gloating at him as if he were a prize turkey. Penlorian met Lucius' gaze, fearful but resolute.

"Don't bother lying to me; you and I both know I won't be leaving here alive," he said with all the dignity he could muster. "I have always been prepared to die for my king; do what you will!"

Lucius smiled at him. "Oh, I intend to," he hissed, cupping Penlorian's chin in his hand almost lovingly. "But thy death shall be neither swift nor merciful, little one, and thy brother shall know of every last gory detail," he hissed, his face inches away, his breath foul. *"Scream as loud as thou wilt, Penlorian ... there shall be none to enjoy it but I!"*

Chapter Seven

olbreth stood before Lucius with several other men, modeling the raiment they had stripped from Eloth's knights.[22] "Are we comely or are we comely?" he drawled, twirling around and batting his eyes as though he were a simpering maiden.

Lucius stared at him, one eyebrow lifting. "Their bodies have been disposed of where they can't be discovered?"

"Aye, mi'lord. We fed the lot of them, save the one, to your hounds ... you should have heard them laddies screaming!"

"I just hope for thy sake no one else did," snapped Lucius. "Now, if thou art through showing off, take thy men and commence posting the edicts. Be prepared, the villagers will be angry but thou knowest what to do."

"It's all arranged, just as we planned, my lord," replied Borgreth, girding Penlorian's sword about his waist. "C'mon men, let's give these peasants a taste of the new Elliothian chivalry!" They filed out and eventually marched into the market square where their arrival was met with many raised eyebrows. The *Eden Mist* had departed hours earlier, so the appearance of Eloth's knights caused all to wonder what they were still doing there. Borgreth shouldered his way up to the door of the Boar's Head Inn, tore down several old proclamations and nailed a new one in place while the curious villagers gathered round.

At that moment Dwayne exited through the double doors, saw whom he took to be Penlorian (by the gold border on the cape), and slapped him heartily on the shoulder. "Come to buy me that mug of ale now, eh?" he chortled.

Borgreth rounded on him with such a snarl that Dwayne hopped backwards in fright. "Watch who you clap on the shoulder, laddie, or next time I might take your bloody head off!" he snarled, his knife already drawn.

Dwayne stared at the unfamiliar face in dumbfounded amazement, running his eyes up and down the length of his clothes. What was this man doing in Penlorian's raiment? He glanced sideways as two additional "knights" came up to stand beside their comrade, scowling at him in a most threatening manner.

"What's the problem here?" one of them asked menacingly, fingering the dirk in his belt.

Dwayne was speechless with shock, his eyes growing even larger when two more knights added their number to the group, bringing the total to five. He looked at each face one by one, his fear and confusion growing by the minute. Eloth's knights had changed identities overnight, becoming much larger, and significantly more ugly and intimidating.

Dwayne turned back again to look at the knight in Penlorian's clothes and found him staring right back, a nasty suspicious look growing in his eyes. "I'm so-sorry," he managed to stammer, silent alarm bells going off in his head. "I g-guess we can have that drink la-later." Mercifully, the answer seemed to satisfy him. With a final parting glare, Borgreth turned and swaggered off with his other men in tow, shouting to the crowd to clear a wide swath for "Eloth's noble knights." It wasn't until they were well out of earshot that Dwayne allowed himself the luxury to exhale in relief, feeling fortunate to still be alive. He thrust his trembling hands deep into his pockets and turned about to read the edict with the others who had gathered around him.

> By Royal Decree of His Majesty, Eloth and Joshua, Lord of Shiloh:
>
> Be it known this day, that at the time of the next full moon, and every month thereafter, a tax of 25% will be levied upon all proceeds resulting from the purchase, trade or sale of all goods in Shiloh. This tax will be due and payable in full, by coin of the realm, to be collected by my Royal Knights, the Seraphim.
>
> Those who fail to pay their taxes will become indentured to service of the crown until the debt is fully paid. Those who refuse either by word, inference, or deed to comply most loyally with this edict will be subject to the full weight of the law, including confiscation of property, permanent loss of freedom, debtor's prison, or capital punishment.
>
> Long live His Royal Majesty, Eloth, Sovereign Lord of Ellioth and Shiloh.

"This is thievery!" exploded the blacksmith. "None of us can pay these taxes and well he knows it! What is the king thinking? Has he gone mad? We were told before we came here that no taxes would be due for the space of five years and then only one-tenth! This will enslave us all!"

"*SSSHH!*" hissed his wife, looking about fearfully. "Do you want them to come back and arrest you for speaking this way?"

Loud arguments broke out, causing larger and larger crowds to gather in the growing commotion. A few blindly defended the actions (they assumed to be) of the king, saying that he had every right to raise taxes after so many years of peace and prosperity, but more denounced him, feeling totally betrayed.

"I should have known this would end up as a miserable trick! It was just too good to be true!" spat the cooper. Many nodded their heads in agreement.

"Eloth was only interested in one thing! Accumulating power and riches from our blood and sweat! We're little more than beasts of burden to him!" added another loud voice.

"Wait a minute! Wait a minute!" exclaimed Dwayne, shouting to be heard above the din. "All of this is totally uncharacteristic of our king! Am I the only one here who has noticed that those knights are different from the ones who arrived yesterday?"

"All we saw were their uniforms and that makes them knights!" answered someone.

"The Steward's seal is upon this bloody edict!" came another in response. "If you have a better explanation to offer then let's hear it!"

Dwayne stood aghast, at a complete loss to account for the seemingly authentic seal upon the edict. But if those men were knights of Ellioth, he was a billy goat! "I don't know what's happening nor can I explain my doubts, but I can say that those knights are not the same men who came from Ellioth!" he insisted. "Especially the one with the gold edging on his cape who almost took my head off!"

"Can anyone else verify this claim?" shouted the blacksmith, looking about. No one could. "Seems you're the only one, laddie. You'll have to do better than that!"

Dwayne bristled with anger. "Then let us go address Lucan and get this business straightened out once and for all!"

"Let's go!" they agreed.

In one accord, they rounded up their brethren from their shops, stalls, fields, and cottages and marched up the hill paying little attention to the horn blasts which began issuing from the gatehouse. When they reached the gates, they were astonished to find them closed and locked against them. Even the new drawbridge had been lifted.

"Now what is the meaning of this?" swore Damien in disbelief, innkeeper of the Boar's Head Inn, under his breath. He glared at the knights posted atop the gatehouse with their crossbows, longbows, and arrows already fitted to the string.

"What seek you?" cried out Borgreth in a loud voice. "Why do you gather before the gates? Have you no fields to plow or livestock to tend?"

"We wish to speak with the steward!" shouted Damien, shaking the crumpled proclamation in his fist.

"I am Eloth's knight and Captain of the Guard, appointed for the defense of Shiloh," shouted Golbreth arrogantly, stepping into view. "Eloth himself sent us with these edicts to ensure that they are carried out. Whatever you have a mind to tell Lucan you can bloody well say to me!"

This did not bode well with the villagers who eyed the "knights" with wary eyes. Why were they attired as if for battle and why was their manner so surly? Surely they could see that they only desired to talk, not do battle!

"Our business with Lucan does not require battle arms!" said the blacksmith. "Why do you greet us as though we come to a siege?"

"By order of Eloth himself," replied Golbreth. "We have been instructed to arrest any who protest his royal decrees."

An alarmed murmur swept through the crowd in response. *Arrested? For simply voicing a complaint?* "This is absurd!" whispered the blacksmith to Dwayne, fearful of being overheard. "They can't arrest us just because we want to talk!"

"I don't think *they* would agree with you!" replied Dwayne in a hoarse whisper, eyeing the knights with a fearful eye. "That one there nearly took my head off a moment ago for clapping him on the back!"

The villagers looked back up at the knights who glared right back at them their malevolent silence defying one and all to say or do anything that would give them an excuse to shoot.

"We wish only to clarify the meaning of this tax," faltered the blacksmith.

Golbreth stared at him menacingly. "Precisely what do you find difficult to understand?"

A long silence ensued in which the blacksmith weighed the risk of whether he should respond and get an arrow in the throat for his trouble or leave well enough alone. A shadow of a nasty smile ghosted the knight's mouth as he raised his bow in reply and leisurely took aim upon him. The blacksmith backed up in a hurry. The knight was actually going to shoot him! Without further delay, he turned away and fled, shoving people out of his way in his haste to get through the crowd and out of bow shot. Golbreth sneered at his departing figure then waved them off. "All of you! Disperse and go back to your work!" he shouted.

"But why can't we just speak with him?" protested the miller, ignoring his son who was tugging desperately on his arm to keep quiet. "Surely there is no crime in such a request!"

"Disperse I say, *disperse!*" shouted Borgreth, lifting his crossbow and taking aim upon the miller. He let the arrow fly, penetrating the ground right between his feet. A few more inches and he would have been skewered. The miller paled, unsure if he owed his survival to bad aim or if it had only been a warning shot. Either way, he did not want to risk it a second time. The entire crowd backed away with him, murmuring in alarm as Borgreth took aim again upon them. Just at that moment Lucius appeared, stretched forth his hand and forcibly lowered the crossbow before he could loose a second arrow.

"Peace, good knight," he said in a loud, calming voice. "Let me address them; the voice of reason shall surely prevail." Golbreth and Borgreth both stared at him menacingly for a long moment (as rehearsed) then "reluctantly" nodded. Lucius turned to the crowd below, his voice dripping with empathy. "Good people, I share thy genuine dismay over the proclamations posted today, but I am not responsible for issuing them. It is the knights of thine own king which brought them and charged me with their strict enforcement. Is it not thy duty, as his loyal subjects, to obey all his edicts?"

"But none of us can pay these taxes!" protested a woman from the crowd.

"Then I fear his knights will take matters into their own hands," sighed Lucius sorrowfully, allowing the unspoken threat to have its effect. "I am merely an appointed servant, a messenger, I can do nothing."

"Get ye gone, all of you!" shouted Golbreth again, raising his crossbow. "You'll never be able to pay your bloody taxes if you continue to stand around all day gawking before the gates! *Disperse!*"

With angry faces and anxious murmurs, the crowd slowly drifted away, dejectedly returning to their shops and fields, frustrated and very disheartened. Dwayne hesitated and was one of the very last to leave. He could feel the knight's deeply suspicious eyes on his back with every step, his neck hairs bristling in alarm. Any moment he expected to hear the *twang* of the cross-bow and feel an arrow between his shoulder blades. He didn't feel safe until he was all the way down the hill and well out of bow shot. Not for one instant did he believe a word uttered by Lucan, of whom he was now thoroughly suspicious. He had no doubt that the high taxes were but the beginning of their sorrows.

People began to disappear the following month, usually during the wee hours of the morning. Neighbors would awake to find other neighbors suddenly gone, their home and property either in smoking ruins or with a notice posted upon the door that read *"Confiscated by order of the Crown."* It became the primary topic of discussion behind closed doors and in the back rooms of inns and always in hushed whispers because it was uncertain as to what unfriendly ear might be listening. While most of the villagers grew ever more destitute, a select number actually became wealthier, fueling the rumors that they had become informants in the pay of the "crown." Old friends began eyeing each other with distrust and relationships even amongst members of the same family became strained. As time wore on Eloth's "knights" grew increasingly more brazen in their dastardly deeds.

Dwayne bent over the millstone, inspecting the texture of the grain underneath when a shadow fell across him. He turned around, expecting to see a customer and felt the blood drain from his face upon finding two *knights* blocking the doorway.

"You are the miller's son," stated Golbreth, frowning at him. "Where is your father? He's under arrest."

"Bu-but why? We just gave every last farthing we had to pay *your* taxes!" Dwayne answered.

For an instant, the flicker of a smile passed over Golbreth's face, as if to plainly say that he knew it as well. "Not according to my information, he hasn't," he drawled, plucking an apple from the top of a pile and biting in with relish. "Now tell me where he is and maybe I won't set torch to your mill!"

Dwayne was at a total loss, watching in silent rage as the knight flung the once bitten apple onto the floor in disdain.

"What's going on in here?" demanded the miller angrily, suddenly stepping into the room. He glared at Golbreth. "What are you doing here? I just paid your bloody taxes last week! Every last farthing I had *and* my last milk cow! I owe you nothing more!"

"Not by my figuring, old sluggard!" countered Golbreth. He looked around, seeking something of value. "If you give us those ten sacks of meal there, I might be persuaded to forget this little conversation."

"Father, please ... " whispered Dwayne, watching the telltale signs of rage spread over his father's face. "*Don't—*"

"*You bloody leeches!*" exploded the miller, reaching for a razor sharp sickle. "Get out of my mill!"

Golbreth unsheathed his sword. "You just forfeited your precious mill, you scum! Grab him, men!" More knights marched into the room. They forcibly took hold of the miller and wrestled him onto the floor, pressing him down cruelly with their boots. Dwayne stared aghast in mounting panic, helpless to do anything while he watched them beat and kick his father to a bloody pulp. At that very instant, his mother ran in, took one look and screamed. "Are you all mad? What are you doing? Get off of my husband at once! Dwayne, help him!"

Dwayne looked up. "Mother, *run!*" he screamed, but it was too late. Two more knights appeared out of nowhere from behind her, cutting off her only means of escape. The larger and uglier of the two grabbed her and threw her bodily against the wall, pinning her against it. He looked her up and down very slowly and leered, his mouth close to hers. "It's been a long time since I had a woman," he grunted, fumbling with his sword belt.

Without further thought for his own safety, Dwayne leapt forward, trying to insert himself protectively between his mother and the knight. "No," he pleaded, his eyes beseeching.

"Please just take the grain or whatever else you want and leave us alone!"

The knight roughly flung him aside and pulled his knife. "That's just what I intend to do, laddie," he smiled and let fly.

Dwayne saw the flash of the dagger and ducked in the nick of time, hearing it whoosh over him as it embedded itself into the wall where his head had been only a moment earlier.

"*Run, Dwayne! Run!*" screamed his mother. Moving purely on terror and instinct, Dwayne flung himself out through the window, falling onto the flume which hung over the waterwheel. His last glimpse of his father was a grisly one. He lay as if dead, blood seeping from his nose, ears, and mouth.

"*Kill him!*" someone shouted from within. Two knights came out after him, forcing his limbs into action. Dwayne struggled hysterically out of their grasp, rode the waterwheel down into the pond, and swam for his life. Arrows whizzed past his head, missing him by bare inches. He took in a great gulp of air and dove for bottom, stroking beneath the surface until his lungs were ready to burst. Their arrows spent, the knight cursed and returned inside. A few moments later, Dwayne resurfaced, spitting and coughing up water even as he sobbed with rage and despair. He crawled up onto the opposite bank into the shelter of the surrounding reeds. Despite the horrific screams of his mother, no one had dared to come out to see what was going on or to help her; too fearful of becoming the next victim. He screamed silently in rage, beating his breast in agony. *These knights were not from Ellioth! They would never have done such things!* These men were monsters spawned from the very pit of hell! Something had to be done! *Something had to be done!* He scrambled to his feet with an anguished sob and disappeared into the woods, never to be seen in the village again.

Lucius' men continued to pillage the lives, homes, and storehouses of Shiloh's inhabitants until they had nothing left to claim as their own, always claiming that what was done had been all in the name of Eloth. Shops and cottages were regularly ransacked, put to the torch, or replaced by businesses of a more unsavory nature, mostly taverns or brothels with names such like "Goat's Head Tavern, Dragon's Lair or Hen's Coop," where gambling, drinking, and brawling became the primary source of commerce. It didn't seem to matter if taxes had been paid or not: more and more was demanded until everyone had become indentured as slaves to Shiloh's government. If anyone so much as whispered a word of complaint they were somehow found out and taken away, or murdered in plain sight. Fear fell like a vast shadow upon all. And while the whole of Shiloh's society steadily deteriorated from within, Lucius' finger of accusation continually pointed west, to the land of Ellioth shamelessly declaring that all was the fault of Eloth who refused to withdraw his knights or reduce their taxes.[23] There were some lone voices which contradicted his diatribes against the crown who tried to convince others that it was Lucan who was really to blame, but they became fewer in number each year and were persecuted as extremists and fanatics by the majority of those who had succumbed to Lucius' relentless lies. Desperate to protect their children from becoming either victims or pawns, parents sent them into hiding, secreting food and clothing to them at night.

Chapter Eight

Navigating into port by moonlight was dangerous, but Captain Joseph Fitzbaton was familiar with Ellioth's harbor and had no other choice unless he wanted his throat slit. His neck was already raw from the knife which had been held to it for the past twenty minutes to discourage any ideas he may have entertained of giving warning to those in Ellioth. But his eyes were free at least and he glanced about, wondering what mischief Lucius' men were up to as they began clambering out of the hold like rats from a sinking ship. All was dark and perfectly still as they glided past with not a soul in sight; dashing his hopes that anyone would see their arrival and sound the alarm. His expertise no longer needed, a heavy blow caught him upon the head and Joseph fell with a heavy thud onto the quarter-deck. He was then lifted, carried off the ship and deposited next to a wooden cask a good distance from shore.

The tranquility of the night was instantly shattered by the explosion of cannon fire from the *Eden Mist* as Lucius' men rained destruction upon Ellioth. Cottages and business alike erupted into billowing flames and smoke, instantly alerting the entire kingdom. Men, women, and children spilled out of their homes, frightened and injured, oblivious to Lucius' men who had swarmed onto the other ships in the harbor with knives, casks of oil, and lit torches. The castle had awakened also and knights were streaming down to the harbor to assist their kinsmen. All were too busy tending to the injured and dying to pay much heed to Eloth's fleet until it was too late and by then all six ships were completely engulfed in flame. Unnoticed in all the commotion, the Eden Mist sailed back to Shiloh under cover of night where Lucius would soon learn of his men's success.

The ships went up like dry kindling with a mighty roar, awakening all who dwelt closest to the harbor. Alarm bells rang out furiously, summoning all to douse the flames which were spreading quickly from pier, ships and to the village. Without Eloth's merchant ships, Ellioth would be virtually cut off from all other lands. Before long, the entire village had formed a bucket brigade to put out the flames, but it quickly became horrifyingly apparent that they could do nothing to salvage their ships. Efforts were then redirected to keep the flames from spreading into the village. People ran up and down the streets with sloshing water buckets to soak the thatching on their roofs lest flying embers set them alight, pausing only now and again to glance in awe at the mighty ships bobbing like lit bonfires upon the waves. The flames lit up the sky for miles in every direction and the crack and pop of burning timbers and roar of greedy flames was so loud, it almost drowned out the cries and shouts of those who sought to beat the flames down that had erupted on shore.

Even from a safe distance away, Penloth could feel the intense heat on his face as he feverishly worked to direct the efforts of his people. Suddenly a cry went up and people were pointing off into the distance. Penloth straightened, struggling to see through the acrid smoke as two riders approached Ellioth from the north.

"Who comes?" Penloth shouted, immediately suspicious. "Who rides upon the road to Ellioth at such an ungodly hour?" His ever present sword was already drawn, thinking the horsemen were the culprits who had set the fire.

"It's I, Joshua!" shouted the rider. "Put down thy sword, Sir Penloth!"

Penloth obeyed for there was no mistaking the gleaming white mane and coat of Paracletis as the stallion thundered toward him through the black smoke. Joshua drew reign and dismounted. "I saw the flames in the distance," he said breathlessly as the other rider drew abreast. "I was already on my way back and thought all Ellioth was ablaze! What deviltry is afoot?"

"Joshua!" cried a voice behind them.

Joshua and Penloth both looked around to find Eloth striding toward them from the docks. His face, hair, and clothing covered with soot. Father and son clapped arms about one another in a brief embrace.

"You come at an hour most unexpected," said the king, releasing him. "The entire fleet is lost, burned below the waterline." He brushed at his clothes and hair then ceased, realizing it was useless. "This was no accident; 'twas deliberate sabotage. The bodies of those who did this are probably burnt amongst the wreckage."

"Sabotage, but who?" began Joshua.

"I know not," sighed Eloth. "I questioned the harbor master and his family, but they know nothing. By the time they awoke, the entire fleet was already ablaze and the sentries murdered. I've already directed my steward to inform their families and make provisions for their care."

Joshua pointed to a knot of people that had gathered down near the sea wall. "What is going on down there?"

They hurried forward arriving just as Captain Joseph Fitzbaton was brought back to consciousness.

"Joseph!" exclaimed Joshua in surprise, kneeling beside him. He gently lifted him to an upright sitting position. The captain tried to open his eyes but was coughing too violently to do so.

"Penloth, some water if you please," Joshua said, propping him up in his arms so he could breathe easier. Penloth left and swiftly returned with a dipper of water. Patiently they waited as Joseph sipped at it until it was empty, his coughing subsided.

"Forgive me, my lord, for failing you," he rasped finally, tears seeping down his craggy cheeks. "I wanted to give warning and would have but for my cowardice and the message I was instructed to bring!"

"What mean you, Joseph?" demanded Penloth anxiously. "Who held a knife at your throat? What message! Who set our ships ablaze?"

"Lu-Lucius," he choked, erupting into another spate of coughing.

"Lucius!" all three echoed in disbelief, wondering if he had taken complete leave of his senses. Lucius was surely long dead, banished years ago! Joshua lifted the dipper up and encouraged him to drink more so he could continue his story.

A voice suddenly called out to them from the shoreline. "Sir Penloth, this cask here is addressed to you!" This announcement evoked a violent reaction from Joseph. He seized hold of Penloth's jerkin, his eyes wild with fear and alarm. "Heed them not! *Do not go near it!*" he commanded, his fingers tightening to make sure Penloth remained where he was.

"Why, Joseph? What is wrong? What is in it?" Penloth demanded, struggling to pry the man's fingers loose. A strange fear gripped his heart. "Where are the knights who sailed with thee? *Where is my brother, Penlorian?*"

Joseph stared at him in silence, but the look in his eyes struck terror into Penloth's breast he had never known before, not even in all his years of battle. His heart began to pound so hard it hurt. Penloth shoved Joseph's hands away, ignoring the loud rip as his tunic tore away in his hands and marched with mounting panic toward the shoreline, the light from the flames clearly silhouetting the barrel.

"Penloth ... wait!" Joseph shouted, struggling to his feet. Sharing the captain's alarm, Joshua jumped up and ran to Penloth's side, grasping hold of the knight's arm. Whatever lay inside the cask, it was obviously something Joseph feared Penloth seeing. "Penloth," said Joshua, trying to keep his voice calm and steady. "I pray thee, do not open the cask until we have spoken more with Joseph—"

Penloth shook him off. "Leave me," he growled, refusing to look at him as he continued toward the barrel. Eloth also stood to his feet and called out for Penloth to return, but the knight refused to listen, marching up to the cask which sat within a ring of curious onlookers like a malevolent presence. Penloth grasped hold of the lid to yank it off, causing the villagers around him to back away, fearful of what might lay within. There was a horrific creaking but the lid was stuck fast. After several more futile efforts to pry it off, Joshua breathed a quiet sigh of relief, hoping the obstinate knight would give it up. He was wrong. Penloth cursed, his desperation and panic growing by the moment. He would have that lid torn off if it took all his fingers and blood to do it and let the devil be hanged! He searched the debris littering the ground briefly for something he could use as leverage, but when he found nothing, he cursed again and finally withdrew his cherished sword.

"Penloth! *NO!!*" exclaimed Joshua, horrified. The knight shoved the gleaming blade tip under the lid and worked it back and forth until it was several inches in. Leveraging his weight upon the hilt until it bent almost in two, he forced one end of the lid up. With a scream of splintering wood, the lid began to lift. Penloth slid his blade in further and continued pushing and working it like a can opener. The sword was one of the finest blades ever made and considered priceless, but it had never been created to function as a pry bar. With a loud *SNAP* his ancient sword, Zhalifwyr, broke asunder. Joshua stared in horror, watching Penloth fling away the useless shards as though it were nothing more than refuse and with another string of curses, grappled again with the lid, this time using his bare hands. Finally it began to lift away.

"*Penlorian ... Penlorian. ...!*" Penloth sobbed aloud, turning his face away from the rising stench as he continued yanking. With a last yank, the lid came free and the overwhelming smell of rotting flesh filled the air, washing over all who stood near. Penloth reached into the cask, already knowing what he would find inside. A head of curly brown hair matted with blood greeted his eyes.

"*Noooooooooooooo!*" he wailed, falling to his knees beside the cask, overcome with rage, anguish, and nausea. "*Penlorian is cut to pieces! He cut my brother into pieces!*" he roared in agony. Joshua's arms went about him and held him fast. Penloth wilted like a child in his arms. Eloth approached the barrel and looked within, his face creasing with anguished grief. Without bothering to cover his nose or mouth, the king reached inside and withdrew a bloody dagger with a note impaled on it.

"Penloth, you should never have sent a boy to do a man's job ... Lucius."

He immediately crumpled the parchment in his fist, instantly recognizing the handwriting of his former steward.

"Damn him! Damn him to hell!" Penloth choked. He turned his head and doubled over, finally succumbing to nausea; retching uncontrollably between roars of grief. Joshua knelt beside him, fighting back his own tears and wishing he could forget the horrific image of his friend's body. Together he and Eloth lifted Penloth gently onto his feet, tucking their arms under his armpits to keep him semi-upright. They paused but once for Eloth to give orders that Penlorian's remains be removed and buried with all the honor and glory due a knight, then they half-walked, half-carried Penloth back to his chamber and put him to bed with drugged wine. Despite his exhaustion from having ridden almost non-stop for two weeks, Joshua sat watch over him throughout the night, holding his hand as he wept and moaned in his sleep.

"How fares our good Penloth?" asked Eloth, welcoming his son into his council chambers early the following morning.

"Not good," replied Joshua wearily, running his fingers through his tangled hair. "He blames himself for allowing his brother to sail to Shiloh despite his dark premonitions. Lucius' message was intended to injure him deeply and so it has. I'm not sure Penloth will ever find it in his heart to forgive himself for allowing Penlorian to go."

"My heart weeps for him," Eloth murmured, having not slept all night for wondering how he was going to relay the additional dark tidings of Ardon and his family's fate to his son in addition to Penlorian's monstrous death. Joshua had loved Ardon as much as Penloth loved Penlorian and no doubt was already exhausted both in body, mind, and soul. His own heart was sore with grief and felt as though it had been trampled upon with nail-shod feet. How many times could the same heart be broken and yet continue to beat?

"My son," he said, tears spilling down his cheeks as he took Joshua's hand into his. I had sent forth messengers to summon thee long before word came that the *Eden Mist* had returned."

Joshua stiffened with fear at these ominous words then suddenly noticed the parchment in his father's hand. Reluctantly he took it and read the letter containing Ardon's last words. Eloth felt his own heart break anew as he watched disbelief, anger, and then unfathomable pain pass in quick succession over his son's face. Joshua closed his eyes and bowed his head, overwhelmed with grief.

"There is more," Eloth said softly, knowing that no matter how gently he broke the news, Joshua was going to be devastated. "I have spoken with Joseph Fitzbaton throughout the night and he has related to me all that has been told him by Lucius."

Joshua stared at him, not daring to breathe or move.

Eloth continued. "As you learned last night, our adversary is alive; Ardon and Zarabeth art dead and Lucius is holding our people hostage. Ephlal remains in Shiloh, but he cannot yet make use of it."

"There is a matter dearer to my heart than all else, father, and yet thou speakest not of her," said Joshua, his heart clenching with fear. "Is there naught you can tell me of my Llyonesse?"

Eloth's shoulders sagged and he shook his head unable to speak anymore. In the end, he could not find the strength to say the words that would break his son's heart beyond all recall. Joshua went rigid with fear, all color draining from his face. He closed his eyes, struggling to maintain his composure.

"*Llyonesse is no more?*" He asked of his father. Eloth nodded, his shoulders heaving.

Joshua swallowed, lifting anguished eyes full of tears to his father. "Lucius did not prophesy in vain when he said we would rue the day we showed him mercy," he whispered then began to shake with silent sobs of grief.

A knock came upon the door. Squeezing his son's shoulder for a brief moment, Eloth responded. Gabrielle, his steward, stuck his head through. "They're here, mi'lord," he announced, pretending not to see the prince wiping tears from his face with his sleeve.

"Send them in," Eloth replied, standing to his feet. "I have summoned a council to decide our next course of action."

Joshua nodded, too choked up to speak, wishing he could have had some time alone in which to grieve. His heart felt as if it had been torn to shreds.

The double doors opened wide to permit his knights, advisors, servants, Joseph Fitzbaton, and last of all came Sir Penloth, looking like he had aged into an old man in the space of a single night. Everyone who saw him for the first time was taken aback and greatly appalled but took great care not to draw attention to it out of respect for his grief. To each side of him were Sir Bors and Sir Luther, his closest friends among the seraphim.

Eloth waited for them to take their seats around the council table then spoke. "As you all have certainly heard by now, great evil has befallen us," he said by way of introduction. "We have lost Ardon, Zarabeth, Llyonesse, their unborn child, and now Penlorian along with our best and brightest young knights."

At this, Sir Penloth, who had been silent since the night before, looked up in surprise, his eyes wide with surprise. It was the first he had heard of the news of Llyonesse. Joshua gave no outward reaction, but Penloth's keen eyes did not miss his involuntary flinch. Despite his own grief, his heart wrung anew with pity for his prince.

Eloth continued. "The *Eden Mist* returned late last night and was used to distract us with her cannon fire while they set our fleet ablaze."

"*Lucius!*" came back the surprised response from those gathered who did not yet know.

"Joseph," Eloth continued, turning to the Captain, "please tell this council now the message given thee by him."

Joseph nodded, visibly trembling with the strain of keeping his emotions in check. "Mi'lords," he began, feeling a great measure of personal guilt at having been used as an unwilling accomplice in Lucius' crimes. "The men who sailed hither with me were the very same rebels you banished from Ellioth many years ago. They came by order of their master, Baron Lucius of Northumberland, who himself somehow engineered Ardon's death, murdered Penlorian and the other knights, put Llyonesse to the sword and who now holds all in Shiloh as his hostages. Upon my departure I was given a warning directly from the viper's mouth."

The silence in the room was profound, all eyes fastened upon him in numb horror.

"Speak, Joseph," said the king, "and let all within these walls pay heed."

Joseph swallowed and nodded, closing his eyes as he recited word for word Lucius' malediction.

"Beware, Eloth! All who dwell in Shiloh are my hostages. The cannon from the Eden Mist are mounted on the bluffs in my defense and shouldst you be foolhardy enough to attempt any assault or rescue, I will blow thy ships from the water and put every last man, woman, and child to the sword! Think not to sail here and recover thy sword, Ephlal, for it lies safely within my possession and there shall it remain until it disintegrates into rust!"

Joshua took a deep breath, forcing the torturous doubts from his mind. "How long before more ships could be built?" he asked the steward.

"More?" repeated the steward, shaking his head. "We would be fortunate to find wood sufficient for one and even that might take years, my lord," he replied, looking over a sheaf of papers. "That last lightning storm which burned our groves all but destroyed the old growth we used for timber."

"Cannot adequate timber be salvaged from the burnt ships or cannibalized from present structures to build another?" asked Eloth.

"Nay, they all burned down to the waterline and below," he replied. "Even if we could salvage sufficient timber from other sources, there is still the matter of the keel to consider. It must be of oak or mahogany and very strong. There is but one oak remaining which might serve as a keel, but it is many years from the needed maturity."

"Of what use is one ship to us at any rate?" interrupted Sir Penloth. "The captain here has said that Lucius has cannon pointed out to sea. It would take an armada to get through his defenses and by then all our kinfolk will have been slaughtered like sheep!"

Joshua cleared his throat. "Gentlemen, it matters little whether we have few ships or many for we now have none. Let us concentrate on the task of building *one* ship which can take me to Shiloh."

"We shall scour the realm and use every bit of lumber salvageable," said the steward, standing to his feet. "I shall not rest until there is a ship seaworthy enough to sail!"

"That may be many a year; what will become of our countrymen in the meantime?" asked Sir Penloth, voicing the thoughts of all those in the room. No one answered his question, but the thought of Lucius reigning unchecked, unhindered and confident of his autonomy to destroy without fear of retribution, was unthinkable![24]

Chapter Nine

*L*lyonesse stood with her arms crossed over her chest, fighting back tears of fear and frustration.

"I don't know where it is!" she repeated for what felt like the millionth time. "I searched and searched as you bade me and it is lost!" She widened her eyes accusingly. "You took it, didn't you?"

Lucius regarded her with slitted eyes, his suspicions dwindling slightly. "If I had taken it then what, pray tell, would be the logic in my asking you where it is?" he retorted.

"To plague me!" replied Llyonesse in a small voice. She knew she could only provoke him so far and then he would completely lose his temper. She held out her hand out, palm up. "Please give it back to me," she whispered in a pleading voice, allowing genuine tears to flow in the hopes it would convince him of her sincerity. Lucius continued to stare at her, his right eye twitching as he sought to determine her honesty. She seemed earnest enough, but he suspected she had succeeded in duping him before without his knowledge. Perhaps she had indeed lost the locket; she had lost many other things much more valuable, mostly the expensive gifts he had given her over the years. He sighed in sudden exasperation, losing all will to push the matter further. "Why dost thou hate me so?" he questioned softly, pushing the curls away from her forehead. "Do I not always bring thee pretty playthings? Art thou not always well fed and attired in the very finest clothes?"

"Yes," Llyonesse mumbled, leaning as far away from him as she dared. He was always trying to pet her like she was some cat and she hated it! But Lucius had long ago tired of her elusiveness. He grasped her chin and forced her to look him in the eye. Llyonesse flinched at his touch, feeling her heart pound as his beady, black eyes smoldered upon her.

"Let me go!" she pleaded.

He frowned at her, very displeased. "Very well," he snapped in exasperation, releasing her arm. "Thou art a spoiled little minx, but I suppose that I am to blame for that. Just have a care thou dost not push my patience too far, Llyonesse. There is a limit, even for thee."

The warning was softly spoken but the hard edge to his voice clearly warned her that her days of resisting his wishes were short-lived. He stood and marched from her chamber, closing and locking the door behind him. Llyonesse took a deep, shuddering breath, relieved to be rid of him at last. She felt like a caged bird or one of his prized falcons whom he kept hooded and tethered to a post in the mews until he wanted them for sport. Even they enjoyed more liberty than she for at least they were permitted to fly free during the hunt while she was ever kept locked away in her wretched chamber, seeing none but him and Clotilde, her nurse. She put her ear to the door, listening intently as his footsteps faded away down the hall then waited a bit more. Only after she was convinced that he was truly gone, did she fall onto her knees and squirm under her bed, getting dust onto her expensive brocade dress and petticoats. With nimble fingers she removed a small chink of stone from the base of the wall and slipped two fingers inside, withdrawing a small package wrapped in waxed cloth. It had taken many weeks, broken utensils and torn fingernails, but it had been well worth the effort to safeguard her most precious possession. With shaking fingers she folded back the wrapping and withdrew a small golden locket. She snapped it open, gazing longingly upon the tiny portrait inside.

"Please, Joshua," she whispered, unable to fight the over-whelming loneliness any longer. "Please come for me...please take me away from here." She lay her head upon the cold stone floor, hugged the locket close to her heart and fell fast asleep, trying to remember the fair land of her birth and the voice of the boy which had faded to a distant memory.

Lucius returned to the salon where two of his men were waiting for him. "Well?" he demanded, pouring himself a cup of wine. "Any success in routing them out yet?"

Ranulf and Findalf exchanged nervous glances. "No, my lord," they responded, fearing his reaction.

Lucius swept his gaze over them in disgust. "I fail to under-stand how men who are supposedly renown for their cunning and savagery can have such great difficulty tracking and captur-ing a few ill-fed boys. Hast thou not seized even one?"

"Nay, my lord. They may be *mere boys* but they're crafty as foxes and have many friends amongst the villagers. They either aren't lured by the bait or they figure out how to spring the traps without getting caught."

"Then start rounding the villagers up! Question and torture each one until someone squawks! Set better traps! Use more enticing bait! I want this underground movement exterminated immediately!" Lucius shouted, flinging his goblet against the farthest wall. He pointed his finger in their faces. "Fail me again and I'll have thee disemboweled in the public square like those tanners last month!"

Ranulf and Findalf fled.

Dwayne crouched low in the bushes, his lean face caked in mud for concealment, leafy twigs secured to his tattered clothing and sticking out at odd angles throughout his matted hair. Penlorian would not have recognized his old friend were he alive to see him now. Years of unending hunger and constantly being hunted had done their damage. Gone was the mischievous twinkle that once sparkled in his gray eyes. They were sunken now and ringed with dark circles from lack of sleep. His once full, ruddy face had become a deep bronze and was gaunt and tough as leather. Dwayne had become one with the forest that fed and protected him. He had learned to pass through tall grass and bushes as silently as a butterfly on the wing. Twigs did not snap under his bare, heavily callused feet, nor did birds or insects move to avoid him, so silently did he pass before them. The creatures of the forest had become his allies; they were his meat, companions, and perhaps most valuable of all—his servants. Dwayne smirked with disdain, watching Lucius' men set yet another worthless trap. They worked less than a furlong away in a clearing, grumbling loud enough for his people to hear them from the other side of town. The two men worked quickly, oblivious to the hungry eyes scrutinizing the loaves of bread, wheels of cheese, fresh fruit, and strips of meat laid tantalizingly within a basket. Dwayne grinned. He and his comrades would feast well tonight and laugh over the fools they had made of Lucius' lackeys. They were almost done, their backs turned to him in a dangerously vulnerable position.

Dwayne raised his arm..."*Go!*" he signaled, pointing to Lucius' men. Two large gray wolves leapt silently into the clearing, galloping straight for the basket. Findalf and Ranulf whirled about and screamed with fear as the snarling wolves launched themselves at them. They landed against their chests, knocking both men onto their backs. Two sets of mighty jaws clamped upon their throats and tore them out. After a few jerking motions, the struggling men went still.

"*Penlorian, Penloth. Come!*" Dwayne signaled again. The wolves let go their death hold, snatched up the handle of the heavy basket in their teeth, and trotted awkwardly back to their master with wagging tails. "Well done!" whispered Dwayne aloud, patting and scratching them affectionately about the ears. Penlorian nuzzled Dwayne's neck, licked his face happily then yipped, sniffing excitedly as Dwayne tore up a large hunk of meat and gave each wolf his fair share. He straightened, hefted the basket onto his arm and faded back into the cover of the forest, smirking to himself and wondering what Lucius' reaction would be when he discovered that not only had another one of his traps failed but that he had also been deprived of the satisfaction of executing his men himself.

Lucius didn't let the fact that Findalf and Ranulf were already dead prevent him from hanging their corpses from the town gibbet as a reminder of the price of failure. It effectively served to redouble his men's efforts to attempt trapping the increasing number of outlaws running freely throughout the forest, but they were no more successful than before. Through fall, autumn, winter, spring, and summer they set traps at least one per week, each one more crafty and lethal than the one before, each less and less successful. As far as Dwayne and his comrades were concerned, it had become a game of wits in which they took sadistic pleasure in thwarting Lucius each and every time. Even when he ordered the food poisoned, the rebels somehow figured it out and managed to secret it back into the kitchens where it resulted in the poisoning deaths of his own men, including several who tasted all his food for him. The only rebel he had ever managed to bring into captivity had already been dead of natural causes. He was a young boy whose naked chest had been tattooed with the image of Eloth's sword point down and below it the words: *He shall triumph.*[25] He ordered the body slashed to ribbons then burned with the refuse in the market square.

Year after year the outlaws plagued him, gathering more and more malcontents to their number, forging secret allies amongst the villagers; and, he was sure, even winning over a secret few who served in the castle. No matter how he persecuted or vilified them as wanton criminals, sympathy for them grew as steadily as their numbers. The harder he hunted them, the more elusive they became. They were as wily as foxes yet possessed of the fanatical belief that someday Eloth would come to deliver them. It wasn't until he changed tactics and began painting them as sincere but misguided zealots who had gone astray that he began to win away some of their support from the populace.

Llyonesse and Clotilde sat together in a small patch of warm sunlight that had managed to sneak its way into her little chamber, embroidering in tense silence. Many long years had passed in agonizing slowness since Lucius had taken control; years in which Llyonesse had blossomed into a young woman of incredible beauty. Her auburn hair, once a crown of bobbing ringlets, now cascaded in heavy curls down to the small of her back and curled in gentle wisps about her winsome face. Her expansive blue eyes were fringed above and below with jet black lashes over which arched dark, winged eyebrows. Beneath her upturned nose were very full, pink lips and dimples in each cheek. No longer was she the chubby little girl with tangled locks, scraped knees, and dirty hands; she had grown tall, graceful and thoroughly feminine. Lucius had not been blind to her progressing maturity; indeed he had been anticipating it eagerly and marked the changes in her with increasingly obsessive interest. His baleful black eyes never left her for a moment when in her presence, following her every movement like wanton slaves. Llyonesse had not thought much of it at first, attributing his queer behavior to just another one of his growing list of eccentricities, but earlier that morning her annoyance turned into terrifying alarm as he revealed his plans for her.

She had been walking in her little walled garden, where she was allowed out for an hour each day, when she felt hackles rising on her neck. Before she could turn around to see what evil presence had entered her haven, she suddenly felt herself pushed against the wall and a hot breath in her ear. She stiffened and had tried to break free, crying aloud for help, thinking a criminal had entered her sanctuary, but none could hear her.

"*Ssssssssssshhhhh, resist me not!*" she heard Lucius' hissing voice command her harshly, his hands digging into her flesh. Terrified, Llyonesse obediently went limp, squeezing her eyes tightly shut as he turned her around in his arms. "Look upon me!" he commanded. Llyonesse opened her eyes, her chin trembling with a fear she had never known before. Now she saw something entirely different in his eyes: a strange burning hunger. A sly, cruel smile spread itself over Lucius' face as he slowly looked her up and down then he grasped her head in his hands, entwining his fingers in her hair so she could not turn away. He leaned in toward her.

"No, no!" Llyonesse whimpered in sudden alarm, struggling against him.

"I have waited long enough for you to become a woman, Llyonesse," Lucius growled his bearded mouth bare inches from hers, his breath foul. "But I shall wait no more! I have been in torment since the day I laid hands upon Eloth's sword, but when I touch thee, I find the pain strangely diminished. It makes me wonder what blessed release might be mine after we are wed?"

"W-w-wed?" repeated Llyonesse in complete horror.

"Yes," smiled Lucius wickedly. "You do not think I spared thy life out of the sheer goodness of my heart, do you?" He threw back his head and laughed briefly then redirected his smoldering gaze upon her, flattening her against the wall. "I have saved you for but one purpose, my sweet, and one alone: to take Eloth's sword. But that can only be achieved by becoming a joint heir through a legal union with you. Once that is done, I shall gain the power of the sword and perhaps relief from the incessant agony it has left me in." He gloated at her, a new thought coming to him. Her eyes widened in horror as she perceived his foul thought. "Perhaps I need not wait for a wedding at all," he finished, bending over her.

"Perhaps it will become *much* worse if you *don't!*" Llyonesse retorted with false confidence, bringing him upright in momentary fear and doubt. She stared him squarely in the eye hoping to convince him that she knew something he didn't.

Lucius laughed in response, but it rang hollow and in his eyes she clearly saw doubt and uncertainty. He scowled then took her by the shoulders and shook her hard. "Accept this fact, then, milady," he said, his voice biting hard, "we *shall* be wed and will you, nil you, I intend to lay *full* claim to both you and Eloth's sword!"

She stared at his departing back in impotent horror until he was gone, not realizing until she was completely alone that she was shaking uncontrollably and had gouged bloody half-moons into the palms of her hands.

Clotilde sat embroidering watching Llyonesse out of the corner of her eye in pity as she sat is stony silence, picking at a knot that had worked its way into her thread. Tears of anger and frustration spilled down her cheeks as she tugged harder. The last tug resulted in a loud *riiiiip*. Clotilde looked up in time to see the fabric, hoop, needle, and thread fly across the room. Llyonesse was covering her face with her hands struggling valiantly not to cry aloud. Clotilde laid aside her own sewing and gathered her into her arms, cooing to her softly. Llyonesse's entire body trembled violently within her arms.

"There, there dearling," she whispered, smoothing the hair away from her flushed face. "Tis only a tiny knot ... "

"Oh you know well tis not the stupid knot!" hissed Llyonesse, wiping viciously at her eyes. She then related to her all that had transpired earlier that day. "*I have to find a way to escape,*" she wept angrily when she had finished. "*But how? If I cannot escape, I swear I'll die by my own hand before I let him touch me! I'll make certain he'll never have me nor the king's sword!*"

Clotilde was distraught with fear at Llyonesse's words, fearful it would bring the guards into the room. "Ssshhh, dearling, do not threaten such things."

Llyonesse straightened and stared at her, her eyes tormented. "Nana! My time has run out! In two days he intends to marry me and force himself upon me in the hopes of taking the King's sword! Oh, what are we to do, Nana? *What am I to do?*"

"Do not give up hope yet, sweeting. We have a chance if I can reach those in the underground movement. I have been trying for weeks, but they have gone very deep into hiding of late and mind you, it is a dangerous undertaking when I am watched so closely. I will try again tonight and not return until I have found them. Lucius wants me to go into the village to buy cloth for thy bridal dress. If I do not return, you will know that I have been caught." Her voice failed, unwilling to think of the consequences.

Llyonesse laid her head upon Clotilde's lap and shut her eyes.

"Oh, Nana, if only Joshua would come! If *only* he would come! He would set everything to right, wouldn't he?"

"Yes, he would; he would indeed!" Clotilde agreed, hugging her close.

Lucius' mouth curled into a smile as he stepped away from Llyonesse's door, his suspicions finally confirmed. So the brat's nurse was in league with the rebels after all! Everything had worked out perfectly. Though his physical assault upon Llyonesse earlier that day had been preplanned, he was surprised at just how strongly he had been affected by her. The threat of their imminent marriage had now made it possible for him to root out and exterminate the rebels once and for all. By the time Eloth could build and sail another ship to Shiloh, Lucius would have an army waiting to grind him into dust with Ephlal at his command!

Unaware that her escape from her guards in the jostling marketplace had been orchestrated by Lucius, Clotilde made haste to the edge of town, eventually reaching the forest where she slipped into the concealing shadows of the trees. The shrubbery was so thick it seemed as though she had walked from day into night. Relying solely on memory, she tread the barely perceptible path into the thick of the forest, walking and stumbling over roots and rocks for what seemed an eternity. After getting a number of scrapes and bruises, she finally came upon a cave with a low, overhanging canopy of ivy. Only a select few knew how deeply these caverns delved into the heart of the earth and of the fresh flowing spring which ran deep within, or the many rebels it frequently sheltered. They had dwelt there not long ago yet now it seemed vacated and smelled of mold and rotting leaves. She knelt on all fours and began crawling inside whispering the password so any within would know she was a friend and not take her out with a poisoned arrow. She listened intently for several moments but received no answer and continued crawling, forced to feel her way forward with one hand which she could not even see herself. She inched quite a ways in, hoping she would not accidentally fall into a bottomless pit, fearful she had dared all for nothing. With sinking heart, she finally turned about to go back, wondering what she was going to do next. Except for this one place, she knew of no other way to find Dwayne and his people and there was no time left to find them and elicit their help. In two days the wedding would take place. She turned away then suddenly froze, feeling a hand touch her shoulder then slide down her arm to take her hand.

"Dwayne? Bedwynn? It's me, Clotilde," a soft voice answered her.

"Hush! You've been followed!" it hissed.

Clotilde went immediately still, silently cursing herself for being gullible enough to believe she had actually eluded Lucius' guards. Far down the tunnel she heard the faint sounds of voices then fierce growls. Gooseflesh crawled over her entire body, her hair standing on end as the voices erupted into bloodcurdling screams. *What had she done? She had betrayed and doomed them all with her folly!* A sob caught in her throat.

"Fear not," whispered the quiet voice next to her. "It is Lucius' men who scream."

Clotilde erupted into sobs of mingled fear and relief. "I thought I had betrayed you all!" she choked, guilt-ridden. "He used me to get to you, knowing I would do anything to save Llyonesse."

Torchlight suddenly filled the chamber, momentarily blinding Clotilde. When her eyes adjusted, she found herself ringed by Dwayne and the other rebels. All of them were filthy and half-starved but possessed of the same fire in their eyes. These were the faithful remnant[26], the few who had not given themselves to Lucius in return for his meaningless title's and fickle favoritism. They were destitute in goods but rich in loyalty, calling none lord save Eloth and his son, Joshua, for whom they would gladly die.

Dwayne's arm went about her shoulders, his voice gentle.

"How could you possibly have known?" he said, hugging her close. "It was his most ingenious trap yet and it almost worked but for our sentries who stand watch. We had but a few minutes warning of thy coming but it was enough. The two who followed thee are slain and tonight we shall already be in another place before his messengers can return with his army! Now, my lady, you must remain with us for it is no longer safe for you to return to the castle."

"No!" Clotilde said, immediately alarmed. "If I do not return, there's no telling what he will do to Llyonesse! I dare not leave her alone!"

"He already knows you are one of us!" argued Dwayne. "What comfort can you be to her now if he tortures you for information?"

"None...except maybe to perish with her," Clotilde said stubbornly. "And what could I possibly tell him? Maybe the best plan of all is to simply tell the truth."

"*What?*" exclaimed all around her in horror.

Clotilde looked at them. "It is useless to lie and he wouldn't believe it anyway. When he questions me, I will tell him exactly what happened: I came here, his men were killed, and you have moved on to I know-not-where. You will be in no more danger than you are now!"

"This is true!" nodded Dwayne in agreement. "But you must return at once and we must make our escape!"

"But Llyonesse!" Clotilde protested, determined to still save her. "You must help her to escape! He plans to marry her to get Eloth's sword!"

"That is impossible!" said Dwayne. "We must leave now! Lucius' men may already be on their way here!"

"We can't abandon her to that monster! If he gets the sword, it'll be over for all of us!" Clotilde opened her mouth to protest further but was interrupted by Bedwynn who had stood silent throughout their debate.

"Wait," he said calmly, a smile spreading over his face. "I have an idea. ..."

The instant Clotilde stepped out from the forest with her two escorts she was immediately surrounded by Lucius' knights. There was fully fifty of them in number, all armed for bear with torches already lit and kegs of oil ready to pour down into the cave to incinerate his enemies.

"Halt, traitor!" they cried, aiming their bows at her. "You've tasted the last of your freedom! Good job, men!"

Clotilde's escorts tightened the rope they had looped about her neck. "We searched the entire cave, captain, but it was empty...vacated some time ago. We thought it best to bring her back immediately for questioning," replied Bedwynn, giving no indication of how hot and stifling he found the itchy woolen uniform to be. No wonder Lucius' men were in such surly moods all the time! The disappointment on the other knight's faces was easily apparent. They had been spoiling for years to lay hands on the rebels and had finally thought them in their grasp only to be let down again.

"Take her back to Lucius immediately!" growled the leader, oblivious to the fact that their captive's escorts were not the two they had sent out earlier that day.

"Yes, mi'lord," saluted Bedwynn, tugging on her rope. He needed no further prodding and immediately mounted the horses provided them, galloping all the way back to Lucius' fortress. Once inside the castle, he, Justin, and Clotilde availed themselves of the secret chambers and hidden passageways Lucius had built for his own use, effectively disappearing "into the woodwork." Justin had been one of the chief architects when the castle was built and his knowledge of the castle's floor plan ensured they would never be found by those in Lucius' service.

When Lucius found out how he had been tricked, he went berserk with rage. Every single one of the knights who had allowed the impostors and Clotilde to go free were executed before the entire village. The castle was immediately scoured from top to bottom, turret to dungeon throughout that night and into the next afternoon but not a trace could be found of Llyonesse's nurse or the two impostors who had disappeared with her.

Llyonesse was told nothing save that her nurse was dead and that the marriage would occur as scheduled. There would be no gown, no flowers, no music, no exchange of rings nor vows. Scheldrake would marry them to make it sufficiently legal and then Lucius would take her to gain possession of Eloth's sword. Llyonesse was overcome with guilt and grief over her beloved nurse, feeling totally responsible. She had lost the one person in Shiloh who loved her and now she was left to face her doom completely alone. Her frail hopes, at last, were finally crushed. There would be no miraculous rescue, no escape... not even through suicide for Lucius had anticipated such an attempt on her part and ordered her room stripped of all except a thin blanket. With aching heart she curled into a corner, hugged Joshua's precious locket close to her breast and waited with cold dread for morning to come.

Of all the guard positions in Shiloh, the night watch on the docks was the most tedious. Watching long, hard hours in the gripping cold with nothing to do but pace back and forth, (while trying to stay alert and warm) easily lent itself to apathy. A full moon hung low in the sky and the moist air was so bitterly cold that the breath issuing from their nostrils and mouths came forth as white billowy clouds of smoke. Irrespective of how many layers they put on, the cold permeated their clothing and chilled them to the marrow, a sure sign that winter was fast approaching.

"Ho, now... what's this?" drawled Bryanston aloud, watching a group of giggling young wenches advance toward them. Women were always a welcome distraction and whenever they could manage it, they made arrangements for such visits as frequently as possible.

"Perhaps they're rewards for good behavior!" grinned Dywiddan.

"Whatever the reason, the buxom redhead is mine!" growled Terrille, stepping forward to lay his claim immediately. The maidens greeted them with broad smiles, whispered invitations and jugs of warmed wine. Some of the newer guards hesitated, nervous about abandoning their posts but after receiving several dirty looks from their comrades, they readily gave in and followed the women into the woods like hypnotized little boys. When the last of them had vanished from sight, a small group of cloaked figures crept out from various cottages and shacks, climbing silently onto the ships, two to each. While Justin and Bedwynn readied *The White Stag* to set sail, the others poured oil across the decks of the remaining ships to prevent pursuit. Two small cloaked and hooded figures boarded *The White Stag* as they worked, watching Dwayne feverishly unfurl and secure the sails and untie the mooring lines. One looked back to where the guards had vanished, fearful they would emerge and sound the alarm at any moment. When all was ready, Dwayne let out a soft whistle, his knife poised to cut the last mooring line which was stretched taut. All froze, wondering who would emerge from the bushes, the guards or their comrades? Seconds later the maidens ran to them minus their male companions. Not until every last one was safely aboard did they allow themselves the luxury of a relieved sigh. Dwayne severed the mooring line and *The White Stag* pulled away. Once they were at a safe distance, several bowmen kindled arrows dipped in pitch and shot them onto the oil slick decks of the other ships. They alighted with a loud *whoosh* of flame. Now it would be only a matter of moments before their escape was discovered. By the time the alarm bells started ringing, *The White Stag* had already reached the mouth of the harbor. All onboard watched with anxiety and mounting excitement as people hurried out to the docks to watch the fiery spectacle, unaware of the ship that was already navigating out to open sea.

"Lucius is going to explode when he learns his ships have been torched!" said Llyonesse to Clotilde and Dwayne, unable to stifle a dry laugh.

"What's sauce for the goose is gravy for the gander!" retorted

Justin, a satisfied smirk on his face. "I got the idea from the old viper himself."

Llyonesse smiled, unable to believe she was finally free and feeling only a little chagrined at how she truly wished she could have been in the same room with Lucius so she could see the look on his face when he learned she was gone.

Lucius heard the crack and pop of burning timber in his sleep, annoyed that someone had selected this particular moment to split firewood beneath his window. He sat up and threw off his covers, marched to the window and hefted his chamber pot, ready to dump it on whoever was disturbing him. He parted the heavy drapes with a snarl and froze, gawking at the harbor which was fully engulfed in flames. The chamberpot fell onto the floor, splattering its contents everywhere. Lucius ran to his chamber door and yanked it open, looking up and down the passageway. Servants were running to and fro, shouting orders at the top of their lungs and snatching every water-bearing vessel at hand.

His chamberlain suddenly appeared before him, his face blackened with soot. "The ships have been torched, my lord," he gasped, fighting to catch his breath.

"*I can see that!*" bellowed Lucius angrily. "Get everyone down to the harbor to douse those flames and find out who is responsible!"

"Yes, mi'lord! I've already done so, mi'lord!" he gasped, then vanished down the hall.

Where is Scheldrake? Lucius wondered angrily, pulling on a shirt and breeches before marching down the hall toward the tower stairs. He wanted the advice of his necromancer! He stopped in midstep before Llyonesse's door and paused, uncertain as to why. A strange feeling came over him, a nagging doubt that would not go away as he continued to stare at her door. She was always kept locked in, but the queer feeling that something was very wrong would not leave him. He fumbled about for a moment for the key then swiftly unlocked the door. The glow from the fires lit the chamber with an eerie orange light, revealing that all was entirely too still for his comfort. With an angry curse, he strode to the bed and flung back the bedcovers. Where Llyonesse should have been lying were several bolsters arranged to look like a human shape. He whirled about, searching desperately. The chamber was empty! Llyonesse was gone! His only chance to possess Ephlal and challenge Eloth was gone! With an angry scream of rage, he withdrew his dagger and ripped the bolster from top to bottom, gutting it as though it were an animal. Finally exhausted, he stumbled out onto the balcony and almost collapsed with relief when he saw that Ephlal was still buried within the cornerstone. Its guards were still at their post knowing it would have meant certain death to leave despite the fires raging in the harbor. Llyonesse had not taken the sword, but she *had* provided Eloth with a ship. It was only a matter of time now before *He* came to Shiloh to reclaim it and then there would be no escaping his wrath this time. … Lucius' knees gave way beneath him.

"*Schelllllldraaaaake!*" he screamed.

Chapter Ten

*L*yonesse stared out across the turquoise sea in pensive silence, her face moist with sea spray. Somewhere out beyond the horizon lay Ellioth and ... Joshua. For the past week, she had awakened each day with mingled dread and terrible longing, worrying if he had truly believed Lucius' lies that she was dead.

Ellioth seemed little more than a faded dream and Joshua a distant memory, kept alive only by her own imagination and her locket. Had he believed her dead and married another in her place? Lucius had taken great pleasure in frequently reminding her that Joshua would no doubt grieve for an appropriate amount of time then would try to forget her in the arms of another woman. After all, he was the Crown Prince and was expected to wed and beget heirs. The words had sliced through her heart like cruel knives and she had cried bitterly for weeks afterwards, but Lucius had merely laughed at her tears and kept her locked within in her room so he would not have to listen to her weeping. Now she truly wondered, would Joshua greet her with surprised joy or shocked dismay because he already possessed a wife and sons?

She had received but two letters from him after first coming to Shiloh; both within the first two years before her father's death. The first was to tell her that he had just become Penloth's squire and the second which had besought her to attend his knighting. She winced at the painful memory, remembering how her mother, then great with child, had read the letter aloud only a month before she had died, promising to have Clotilde take her back to Ellioth in her place. Shortly after Eloth's knights came, commerce between the two kingdoms had abruptly ceased. There was no more trade, no more visits between kinfolk, and no correspondence. It was as though Ellioth had ceased to exist. Lucius often told her it was because Eloth no longer cared for his people (save for the taxes which could be gotten from them), but this Llyonesse had always seriously doubted. If what he said was the truth, then how were the taxes conveyed back to Ellioth? Certainly not by merchant vessel for the ships continually floated unused in the harbor and were meticulously maintained under constant guard for years.

Llyonesse returned to the present, shivering with cold as she wrapped her arms about her shoulders, trying to ignore how bony they had become. She had succeeded so far in concealing her weight loss from Clotilde, but she had been found out anyway. She could no longer hide the dark circles under her eyes from crying herself to sleep every night, her sallow complexion, sunken cheeks, or ravaged fingernails which she had bitten down to the quick. It was getting very hard to ignore how everyone stared at her in embarrassed silence no doubt wondering if she had contracted some exotic wasting disease when she was actually eating her heart out with worry! Clotilde was worried sick about her and made no pretense of ignoring the additional layers of clothing she was putting on to keep herself warm and to hide the fact that she was wasting away. She nagged her unceasingly to eat but the enormous lump in her throat made it impossible for her to swallow and her stomach cramped with nausea each time she laid eyes on food. Rather than choke on it any longer and waste their meager stores, she pretended to take her meals in her cabin where she instead gave them to a young boy who had sworn not to reveal her secret. *Someone might as well at least derive some benefit in her lack of appetite.*

"*Llyonesse!*" snapped Clotilde's voice behind her. Llyonesse jumped and gave a little scream, exceedingly startled. Clotilde was staring at her, a very worried expression on her face.

"Did you not hear me approach, child?" She touched her shoulder, horrified at feeling her bones so easily beneath her skin. "Good heavens, Llyonesse! Do you wish to die before we even step foot in Ellioth?"

"Oh, Nana ... " Llyonesse whimpered, eyes filling with desolate tears. "It's not that I have wanted to ... it's just that I can't seem to swallow."

"But why, child? Why? What has been vexing thee so?"

Llyonesse's lower lip trembled. "What if he has married? What if I have lost him?" It was barely more than a whisper, but it was heartbreakingly plaintive.

Clotilde folded her compassionately into her arms, hugging her close. "Hush, little one! No more of this! We have at least another fortnight before we sight land, but you will not live to see the morning if you don't start eating and resting properly! Joshua will not have forgotten you and if he has married another. ... well. ... we will deal with it together if it comes to that. At the very least you should be rejoicing in thy freedom and mustn't lose hope! Not until you see the ring on his finger and his wife on his arm, do you hear me?"

"Yes, Nana," whispered Llyonesse, hanging her head in shame, unable to admit that it would be more bearable to go on living with the fantasy that nothing had ever changed between them than to confront such an awful possibility. But Clotilde was right; she shouldn't think of it! Not yet. She mustn't think of it. She withdrew her prized locket seeking the comfort and solace of Joshua's image. *Remember the happy times* she sternly commanded herself. *Remember when he proudly showed off the "whiskers" he was so sure he had grown on that silky-smooth chin of his and all the flower crowns he used to make. Remember your betrothal at the Mid-Summer's Faire, and that morning long ago when he gave you this very locket ... the only treasure you saved from Lucius' clutches.* She smiled. That too, at least was comforting. No more imprisonment in that horrid, stifling room with the secret door she had never been able to use to her own advantage until last night when Dwayne and Justin had come to rescue her. Come what may, she would again be in Joshua's land, safe from all harm and that at least was a lot to be grateful for. She took a deep breath and turned her face westward, wondering if he would recognize her and what he looked like now that he was a man of three and twenty.

"Land ho! Land ho!" cried the lookout from high atop the crow's nest. The passengers of *The White Stag* rushed to the ship's railing, jockeying for room to scan the horizon with anxious eyes. Their food stores had run out two days ago and what little water was left was going bad. A few more days and many of them might not have lived to see Ellioth's fair shores again but each swell that bore them heavenward confirmed that they were only hours away from their destination. They could clearly see the distant outline of Ellioth's majestic peaks upon the horizon and the white mist upon her shore. Sunlight was glistening upon the golden spires of the palace and the air was filled with the distant perfume of plant life and growing things.

"Look!" Clotilde cried aloud, pointing to the water beneath them. Speeding upon either side of their frothing prow were dolphins. Llyonesse leaned forward to watch them frolic before the ship, their smiling faces and lively chatter filling her heart with joy.

"Only a few more hours now," she whispered, clutching her locket in her fist.

"One more match!" coaxed Joshua, springing up and down on the balls of his feet, wind milling his arms while he waited for Sir Eric to stand erect once again.

"Haven't you had enough yet?" responded the knight, managing a painful squat. He paused and looked up, regarding Joshua with dismay. Ten years had passed since the prince had first become Penloth's squire and in that time he had grown as tall and muscular as a tiger and every bit as deadly in battle. Despite his gentle manner, Joshua was an intimidating sight (even without his armor) for he towered above most in the kingdom by at least one head. In armor, his opponents would just as soon run in the opposite direction as take him on.

It wasn't the first time Sir Eric found himself grateful they were on the same side, even though their frequent practice sessions often left him wondering if it wouldn't be safer to have been an enemy. At least that way he wouldn't have to drill with him on such a regular basis. Despite Joshua's best attempts to be "gentle," he always ended up turning his practice opponents black and blue.

"Could we not continue this... another day?" Sir Eric asked hopefully, accepting Joshua's hand of assistance up.

Joshua's countenance fell with genuine disappointment. He had just been working up a good head of steam and Sir Eric wanted to quit already! Sir Penloth would never have given up so quickly, not even if he had several broken ribs and were twice Eric's age!

"Of course, Sir Eric," he agreed, not wanting to bruise the knight's ego. "I am feeling rather weary myself. What think thee of perhaps after another two days time?"

"A fortnight," countered Sir Eric, knowing he would need at least that much time to recover from the beating he had taken. He wasn't sure but he suspected one of his ribs had been broken. It was going to take a week alone just for the black and blue marks to fade. "Perhaps I can persuade, er- ask one of the other knights to take my place," he offered. *Which is going to cost me dearly,* he thought silently.

"As you wish—" grinned Joshua, then fell immediately silent when the sound of distant bells reached his ears.

"That's the signal for an approaching ship!" exclaimed Sir Eric, his eyes growing round with astonishment. It had been years and years since a ship had been sighted.

"I want a better look!" Joshua said, searching the tiltyard for a better vantage point. It had been over seven years since the last ship had sailed into Ellioth, the one bearing Penlorian's body.

Since then they had been completely cut off from the outside world. Not even a single merchant ship from other lands had ventured into their waters in all that time. Perhaps they could negotiate with the captain for passage to Shiloh. He spotted a large spruce tree which rose in height well above the bailey wall and with great springing steps he ran toward it and launched himself onto the lowest branch, expertly catching it with both hands. Using the momentum, Joshua swung his legs forward until he rose high enough to curl them up and around the next highest limb. With a grunt, he pulled himself up to a sitting position then stood upright again. *All this in a full suit of armor.* Sir Eric shook his head in disbelief and amazement, wondering how one so large could, at the same time, be so bloody graceful. Joshua continued climbing until he reached the topmost branches, pushing down on the limbs to see over the thick foliage.

"Careful, my lord," he heard Eric caution far below him when the branches he stood on bent precariously under his weight.

Joshua climbed up onto a stronger limb, shaded his eyes and gazed toward the harbor, straining to see what manner of ship was approaching. The sail was definitely white with a device of some kind, but was still too far out to discern what it was. If he wanted a better look, he would have to go down to the harbor and borrow Joseph's spyglass. With practiced ease, he jumped outward, just clearing the tree limbs, tucked in mid-air and somersaulted forwards onto his shoulder, rolling back up to a standing position in one swift motion like an acrobat.

"Oh bravo! Bravo! *Well done!*" chortled a painfully familiar, whiny voice.

Joshua and Sir Eric turned around to find a young woman running toward them, clapping her hands in pleasure. "Oh, Joshua!" she chortled. "You are just too agile! Had I not known it was you, I would have mistaken you for Tortuga the Magnificent!"

"Who?" chorused Joshua and Sir Eric simultaneously.

"Tortuga!" she repeated, surprised they had not heard of the famous acrobat. "He's the greatest tumbler in all Ellioth! Really, you men just spend too much time at sword play and not enough time cultivating the finer arts, but I will soon remedy that situation, when we are wed!" She tucked her arm through Joshua's and began steering him back toward the castle, oblivious of Sir Eric who was smirking at Joshua behind her back.

Joshua gently extricated his arm, trying not to show his impatience. "There is a ship off our coast, my lady, so if you will permit me—"

"A ship!" exclaimed the Earl's daughter, her green eyes growing large with excitement. "Is it a merchant ship, do you think? T'would be such wonderful timing and oh so fortunate if they carried bolts of suitable cloth for my bridal gown."

"No formal agreement has been made yet, Marguerite," Joshua reminded her with as much grace as he could muster. His comment did little to hamper her enthusiasm. Marguerite had already convinced herself that the marriage contract was already a done deal and that this particular ship had sailed into Ellioth's harbor solely for the purpose of providing her with wedding fabric. She rewound her arm about his like a boa constrictor and tossed her head. "Mere trivialities … " she sang out, smiling at him in a disturbingly vapid manner. "My father shall offer a *very* large dowry; I am of marrying age, pleasant to look at, highly cultured, bred to high position and what's more, thy father wishes you to produce an heir! I need not remind you of the *long* history of sons and twins born to our family so, as you can see, mi'lord, I am most suitable in every respect! Only a few last details to iron out and I shall be all yours!"

Joshua did not respond but glanced back out to sea, hoping the incoming ship contained pirates that were in great need of very rich, vain women. He had no desire to marry whatsoever, let alone the Earl's daughter, and had so far been successful in thwarting all other attempts, preferring rather to remain a bachelor to the end of his days. Even though Llyonesse had been reported dead for many years, he still felt in his heart of hearts that it would be a betrayal to marry another. Yet, Marguerite spoke truly. If he did not wish the line of Eloth to end with him, he would have to marry and sire at least one son. Out of love for his father and his sense of duty he would have to marry; he only hoped it would not be to the Lady Marguerite who loved him not for himself, but for the status of becoming a queen.

The White Stag's passengers could barely contain themselves for joy as they crowded against the rails, weeping and waving their arms as they greeted their kinsfolk who flocked to the harbor to meet them. All of Ellioth was emptying itself into the streets in an attempt to get to the harbor, pointing, shouting, laughing, and weeping as they recognized the faces of those upon the ship as that of their own people.

Llyonesse hung back, away from the press of her excited companions, leaning weakly on Clotilde's shoulder and gazing with grateful eyes upon Eloth's magnificent palace in spellbound awe. She had forgotten how very beautiful it was. Her memories paled in comparison to its actual splendor. The fields, orchards, groves, village, cottages, flower gardens and shops were clean, well-tended, bright and cheerful and the air was filled with the sound of joy and laughter, not heavy with silent fear. The look of enduring sorrow that had become etched on the faces of her sailing companions was replaced with smiles and tears of joy. Even the breeze seemed to sigh of peace and tranquility.

"*Edith*!" cried Clotilde aloud, recognizing one of her oldest friends in the crowd. "Over here!"

The woman saw her and jumped up and down. "Clotilde! Clotilde!"

Llyonesse gave her a nudge and Clotilde ran forward into familiar arms, embraced by those whom she had long missed and faces she had thought never to see again. Dwayne took Clotilde's place supporting Llyonesse against him when she became engulfed by her friends. They were the last to disembark and had just set foot upon solid ground when a chamberlain in scarlet and gold livery rode up on horseback.

"Hail!" he cried, standing in his stirrups to see better over the head of the milling crowd. "Do my eyes deceive me or is this truly *The White Stag*, his majesty's ship? Have ye come from Shiloh?"

"*Escaped* is more like it," confirmed Dwayne. "I am Dwayne, the only surviving son of Elisabeth and the miller, Devin. There are four and twenty of us, including the steward's daughter, Llyonesse."

Upon hearing these words, the chamberlain's jaw dropped open in amazement. "We all thought you dead, my lady!" he exclaimed at last, confirming her worst fears. In his excitement at this discovery, he did not notice how his words had made Llyonesse flinch. "The king and prince will want to see you all immediately," he continued excitedly. "I will escort you to them by the swiftest means possible! Wait here!" With those words he galloped off and went in search of transportation while Dwayne set her down upon a nearby crate.

"Are you all right?" he asked with deep concern.

"I guess it's all the excitement," she lied, managing a wan smile. "I'll be fine; Clotilde will look after me. Go on, I see many friends who are waiting to greet you."

"I'll return her to you straight away before her friends whisk her away!" he said, pushing his way through the crowd.

Eloth's chamberlain found the local farmers and merchants more than happy to donate their wagons, oxen, horses, and mules to transport their kinsmen up the steep road to the castle and insisted on accompanying them in a great procession. The crowds followed behind, cheering them as though they were long-lost heroes back from a crusade. Llyonesse's heart pounded harder with every turn that brought her nearer to Joshua, little realizing that she had become the chief object of intense interest among all who thronged upon either side of the road to watch. Many stared out of simple curiosity, but when they got a closer look at her face their jaws dropped open as if they had seen a ghost. The name of "Ardon" well preceded her arrival to the castle gates. When they reached the courtyard a short time later, dozens of squires were already waiting to attend them. After being lifted out bodily by a strapping young man with brown hair who set her firmly back upon her feet, Llyonesse tipped her head way back to stare up with renewed awe at the golden spires of the lofty palace, the roofs molten from the reflecting sun. She shivered in its mighty shadow, wondering when she would wake up from her dream to once again find herself a prisoner in her bedchamber in Shiloh. Well, she would at least wait to pinch herself until she had seen Joshua!

"Are you coming, my lady?" asked Clotilde, taking her gently by the arm.

"Yes, Nana," she replied softly, her heart rising immediately into her throat. The moment of her reunion with Joshua was swift approaching and she was very, very nervous. Llyonesse lifted her skirts and began to mount the marbled stair, thankful for Clotilde's supporting arm. Each step filled her with more and more apprehension and she cursed herself for not having forced herself to eat all these past weeks! She was as thin as a wraith and probably every bit as white as bleached flour. Joshua would take one look at her jutting cheekbones and ribs and declare her an impostor on the spot. The Llyonesse he knew had been a chubby little girl with bobbing curls, not a bony scarecrow with dull, lifeless hair hanging in matted tangles down her back!

"Wait, I need to catch my breath!" she gasped, closing her eyes and sucking in great draughts of air, lightheaded from climbing so many stairs. It was going to be nothing short of a miracle if she did not end up fainting at his feet. "Okay," she said nodding to those who were patiently waiting for her. "I can continue now."

The chamberlain gave her a smile of encouragement then swiftly led them down a richly appointed hall, halting before two, heavily gilt doors before which stood two guards.

"Please wait here; I shall only be a moment," he said, half-turning before closing the door behind him. Llyonesse nodded, her blue eyes round with fear; trying not to think, or hope just staring at the golden lion's heads which seemed to silently snarl at her.

Eloth stood as his chamberlain entered the room, causing those who stood about the dais to fall silent.

"Is it true?" he asked anxiously, interrupting the earl who had been in the midst of negotiating his daughter's dowry. "Is the vessel truly from Shiloh?"

"Yes, my lord," the chamberlain replied with great urgency. "It is *The White Stag* and it is filled with fugitives who seek an immediate audience."

Deafening silence greeted this news then everyone began to talk at once.

"Have them brought in immediately!" cried Eloth as Joshua entered the room from another door.

"My lord," bowed the chamberlain. "*At once!*"

Joshua stood as though paralyzed, holding his breath along with all the knights, courtiers, and seraphim who had gathered in the throne room in record numbers. All eyes riveted upon the double doors as they slowly opened and one by one, the fugitives filed in, identifying themselves by house, trade, or lineage until twenty-three stood before him.

Llyonesse paused just outside the door, leaning her sweaty forehead upon it for support; her heart pounding wildly, her flesh chilled to the marrow. She knew the door guards were staring at her with pity, but she felt too ill at the moment to bother about them. She only hoped that if she was going to throw up, it would be in the hall and not upon the throne room floor. Would the moment never come?

"My lords," she heard Clotilde's voice through the roaring in her ears. "Allow me the honor of presenting my mistress, the lady Llyonesse, daughter of Ardon and Zarabeth, sole survivor of the house of Tolham."

Llyonesse stepped inside on wobbly feet, eyes glued to the floor, her appearance greeted by deafening silence. Joshua stared at her transfixed, his heart pounding wildly. Against all hope, reason, and heartbreak she was alive! *Alive!* There was no mistaking her; Llyonesse had grown into the very reflection of her father!

With tears of joy sparkling in his eyes, Eloth rushed forward; gathering her into his embrace. "Out of the shadows hast thou returned hither to us, dearer than daughter," he wept, kissing her pale face. "Welcome home!" His eyes closed in quiet joy, tears spilling down his cheeks, wishing with all his heart that Ardon were alive so he could behold his beautiful daughter. "Come," he said, leading her with an encouraging smile toward Joshua. "There is another who has missed thee even more than I."

Docilely Llyonesse allowed herself to be led before a tall, handsome knight who stared at her as if stricken dumb with shock; all the while her eyes darting about the chamber to find Joshua's face in the crowd. Standing next to him was a beautiful woman who glared at her with undisguised jealousy, her slender white arm linked possessively through his. She was the most beautiful woman Llyonesse had ever laid eyes on with hair of spun gold and eyes of palest green. She was almost as tall as the knight and very stately, all aglitter in diamonds and a diaphanous blue gown which displayed her magnificent figure to full advantage; a stark contrast to her wraith-like figure, dark filthy hair, freckled skin, wan face, and dirty clothes.

Llyonesse glanced up at Eloth questioningly, perplexed as to why he would introduce her to one of his knights then did a double take. No, not a knight...*Joshua!* Llyonesse gasped, amazed at how tall, and mature he had become, completely unaware of how she was ogling him or that her mouth had fallen open in unabashed awe. He stood at least two heads taller than she and was impressively broad in shoulder and frame. His armored chest tapered down to a slim waist and long, heavily muscled legs which were also encased in heavy armor. He had become every inch the knight in shining armor she had always imagined him and little resembled the boy she had hero-worshiped as a child, save for his sparkling gray eyes which were devouring every inch of her.

Joshua was completely oblivious to all else, including the

death grip Marguerite had upon his arm. When had the chubby little girl grown into this slender nymph with a face that rivaled that of an angel's? She did not at all resemble the child with the muddied hands, chubby cheeks and mop of tangled curls but had become a young woman lithe of limb with a cascade of dark hair, slender limbs, and pinked cheeks. If he could but touch that translucent cheek and see her dimples again, he would know of a certainty it was truly his Llyonesse and not a phantom come to torment his heart anew.

"Llyonesse?" he whispered, tears filling his eyes as his hands gently cupped her trembling chin.

"Joshua?" Llyonesse gasped, melting beneath his tender gaze. How deep and utterly masculine his voice was! Not at all the voice of her childhood hero and it issued from a face *covered in the most glorious growth of golden-brown whiskers she had ever seen*—the crowning achievement of his manhood. Unable to hide the smile which dimpled her cheeks, she reached up her hand, wondering how they would feel.

Joshua's breath caught with joy upon beholding her smile. It was indeed his Llyonesse! Only she would have been so unashamedly impressed with his growth of facial hair.

"It finally grew in," he grinned, bringing her fingers up to his face to feel his whiskers. Llyonesse had to practically stand on tiptoe to reach him, but with sheer pleasure and reverent awe, she stroked her fingertips through the silky mass, her smile broadening in happy delight. It was very, very soft to the touch and not the least bit stiff or bristly. Joshua smiled at her look of satisfaction, pressing his hand over hers to hold it against his warm cheek. Their eyes met and for a brief instant, they were children once again.

Eloth and the seraphim stood silently, respecting the privacy of that brief, intimate, magical moment, smiling quietly to themselves (or weeping silently) altogether oblivious of the earl and his daughter who had become as rigid as a fence post.

Marguerite's face was aflame with indignation, green eyes glaring daggers at her unexpected rival whilst twisting her kerchief into *itty-bitty* little knots. She had been a handshake away from becoming Ellioth's Queen only to have it all ruined by this little snip of a girl materializing out of nowhere! *How dare the prince humiliate her before all his court by making sheep eyes at a half-starved, filthy nobody! Now what was he doing? Was he actually going to kiss the child's hand in front of everyone as if she were a noblewoman!?* Before her father could stop her, Marguerite re-entwined her arm through Joshua's and cleared her throat loudly for attention.

"My lord?" she said, brazenly nudging him to introduce her.

The fragile enchantment broken, Joshua turned to stare at Marguerite, his face a complete blank. She was aghast. He had quite forgotten she even existed! She gave him a silent but very meaningful glare. Joshua blinked at her, uncomprehending for a moment, then years of ingrained chivalry automatically took over.

"Oh, I beg thy pardon, my lady," he said with genuine chagrin. "Llyonesse, this is the Lady Marguerite, daughter to the Earl of Devonshire. Marguerite, my lady, Llyonesse."

His lady? Well, there it was...Marguerite sniffed and gave her a perfunctory curtsy. "*Lady* Marguerite!" she corrected him and bestowed upon Llyonesse her most brilliant (but hollow) of smiles.

"How delightful to discover that you are not dead after all!" she exclaimed. "It is truly a genuine pleasure to meet his highness' childhood playmate at long last. I do hope you'll forgive my astonishment, for you see, we were just in the midst of finalizing the dowry—"

"Mar-guer-*ite!*" hissed her father, turning crimson with profound embarrassment. Joshua glared at her in astonished horror.

Llyonesse stared at the woman dumbfounded. "Dowry?" she whispered, pierced to the heart. Joshua was making plans to wed? Clotilde's words instantly came flooding back to her mind ... "*If he has married ... well, you will have to deal with it, but not until you see the ring on his finger and his wife on his arm* ... "Well, it seemed as if her ominous words had been prophetic after all. The woman was already hanging onto his arm for all she was worth and judging by what she said, the ring wasn't too far off! Llyonesse's heart plummeted to the soles of her feet. How could he have done this to her? But no, it truly wasn't his fault. It *had* been many years since he received news of her "death," so he had obviously waited till now, to his credit. It was a wonder he hadn't already been married for years! What was he to have done? Die a bachelor and leave the throne of Shiloh and Ellioth vacant? But it was so cruel to have come this close and yet be too late. There was nothing left for her anymore. Lucius had stolen her last dream and ruined her life after all!

Summoning every ounce of strength and dignity she had left, she offered Marguerite a joyless smile and curtsied. "I wish you much happiness," she managed, refusing to look at Joshua's stunned face.

Joshua flushed with anger at the sight of the crushing pain upon his Llyonesse's face. It would have been a joyful reunion were it not for Marguerite! He was sorely tempted to take the earl's daughter over his knee and paddle her in front of the entire court! The sheer effrontery of the woman was beyond description!

"There is much to be discussed as can plainly be seen," interjected Eloth with a stern look in the Earl's direction to curb his daughter's tongue. He hugged Llyonesse close to reassure her that all was truly well. "Take heart, little one. All is not as it appears. Tonight we shall have a feast in celebration of thy safe return. Until then, take rest in the chambers being prepared for thee."

He turned to Dwayne and his comrades. "Glad am I to see you all again as well. Go now and take thy rest. My servants shall tend to all thy needs."

Dwayne looked upon his king with eyes filled with tears of joy, his heart so full of gladness that he could barely speak. He nodded his acknowledgment then glanced with concern at Llyonesse who was growing paler by the moment, then turned and followed the Chamberlain from the throne room, followed by his comrades.

But Llyonesse could endure no more. Before anyone could react to her choked cry of despair, she fled from the room, hand cupped over her mouth, skirts flying. Clotilde hung back for only a moment, just long enough to give the Lady Marguerite a wilting glare.

"Excuse me, my lords," she nodded then went after Llyonesse.

The earl cleared his throat and turned back to the king with supreme embarrassment. "About the dowry," he began.

"Llyonesse," said Clotilde, grasping her by the shoulders. "Come away from the balcony! There is a hot bath, good food, and clean raiment waiting for thee."

Llyonesse did not respond, but bent forward to look far below. It was a very, very long drop to the bottom. She wondered if falling from such a height would hurt very much.

"*Llyonesse!*" snapped Clotilde in a voice that brooked no further disobedience. "March back in here and take off that filthy dress this *instant!*"

Llyonesse slowly turned away from the window, her voice filled with despair. "My worst fear has been realized, Nana; what is to become of me now?"

Clotilde stared at her, not knowing what to say. She had long held out hope that Joshua would not have believed the false reports concerning her death and remained unmarried, but it seemed that fate would have it otherwise. Her heart twisted with fear and pity for Llyonesse, who looked truly desolate enough at the moment to fling herself off the balcony. "There is still hope," she offered, trying to sound cheerful as she began to peel off the dirty clothes. "They are not wed yet; he may call it off now that you have returned."

Llyonesse said nothing and Clotilde knew her words had fallen on deaf ears.

At that moment, there came a knock upon the door. Llyonesse started but did not move to open it. "Get thee behind the changing screen and take off that dress!" Clotilde repeated, striding forward and opening the door just a crack. A young squire stood in the hallway holding a silver tray. Clotilde opened the door wider to let him in, wondering why he was dressed so elaborately. Curiosity overcoming her, Llyonesse emerged from behind the screen, wrapped in a long drying sheet.

The page bowed low before her with a grand flourish. "I bear a gift for the lady Llyonesse from his highness, the prince," he said, removing the silver dome from the tray. Upon it lie a wreath woven of pure white roses and blue Forget-Me-Not's. Clotilde put her hand over her mouth to hide her smile of delight, immediately recognizing the significance of the gift. Llyonesse stepped forward, lifting the wreath gingerly in both hands as though it were a very precious, fragile treasure.

The page continued. "The prince requests that you do him the honor of sitting with him this eventide to share a trencher at the feast which is to be held in thy honor," he continued awkwardly as if he had been hastily rehearsed.

Clotilde gave Llyonesse a look of satisfaction that plainly said she was not the least bit surprised.

"Tell my lord that I would be very honored," replied Llyonesse with a hesitant smile, a bit of color returning to her pale cheeks.

"No," interjected a deep voice, startling them all. Joshua appeared in the doorway, holding forth a pink rosebud. "The honor is all *mine*."

Llyonesse's cheeks flamed with joy at Joshua's brilliant smile. "Thank you, mi'lord!" she said timidly, accepting the rose.

Joshua stepped closer, lifting her chin with the crook of his finger. "*Joshua!*" he corrected her, wagging a teasing finger in her face. "But I warn you, Llyonesse: have a care with thy table manners! I want no more peas dropped down my tunic nor pudding catapulted across the table as you were once wont to do!"

Before Llyonesse could defend herself with the excuse that she had been much younger back then, Joshua took the flower-wreath from the tray and placed it gently upon her head where it perched at a tilt, covering her right eye. "Wear it tonight, that's an order!" he grinned. Then, grasping the sleeve of the giggling page, he swiftly withdrew, closing the door behind them. Llyonesse stood in utter bewilderment, not knowing whether to laugh outloud or weep with relief.

"He certainly hasn't lost his sense of humor!" Clotilde remarked.

Llyonesse removed the wreath to admire it, smiling despite herself. It was just like the ones he used to weave for her when they were children. Perhaps things were not as bleak as she first thought.

Suddenly there came another knock upon the door. Perhaps this time Joshua had returned with a tamed monkey and organ grinder! She flung open the door with a broad smile of greeting only to find the Lady Marguerite standing on the other side with a small lacquer chest in her hands. Llyonesse's smile instantly vanished. *Now what?*

"I do hope that I am not disturbing you!" Marguerite said with a sour little frown. "I've come to see if there is anything I can do to help you dress before the banquet?"

"Oh … how kind," Llyonesse replied with a wan smile, hopping backwards as Marguerite swished past her into the room, her blue gown billowing out behind her like a gossamer whirlwind in her wake. She laid the box upon the dresser and opened the jeweled lid. "I thought you might let me do your hair," she continued.

"It will allow thy maidservant the opportunity to freshen up as well and give us a chance to get acquainted?"

"Very thoughtful of you!" sniffed Clotilde who felt no inclination to make a pretense of courteous behavior. " ... but I think that we can manage just fine—"

"*Nonsense!*" replied Marguerite, who evidently wasn't going to take "no" for an answer. "There is already a bath prepared for you and fresh raiment laid out from my very own wardrobe. Please indulge me. I wish to make amends for my horrid behavior earlier today!"

"Weeeeeeeeeell ... " protested Clotilde, weakening in the face of such frank honesty. She eyed Llyonesse for approval.

"It's all right, Nana," Llyonesse assured her, admiring her wreath with a happy smile. "I'll be fine."

Clotilde smiled in relief. *Bless Joshua for his thoughtful gesture!* "Thank you, my lady," she said, curtsying to Marguerite. "I *could* do with a hot bath." With a last glance in Llyonesse's direction, she followed the waiting page out the door and down the hall. When the door was closed, Marguerite began laying out a variety of scented oils, hair combs, and gorgeous jewelry. Llyonesse placed her precious wreath carefully upon the dressing table then dropped the sheet and lifted her arms so Marguerite could undo her laces and stays.

"How young you are," she said, tugging furiously at the knots."Why, you must be the same age as my little sister!"

"How old is she?" Llyonesse inquired ... *just to be polite.*

"She'll be ten this summer," Marguerite replied.

Six years and she couldn't tell the difference?

Llyonesse said nothing, determined not to let anything spoil her good mood. The laces finally undone, Marguerite pulled the last of her filthy garments up and over her head, accidentally knocking the wreath off the table.

"Oops! What's this?" She scooped it up instantly, studying it with a wrinkle of her delicate nose.

"Joshua made it for me," Llyonesse informed her, retrieving her cherished gift and putting it carefully back onto the dressing table.

"How very sweet of him!" exclaimed Marguerite with false enthusiasm. "Is this the usual custom of greeting long lost playmates in Ellioth?"

"Yes…well, no," Llyonesse corrected herself, momentarily flustered. "He often made them for me when we were children…"

"Well, he obviously just adores you!" exclaimed Marguerite, selecting an ivory handled brush and pushing Llyonesse down into a chair. She vigorously began combing out her long, snarled tresses, trying not to gag at just how filthy and oily they were. "I passed him in the hall on my way here and he remarked how happy he was to have found his little sister alive again…"

"Sister?" repeated Llyonesse, a strange sense of foreboding coming over her. "We are not related by blood."

"Why yes, I realize that!" nodded Marguerite. "But was not thy father his foster brother?"

"Yes, but we were betrothed since I was eight," said Llyonesse.

"Yes, so he told me," replied Marguerite, a very pitying look in her eyes.

"Wh-why are you looking at me like that?" stammered Llyonesse, immediately sorry she had bothered asking.

"Oh, Llyonesse!" Marguerite whispered with a shake of her pretty head. She carefully set the comb and brush down and gathered her into a gentle hug. "You mustn't worry about whether or not Joshua shall fulfill his duty to thee! You, even more than I should know what a very, very honorable and obedient man he is. You need have no fear that he will shirk his duty to marry thee."

"Duty? But, but he loves me…" whispered Llyonesse glancing at the wreath for reassurance, thoroughly confused.

"Indeed he does!" agreed Marguerite cunningly. "I should think that there is a better than good chance that his brotherly affection will one day blossom into a love of…shall we say, a more *mature* nature?"

Llyonesse stared at Marguerite horror-stricken, comprehending at last. The wreath, the invitation, his smiles…they were all brotherly affection…or part of his…*his duty*! Their betrothal was nothing more than a responsibility he was obliged to fulfill! Marguerite had spoken truly when she said Joshua was an honorable man. He was *very* honorable *and* obedient and no doubt would honor a marriage contract even if it meant sacrificing the love of a real woman for the commitment made when they were both children! She might have the prior claim by promise, but it did not mean she had any such claim to his heart as a man. As adults they were virtual strangers! She stared at the wreath with new eyes, no longer able to behold it with her former joy. It was a gift for the child he remembered her as, not for the woman she had become. In his eyes she was still the little girl for whom he plaited daisy-chains.

Nausea swept over her. "Please, go!" she managed to choke out before covering her mouth and fleeing to the privy.

Marguerite waited for a few moments while Llyonesse wretched, wrinkling her nose in profound distaste. When it became apparent she wouldn't be coming out for quite some time, she gathered up her jewelry chest, perfumes, and brush, and tucked them under her arm. "I will summon thy nurse!" she called out, leaving the door ajar behind her.

Llyonesse waited until Marguerite's footsteps faded away down the hall then collapsed fully upon the floor, giving way to great choking sobs which shook her to the marrow, little caring if she died naked in that very spot. *She should have remained in Shiloh. At least there he still belonged wholly to her and she to him.* She lay sobbing for what seemed hours, then lay still, too exhausted and sick to get up, even after a terrible chill set in. What was taking Clotilde so long? Why had she not come? She was trembling violently, the room was spinning and the stone floor was freezing cold. Try as she might, her limbs would not obey her will to rise. Oh how she wished someone would come…anyone! Still she waited, wearily watching her surroundings begin to fade into a black fog. She barely heard the footsteps approaching her chamber from down the hall. She summoned every ounce of strength she had left to call out, but her voice could not rise above a whisper.

The door opened moments later. "My lady?" called out Clotilde, looking about. The chamber appeared completely empty. She looked more carefully, sensing that something was terribly wrong. "Marguerite? Llyonesse? Where art thou?" Something made her look behind her and what she saw made her gasp in horror. Llyonesse lay as if dead upon the floor, her flesh as white as fuller's soap and beaded with cold sweat. She rushed forward and knelt beside her, feeling her neck for her pulse and pushing the sweat-soaked hair out of her face. "Good heavens, Llyonesse! Did Marguerite leave thee in this condition?" she moaned angrily, trying to lift her into her arms. Her skin was hot to the touch. "You're burning up!" she wailed in alarm. "How many times did I warn you against this very thing all those days you refused to eat!"

Llyonesse could barely answer, her teeth were chattering so hard.

"Cold," she stammered, curling into a fetal position for warmth, "... so cold."

Clotilde rewrapped the sheet about her then grasped her from under her armpits, trying desperately to haul her back up onto her feet. The shoulder seam in her beautiful new gown ripped, but she cared not. She was still struggling when a knock came upon the door.

"Help us!" yelled Clotilde, too busy to bother opening it herself.

The door opened. Joshua had come to escort Llyonesse down to the great hall, but one look at her laying half-conscious in Clotilde's arms and he marched in without waiting for a second invitation.

"What is wrong?" he demanded, his eyes filled with concern. "Why is Llyonesse so pale and what in blazes is she doing half naked upon the cold flagstones!"

"The Lady Marguerite left her in this condition, my lord," snapped Clotilde, too upset to speak more respectfully. "She's terribly ill, burning with fever."

"Fever?" repeated Joshua, feeling Llyonesse's flushed cheek. *Fever!* Her flesh was on fire! He bent down and lifted Llyonesse into his arms, cradling her against him. "There's no time to lose!" he said, striding from the room.

"My lord?" cried Clotilde in bewilderment, running after

him. "She's naught but a thin sheet about her! Where are you going? Where are you taking her?"

But Joshua did not hear her in his haste. Servants and courtiers alike cleared out of his way, pressing themselves flat against the walls as he shouted for them to move aside, half running, and half marching through the castle with Clotilde running frantically behind him. Dimly Llyonesse heard his booted feet thudding heavily upon the boards of the drawbridge then the next thing she knew, she was being submerged into ice cold water. Without pausing to remove so much as his boots or sword, and in all his finery, Joshua waded into the stream which flowed from the mountain snows directly above the castle before the startled eyes of all those nearby, plunging both himself and Llyonesse in up to their necks. She moaned aloud as the ice cold water gripped her flesh, squeezing her eyes tightly shut while Joshua struggled to keep his footing on the slippery rocks. In less than a minute his teeth began to chatter and lips to turn blue. Llyonesse wept unceasingly, pleading with him to take her out and it broke his heart to refuse her.

"N-n-not y-y-yet," he replied, his teeth chattering violently. "We m-m-must br-br-bring your fever d-d-down!" The wait was agonizingly long, but Joshua forced himself to endure the bone-chilling temperature until her tremors ceased and she fell into a deep sleep. With every ounce of strength he had left, he waded back to shore where outstretched hands waited to assist them. Llyonesse was lifted out of his tired arms by Sir Penloth who quickly wrapped her in several woolen blankets.

With a reassuring nod in Joshua's direction, he carried her back into the castle. "See to yourself, my Lord!" he called over his shoulder.

Joshua fell onto his knees, numbed through and through, unable to feel his feet in his water-logged boots. His sodden clothes and hair were plastered against his skin. A squire hurried to him with a warm cloak and threw it about his shoulders.

"Thoughtful lad," he smiled wearily, tousling the boy's hair. "Now run and inform the king there will be no banquet until the lady Llyonesse is well. I will join him in his chambers after I have changed."

"Yes, my lord," replied the squire, hurrying off to deliver the message.

Chapter Eleven

Joshua came to his father's chambers an hour later clad in thick, green, woolen hose, a long, brown tunic and heavy cape, hoping the multiple layers would thaw him out more quickly. A warm fire was blazing in the hearth and a bowl of hot venison stew awaited him. Sir Penloth, several of the other seraphim, and the fugitives from Shiloh nodded in greeting as he took his seat before them. Before Joshua could think to ask him, his squire was already at his elbow, pouring him a cup of warmed red wine for which he was rewarded with a grateful smile of appreciation.

"It was told me that you and Llyonesse went for an unexpected swim," commented his father. "How fares she? Is she sleeping comfortably now?"

"Yes and the physician assures me she will be fine," replied Joshua, drinking deeply of the mulled wine. It coursed through his veins, immediately warming him.

"That is good. I do not think either of us could have borne losing her a second time," replied Eloth.

"No," agreed Joshua whole-heartedly. "Knowing she is alive and safe has lifted a heavy weight of sorrow that has long been on my heart."

Penloth turned to him. "We have spoken only a little before you came, but the situation is even worse than we thought.

Lucius has complete control of Shiloh and has a significant following amongst our people. Rebels, like Dwayne and Justin here, are either written off as demented zealots or hunted like animals. What plagues me, however, is why the miserable villain wasn't run off the moment he started pushing his weight around!"

"Why indeed?" agreed Sir Eric angrily.

"Because from the very start he claimed that the insufferable taxes and edicts came directly from Ellioth," replied Arthur defensively. "When we finally did have proof of his duplicity, it was too late and impossible to convince others of what we knew."

"Not to mention dangerous!" added Dwayne.

"Aye, we had to be very careful about whom we told; he had spies everywhere," said Seth.

"His phony knights began arresting any who questioned him, pillaging our homes, and murdering our kinfolk all in the name of Eloth," continued Dwayne. "My parents were two of the first to be murdered—" he paused, choking on the grief he had long denied himself. "They beat my father to death and my, my mother … they … I was barely able to get away—" He closed his eyes, unable to finish.

All in the room stared at him in horrified sympathy. Seth, who sat closest, put his arm about his shoulders to comfort him.

Penloth regarded Dwayne with pity. Though the miller's son was only a few years older than Joshua, he looked much older. He was thinner, completely gray and more battle scarred than any knight he had known. Yet Dwayne had fought his private war with only his cunning and wits.

"Tis evil enough to commit such acts, but to do them in my name!" bristled Eloth, his countenance dark with anger. "Tis the height of wickedness! After all the years I reigned in righteousness, I would have expected them to know better than to believe I would tolerate such evil! Now, tell me of my sword, Ephlal, where is it?"

"It remains in the courtyard of his keep, still embedded in

the cornerstone," Bedwynne replied. "He keeps it under constant guard and none are allowed to get so much as within thirty paces of it."

"The guard will do him little good," said Eloth, smiling wryly. "None save I, Joshua, or Ardon's direct heirs could withdraw it, let alone wield it." He suddenly stopped, staring at his son with sudden comprehension.

"Llyonesse!" Eloth and Joshua exclaimed simultaneously, discovering the missing piece of the puzzle at last.

"So that is why he told us she was dead!" said Joshua. "He wanted to use her to gain possession of Ephlal." He turned to Dwayne. "What knew you of his plans for her?"

"I can tell you," interrupted a female voice.

All in the chamber turned round to stare at Clotilde who stood in the doorway. "He planned to wed her and consummate their union in the hope of transferring her ability to wield Ephlal to himself."

All color drained from Joshua's face and none save Penloth heard the curse he uttered under his breath.

Eloth straightened with rage. "Regardless of what Lucius did, Ephlal would not have suffered his touch!"

"My lord," interjected Bedwynn in exasperation. "Lucius has committed great evil, but he is not alone. We have known betrayal at the hands of our own kin! Many now serve him willingly, completely aware of who and what he is. Lucius is not wholly responsible for all the evil in Shiloh, my Lord; he has merely been the catalyst. Thine own subjects have committed more than their own fair share of deviltry, I can assure you!"

Dwayne stood, no longer desiring to keep silent about his true feelings. "My lord, I counsel thee, forget Shiloh; she is past redemption. Save for those locked away in Lucius' dungeons, we few are all that is left of those who have remained loyal to you!"[27]

"Forget Shiloh? Can a father forget his children, even his wicked children? Art thou of a surety there remain none left who do not cry out for justice?"[28]

"My lord," responded Dwayne with no small measure of bitterness. "I cannot so much as name *two*."

"Yea, even if there remained but only one, I would not abandon them," replied Eloth sternly.

"Then what is to be thy response, my lord?" Dwayne wanted to know. "Will not the lord of Ellioth and Shiloh uphold his law and execute judgment upon the guilty?"

All eyes turned solemnly to Eloth to see what he would say next.

Eloth slowly rose to his feet, his eyes smoldering. "Am I to now remain here and do nothing on the basis that my people are unworthy and deserve their fate?" he thundered. "Art thou aware, my unhappy miller, that Lucius himself once adjured me to do exactly the same and that if I came to Shiloh he would slaughter all within his walls? Perhaps all I need do to ensure 'justice is done' is to accept his challenge! I can sail brazenly into the harbor and sit at my ease whilst that serpent carries out the edicts of the law for me! Is this truly thy counsel?"

Dwayne hung his head in shame at Eloth's biting words, unable to look him in the face as the king continued. "Thieves, murderers, and rebels you call them, but pray tell me, didst thou not steal? Didst thou not murder in order to survive all these years? Deny it not!"

Dwayne shifted uncomfortably and nodded, feeling as though Eloth were peeling his skin away layer by layer.

"Does not my law place *all* who commit such crimes under my judgment, regardless of the reasons or circumstances? *Too easily dost thou demand justice for those in Shiloh! Art thou as willing to fall under the same judgment as they? Wouldst thou not prefer mercy?*"

Dwayne gave no answer, utterly ashamed of how Eloth had laid bare his hate-filled, bitter heart before all in the room.

"How long before the ship we have been laboring on these past years would be ready to sail at the earliest?" asked Joshua.

"At least another month, perhaps more," replied Penloth.

Joshua shook his head; his decision made. "I will not delay even one day longer." he said.

"Then what is to be done, lord?" asked Bedwynn sorrowfully.

"There is only one thing which can be done," Joshua replied quietly. "I take ship upon *The White Stag* for Shiloh and redeem my people."

All in the room turned round to regard Joshua in mute astonishment. All that is, save Eloth, whose face plainly showed that it was an announcement he had long been expecting and also dreaded.

"But did you not hear all that has been said, my lord?" argued Sir Penloth, standing to his feet. "Shiloh is Lucius' kingdom now!"

"No, it is *my* kingdom, Sir Penloth! Mine to rule and therefore mine to redeem," Joshua corrected him sternly.

"But surely he has surmised what your next move will be. We have already lost the element of surprise; you would be walking into a trap!" cautioned Sir Eric.

"I shall enter Shiloh by stealth and reclaim Ephlal. If you can ready the new vessel within a fortnight of my departure, then follow me to Shiloh and await my signal. If I have succeeded, I will fly our standard from the highest tower. If you do not see it, you may assume that I have failed and that all within are condemned to die by your hand."

Penloth stared at him aghast. "'Tis sheer folly!"

"Yes," replied Eloth suddenly. "But oft the foolishness of the wise confounds the wisdom of the foolish.[29] Joshua indeed may be walking into a trap, but it shall be one of his own choosing. Prepare *The White Stag* for departure."

Chapter Twelve

*L*lyonesse sneezed and opened her eyes to find a daisy petal tickling her nose.

"Not sick again I hope!" said a masculine voice.

"Joshua!" she exclaimed in stunned amazement. She looked around and her eyes went wide at finding a multitude of vases with freshly cut flowers filling the chamber. "You have brought the garden in to me!"

"Of course!" he smiled then pressed his hand against her forehead to feel for any sign of remaining fever. He found none. "You had us all very concerned, milady," he scolded her with a crinkly smile that made her heart skip a beat. "…and Clotilde informs me it was all due to self-neglect! How do you think I would have felt after all these years of mourning to discover that you were alive only to have thee die for real within my very halls?"

Llyonesse was left at a complete loss at how to answer.

Joshua hugged her close and gave her a warm smile. "I believe this is the first time I've ever had the pleasure of seeing *you* at a loss for words!" he grinned, remembering how she used to prattle unceasingly about all sorts of childish nonsense. "I have ordered a hearty breakfast sent up (which ye shall eat every bite of) and then perhaps, if you feel up to it, we can go for a walk in the garden … for a good talk. Only I regret to inform you that it is looking rather barren at the moment." With a conspiratorial wink, he rose to his feet, lifted her hand and kissed it gently, his whiskers tickling in a most pleasant manner. "I will be waiting for thee by our rose bush," he said, then left the room.

Llyonesse watched him go with rising excitement. Perhaps Marguerite was wrong after all. Perhaps it wasn't only brotherly affection. Suddenly she felt very, very hungry.

Joshua sat upon a stone bench near a very old but fragrant rose bush, lost in a fair memory when out of the corner of his eye he spied Llyonesse approaching him. Even when she had stood before him dirty from long travel and pale, he had thought her beautiful. Now she was such a vision of loveliness in her pink brocade gown that it took his breath away. Pink flowers were twined throughout her hair which tumbled unbound down her back and glistened in the sunlight and her skin glowed with a happiness that he knew had much to do with him. Joshua gazed his fill at her, marking the uncanny resemblance she bore to her father and wondering if he were but lost in a hopeful dream. Clotilde hung back, allowing Llyonesse to close the remaining distance without her then turned aside and busied herself by picking imaginary bugs off the shrubs.

Joshua held his arms out for her. "Llyonesse!" he greeted her lovingly.

"Joshua!" she smiled, thrilling to the warmth and affection in his voice and manner.

He looked so incredibly handsome in his tunic and cape of dark green wool! They offset his golden-brown beard, hair, and gray eyes to perfection. They stood less than an arm's width apart, yet Llyonesse could feel the warmth from his eyes even at this distance. Her cheeks began to flame under his steady gaze.

"Pink becomes you," Joshua said softly, the compliment making her heart soar. He indicated the rose bush at his side, the one they had planted together as children. "'Twas the only shrub from which I did not pluck blossoms this morning," he said, gazing at it fondly. "It must have known thou wast coming for it bloomed two days before thy ship was sighted, completely out of season. ... is not the fragrance wonderful?"

Llyonesse bent over the bush covered with pale white/pink blooms and inhaled deeply of their perfume. The scent brought back many wonderful memories, not the least precious of which was the day they had planted it together.

"Come," Joshua said, tucking her hand into the crook of his arm. "We have much to talk about. Walk awhile with me." Slowly they meandered among the artfully sculptured hedgerows and sparkling fountains, speaking first of pleasantries, then finally turning to more serious matters. Joshua wanted to know about every moment of her life between their parting many years ago and the moment they had been reunited in the courtroom.

At first she found it very difficult to speak for her earliest memories were of the loss of her parents; a loss she had never been able to really mourn over (for Lucius had forbade her to cry). Many times she stopped in mid-sentence, unable to continue because her throat constricted so in grief. But like a skillful surgeon, Joshua held her close and encouraged her with gentle words to fully unburden her heart. In the comfortable familiarity of his friendship and shared sorrow, Llyonesse finally told him of her life which had been spent locked up in a richly appointed room with only his locket, an ornery cat, and Clotilde for company. She related the many nights she had cried herself to sleep, longing to return to Ellioth, sustaining herself on memories which grew dimmer and more unreal every day, desperate for rescue from the horrors of a man who haunted her every footstep.

At long last Llyonesse gave vent to the full measure of her despair and anger, dissolving into uncontrollable sobs. Joshua gathered her gently into his arms, rocking her back and forth and speaking soft words of comfort, caring little how wet she made his shirt. His own tears mingled with hers as he too relived the grief at the loss of his foster brother, Ardon, Penlorian, and the other young knights whom he had all known well. When she finally calmed and looked again upon him, her eyes were swollen and red, but she felt as though a thousand pounds had been lifted from her heart.

"You must think me a great baby," she said, blowing her nose into a kerchief he offered her. She gasped. "Oh, I have ruined your tunic!"

Joshua looked down, noticing for the first time how soaked it had become. "Nonsense," he smiled. "You have merely christened it for me. Henceforth it shall forever be my favorite."

For a moment, Llyonesse wasn't sure whether to thank him or burst out laughing. She smiled at him, feeling closer to him than she ever had before, even when they had been childhood companions. She looked up, shocked to find that the sky had already grown dark and that the first stars were already beginning to peep out. The entire day had passed, it seemed, in the space of only a few moments. She looked around but saw no sign of Clotilde who had left long ago, realizing that her role as chaperon was completely unnecessary.

Joshua's arms went round her, drawing her close. "Llyonesse," he murmured, lifting her chin to him. "I swore to myself that if by some miracle I ever had thee in my arms again, I would say to you what I have waited years to say."

"What, Joshua?" asked Llyonesse, her heart pounding.

"*I love thee...*" came the whispered reply against her lips. "*Not* as a little sister, *nor* as a fond memory, as Marguerite so jealously inferred." The next thing she knew, his lips were fully upon hers in the tenderest of kisses. It was not the kiss of duty nor brotherly affection, but a kiss filled with such love and passion it made her head swim and toes curl within her slippers. "Come," he whispered his voice suddenly grown very husky. "'Tis getting dark; we must return for dinner." He rose to his feet, pulling her up with him close in his arms.

"Hmmm? What?" Llyonesse's eyes blinked open. "Oh, yes..." she stammered, unable to help but feel disappointed they couldn't be alone longer. She smiled shyly up at him. "I think I shall need you to guide me. I don't remember where anything is anymore."

Joshua slipped his arm about her waist possessively. "I

wouldn't have it any other way," he smiled, walking her back to the main house. "It will give me the excuse of reacquainting thee with Ellioth."

Despite their growing hunger pangs, Joshua walked slowly to the main hall in content silence, reluctant to share her company with a multitude of others, knowing how little time they had together. When they finally entered the enormous hall, Llyonesse felt as though she had stepped back in time to when she was a child. It was even as it was that night so many years before; the hall again ablaze with light, music, and the sound of laughter. It seemed as if the entire kingdom had turned out to welcome her in a great feast. To her profound embarrassment, the enormous room fell silent when they entered. Llyonesse stole a furtive glance at a table as she walked past and went red upon discovering that the food had not yet even been served on account of their absence. Had she known, she wouldn't have allowed herself to cry until her eyes were swollen almost shut. They finally reached the head table where the king and seraphim waited with smiles of welcome, seating themselves only after Joshua pulled out her chair then seated himself to her right. Eloth nodded to the steward for the first course to be brought in.

It was a truly wondrous affair and altogether elegant. Even at Lucius' table (which had been laid with the hoarded wealth of Shiloh), she never recalled dining with such rich and costly platters of gold and goblets of crystal. Nor had she had the pleasure of witnessing such wonderful table manners as those exhibited by the nobility of Ellioth. Lucius and his band of thieves ate like pigs; their most gracious table manners consisting of tossing hunks of greasy meat across the room to one another and spearing them in mid-air with their knives. In contrast, Joshua served and cut her meat for her himself, choosing always the most tender morsels and vegetables from gorgeous silver platters. Her one and only disappointment lay in the fact that the lady Marguerite and Earl were nowhere in sight to appreciate the attention he was overtly lavishing upon her. As if reading her very thoughts, Joshua finally admitted that he had sent both packing the previous day for their own lands back in the north.

"How is it that you made her acquaintance?" asked Llyonesse, her voice unconvincingly indifferent.

Joshua smiled to himself, enjoying her obvious jealousy. "I met her father many years ago, after I was knighted," he replied. "I was journeying through Ellioth's northern realms and was visiting his Keep when word came from Ellioth to return with all haste. As a matter of fact, I left right in the middle of the lady Marguerite's recital."

"Recital?" repeated Llyonesse, her eyes growing large.

"She was playing the lute," Joshua clarified. "I departed rather abruptly and, in my haste to make amends, I invited the duke to Ellioth little thinking he would use the opportunity to try and marry his only daughter off to me. Despite their machinations, I would say that all's well that ends well, don't you agree?"

"Ummhummm," replied Llyonesse noncommittally, her face somber.

Joshua leaned forward, his voice soft but serious. "You needn't scowl so, Llyonesse, I never abandoned hope that thou still lived and would one day return to me. We shall wed in due time, as has always been my heart's desire."

Llyonesse smiled at him, her last doubt swept completely away. Marguerite had lied! Joshua did not think of her as a little sister at all or that it was his duty to marry her! That kiss in the garden should have been proof enough, but now she felt completely reassured. She returned his grin with a smile of such brilliant happiness that Joshua laughed aloud for joy, forgetting for a brief moment the shadow of his imminent departure which had lain so heavily on his heart.

After the main courses were cleared away, trays of wondrous pastries, dates, puddings, comfits, and cordials were served on silver chargers, each creation more fanciful than the last. Llyonesse selected a small tart of dried dates and pears topped with a caramelized crust of various nuts for her dessert. Joshua told her it was known as a "Musician's Tart," explaining it was named so because nutmeats being so costly, they were often used as payment to musicians for their services. As if to illustrate his point, the court musicians broke into loud music, introducing the first amusement of the evening. With loud shouts and beat of drums, a troupe of men scampered into the hall, all attired in outrageously bizarre outfits. With great fanfare, they began performing incredible feats of skill. In one trick, they stood five men high, one atop another's shoulders, adding more and more to their human tower by catapulting members of their troupe from a specially made board which sat like a teeter-totter upon a barrel. Each time the heavyset leader took a running jump onto the board, Llyonesse squeezed Joshua's hands tightly, and released her grip only after the acrobat had successfully landed on the shoulders of the topmost person.

Joshua was torn between watching the performers and Llyonesse's face, which was a study in delight, terror, wonder, amazement, and awe. So many different expressions passed across her features that he soon became fully absorbed in watching only her, delighting in her enjoyment despite the pain her gouging nails were bringing him.

Thunderous applause and gold coins showered down upon the acrobats at the end of their performance. As they ran from the hall, a husband and wife team (and their thirty trained dogs) entered all attired in some sort of human costume, complete with hats, pantaloons, and garters. Llyonesse clapped and laughed until her ribs hurt. The poodles, collies and shelties pranced, capered, jumped through flaming hoops, balanced on empty kegs, and danced waltzes with their masters all the while creating a horrendous din with their loud yapping. The audience roared with laughter throughout the entire performance and when they finally all lined up to take their "bows," they too were showered with gold coin and the dogs rewarded with table scraps and juicy bones. A brief lull ensued, leaving many to wonder what the next form of entertainment would be.

Joshua nodded at Gabrielle who in turn signaled the attending squires. Quickly they dispersed throughout the great hall, dousing candles and candelabrum until the blaze of light had diminished to a subdued, golden glow. Llyonesse craned her neck forward, wondering who would appear next. Then Gillian, Eloth's Bard, strode into the hall carrying his ancient, elaborately carved and gilded harp. The people broke into thunderous applause for Gillian's performances were only granted on extremely important occasions. The Bard bowed in acknowledgment of their appreciation, his long, black velvet tunic with golden embroidery work twinkling fitfully in the soft candlelight. Llyonesse stared at the Bard in awe, having never recalled seeing him during her brief childhood at court. She wondered how old he was for he seemed both youthful and ancient at the same time; his face perfectly smooth and devoid of wrinkles, much like that of a young man, but with deep-set, icy blue eyes that were filled with wisdom and snow white hair which hung to his shoulders. With a nod in her direction, Gillian tilted his harp against his shoulder and set his fingers upon the strings. Suddenly the hall became filled with the strains of hauntingly exquisite music.

> *"How beautiful thou art, my darling, how beautiful thou art! Thine eyes are like those of a dove behind thy veil, thy hair as the color of autumn leaves. Thy lips are that of a scarlet thread and thy mouth wholly desirous..."*

Llyonesse stiffened. This was no lay nor legend, but a love song and Gillian was directing it at her!

> *"Thy temples and cheeks art blushed with the color of pomegranates and behind thy shimmering veil thy neck is graceful and comely, like that unto a graceful swan. Thy smile dazzles as the sun at noonday..."*

His voice was rich and melodious; the notes gossamer threads that wove into a growing tapestry of enchantment. Llyonesse listened, completely transfixed, her heart soaring with each note that filled her soul.

> *"Thou art altogether lovely, my beloved, my darling; thou hast quickened my heart with but a single glance of thine*

sparkling eyes. How beautiful is thy love, my sister, my dar-
ling, much sweeter than fine incense and wine... "³⁰

Llyonesse slowly opened her eyes, dimly realizing that the music had stilled some moments earlier. Her heart ached with emotions too tumultuous to express and tears were flowing freely down her cheeks as she turned to stare beseechingly at Joshua, desperate to convey how utterly humbled and beloved she felt. Joshua nodded at her, for he had no need of words to tell him what she felt. *He knew.* He took both of her hands into his, entwining their fingers so that she could not tell where his began and hers ended and gazed at her with intense love. Suddenly she understood as if she had heard him speak the words aloud. *Joshua* had written the bard's love song, not Gillian!

Those in the hall also sat in awed silence. Applause would have only cheapened the gift they had been allowed to share; and to offer praise to lower it to the level of mortal scrutiny and so they paid Eloth's Bard the highest compliment of all and honored him with their silence lest they break his fragile spell. Gillian bowed low before Joshua and Llyonesse then took his leave.

"Come, Llyonesse," whispered Clotilde, helping the shaken girl to her feet. "I think it is long past thy bedtime."

Joshua also stood to his feet, releasing her hands with great reluctance. "Sleep well, my beloved," he said softly, looking deeply into her eyes. Llyonesse nodded, and then turned, following Clotilde docilely from the hall as though she walked in a dream.

The following morning, Clotilde awakened Llyonesse early, bearing a covered tray, a fresh cake of scented soap, and a clean riding frock of pale yellow. After she had bathed, Clotilde helped her into her clothes then sat her down to arrange her hair. Llyonesse sat quietly as Clotilde wove the thick strands into a single braid down the middle of her back, tying it off with a bright yellow ribbon and sighing with frustration at the wisps of stubborn curls which playfully refused to remain in the braid.

"What think you?" She held up a mirror for Llyonesse just as a knock came upon the door. Llyonesse jumped to her feet.

"Calm thyself!" Clotilde whispered sternly. "Try to behave as the lady he now thinks thee!" Then she opened the door.

"Good morning, milady Llyonesse," said Joshua, entering the room. Llyonesse could already feel herself blushing at his broad smile, quite taken with how handsome he looked in his buff breeches, kidskin boots, and his now favorite, tear-stained cambric tunic. A large picnic hamper was slung over one arm. "Ready?"

Llyonesse nodded, unable to find the courage to look him straight in the eye after the previous night's serenade. Joshua grinned with pleasure; he liked seeing her blush. He turned to Clotilde who had been watching the exchange with amusement. "We are off to the high meadows, my lady, so don't expect us to return until sundown."

"Milady is in good hands," smiled Clotilde, opening the door wide.

Waiting for them in the courtyard was Joshua's white stallion, Paracletis, and a palfrey fitted with a lady's side-saddle. Its pale, cream-colored mane had been braided cunningly with yellow ribbons and wildflowers. Both horses turned their heads when they approached and nickered in greeting. The palfrey extended her face to Llyonesse who petted her with delight.

"Here's a carrot," Joshua said, withdrawing one from the picnic hamper. The horse thrust its nose into Llyonesse's hand before she could even offer it. "Patience, Buttercup!" Joshua chided when Llyonesse stepped backwards, intimidated. "Pay her no mind, she's a regular pig but gentle as a lamb. Carrots are her favorite ... try now," he said, putting his arm about her shoulders encouragingly.

Llyonesse gingerly held forth another carrot and giggled in delight when Buttercup eagerly closed her lips about it and gently drew it out, munching loudly. When the carrot was gone, she butted Llyonesse's hip and whinnied softly.

"She wants more!" smiled Llyonesse, rubbing the soft nose. "May I?"

"Buttercup would eat the entire contents of our lunch if you let her!" said Joshua with a grin, patting the mare. "There will be plenty of sweet clover for her to graze on when we stop to picnic, so she'll just have to do without ours." He handed the basket to a waiting squire, and reached for her waist. "Up we go!" For a fraction of an instant their eyes were bare inches apart and then Llyonesse was balancing precariously in the saddle trying to concentrate on his instructions on how to sit properly. After Joshua had mounted, the squire handed the basket back up to him.

"We shall return by sunset," Joshua told him, turning Paracletis about.

"I'll be waiting mi'lord," the boy replied with a wave and grin.

With a gentle prod Joshua led the way with Llyonesse following close behind. When they reached the outskirts of the village, they rode side by side at a gentle walk through emerald plains of tall grass, green and fragrant from recent rains and through orchards. They soon came upon a flowing stream where Joshua turned them off the road and followed its course several leagues northwest. A half hour later they came upon a small loch nestled within a grove of oak, maple, and birch trees. Clouds scudded across the pale blue sky, making dappled patterns of sunlight and shadow upon the moors which lay beyond. Joshua dismounted first and laid out a large blanket, then reached up to help Llyonesse down. She slipped her leg off the saddle and immediately began sliding downwards. Joshua was quick to react and caught her in his arms. "Careful!" he cautioned her, setting her gently on her feet. "You can turn an ankle that way!" Next he unsaddled and unbridled the horses, allowing them to run free over the grass at will. "Come," he beckoned, patting the place next to him on the blanket. "Let's see what cook packed for our picnic."

Obediently Llyonesse sat down, at a total loss as to what to say or how to act while Joshua pulled out package after package of food. There were a number of dainty sandwiches, wedges of assorted cheese, fruit, and best of all, Prunella's famous almond cakes. Joshua held one up to his nose and sniffed deeply. "If you behave thyself I might let you have one," he said, grinning wickedly.

My goodness, he's handsome when he smiles like that! Llyonesse thought, helping to lay out their feast. Last of all came two wineskins, one filled with mead, the other with dark brown ale.

"How is it that you and Marguerite came to be betrothed?" It was out of her mouth before she even knew it; her undercurrent of jealousy unmistakable.

Joshua paused and sat back on his heels, regarding her with mischievous eyes. So his little Llyonesse was still jealous, was she?

"Well ... ?" she persisted

"Sandwich?" Joshua offered.

"Yes, thank you ... are you going to answer me?"

"Cheese or fruit?"

She glared at him. "*Joshua. .!*"

He peered into the basket and rummaged around. "Sorry, no Joshua's in the basket!"

Llyonesse groaned. Why was he being so difficult? She scowled at him. "You aren't going to tell me what I want to know, are you?"

Joshua looked her straight in the eye and smiled. "Precisely," he answered. Marguerite was a closed chapter and he just as soon forget about her.

Llyonesse sighed; she had forgotten how stubborn he could be and how infuriated it always made her. She removed the stopper from the wineskin, and examined it thoughtfully for a moment. "Ale?" she offered.

"Yes, thank you—"

Llyonesse grinned, pointed the wineskin at him and gave it a big squeeze, squirting him point-blank in the face. She burst into laughter, lurched to her feet and hopped backwards before he could grab her and squirted him again. "Still thirsty?" she laughed, twisting away from his outstretched arms. Joshua shielded his face from another stream of spewing liquid. "Stop this instant!" he said.

"I didn't hear the magic word!" Llyonesse sang out, dancing nimbly out of reach again. Joshua made a weak attempt at another grab, but she managed to evade his grasp again and get in another good squirt at the same time.

"I'll get you!" he shouted, going after her in earnest now.

Llyonesse squealed with laughter and ran away, putting a large bush between them. When he went to the right, so did she and visa versa. "Tell me what I want to know and maybe I'll stop!" she cried. They chased one another in circles for several minutes during which time she succeeded not only in thoroughly avoiding his grasp, but in drenching his face, shirt, and breeches as well. Finally, Joshua had had enough. With a grunt, he leapt over the hedge clearing it completely and grabbed at the wineskin. Llyonesse shrieked, aimed, and squirted again, punctuating her bull's eye with another loud squeal of laughter as she dodged away. Joshua wiped his face. He had to give her credit; her aim was amazingly accurate for someone laughing so hard. This time she put a large boulder too great to clear between them and squirted him until the wineskin was flat as a pancake. Her ammunition gone, Llyonesse dropped the wineskin and ran to re-arm herself with the skin filled with mead, but Joshua was too fast for her and got it first.

"Got you!" he shouted, pinning her arms to her sides to keep her from further mischief.

"Let me go! Let me go! You smell like a distillery!" she laughed, wrinkling her nose.

"So do you!" Joshua replied, yanking the stopper out of the other skin with his teeth.

Llyonesse's eyes widened. "Joshua, you wouldn't! Not all over my beautiful new ... STOP!" Too late, Joshua upended the skin and squeezed, dumping the entire contents in one continuous stream over her head. Mead ran down her face, neck, and into the bodice of her yellow dress. "*Joshua!*" she sputtered, unable to believe he had actually done it. "Now what are we supposed to drink?"

In response to her question, Joshua grabbed her, slung her over his shoulder, and carried her out into the lake until the water reached the top of his boots. "What do you think?" he replied then promptly dropped her in. "Water!"

The backsplash she made upon entry was quite satisfying in size. Llyonesse came up laughing and sputtering. "I'm all wet!" she wailed, pushing her hair out of her face to examine herself. "And to think I spent two hours this morning primping for you!"

Joshua smiled, wishing she could see how fetching she looked with her hair and clothing plastered to her face and body, her thick black lashes separated into starry spikes. Heedless of the floating weeds and water lilies, Joshua waded further in and drew her into his arms, his face suddenly becoming very soft and serious. "Llyonesse," he murmured, looking deeply into her eyes, "when I was told I'd lost thee, my heart was sundered in two."

Llyonesse looked up, observing his raw pain for the first time. How could she have been so self-centered? She had never even stopped just once to consider how he must have suffered. She reached up to cup his cheek. "I'm so sorry," she whispered. "But all that is behind us now. We are together."

"Yes, for now," agreed Joshua, his eyes fastened upon hers. Then with sudden passion, he drew her close in his arms, kissing her with his warm lips. Had he not been supporting her, she was sure her legs would have given way beneath her. How long they kissed she did not know, but when next she opened her eyes she felt as though time had come to a complete stop.

"I daresay you taste even better than Prunella's almond cakes," he whispered softly, kissing her eyelids, nose, and cheeks with abandon.

Llyonesse shut her eyes in sublime happiness. "I'll never leave you again," she promised, entwining her fingers in his. "Never, except perhaps to bathe."

Joshua's body stiffened almost imperceptibly at these words, instantly alerting her that something was wrong. She stared at him, almost afraid to ask. "Joshua, tell me ... what is wrong?"

He stared at her long ere he answered, knowing his next words would wound her deeply. "But we are about to be parted again, my Llyonesse. I sail for Shiloh in two days."

Llyonesse stared at him horror-stricken. She could not have been more devastated had he told her he was marrying the earl's daughter that afternoon. "But, but *why?*" she whispered with rising panic. "*Why?*"

"Can you not guess?" he answered. "You of all people shouldst know me well enough to realize I will not abandon my people to that tyrant. Lucius is bent on their destruction."

"But you cannot challenge him with only one ship!" she cried, desperately seeking a reason to prevent his departure. "His cannon will sink it before you could drop anchor!"

"I will give him no such opportunity," Joshua replied.

Llyonesse became angry. "But, but you just swore we would never be parted from each other again! Were those empty words or did you say them merely to placate me?"

"It was thee who swore never to leave *my* side," he corrected, regretting the words instantly. "I said that no man would ever take thee from me again and none shall. Thou shalt abide here in safety—"

"One word more or less does little to change the fact that we shall be parted, perhaps forever!" she shouted, pushing away from him. "Is this why you brought me out on this picnic today? To prevent a scene before all thy court? *To soften the blow?*"

Joshua gave her an injured look. "I wanted you all to myself for at least this one day ... should the worst befall me ... "

Llyonesse's eyes widened in alarm. "You speak as a condemned man!" she whispered. The answering look on his face was her undoing. "*Nooooo ... !*" she wailed, covering her face with her hands. "*Not when we've just been reunited!*"

Joshua pulled her to him. "*Lessie, Llyonesse!* Think ye not that if there were any other way that I would do so?[31] It breaks my heart to leave thee again! Canst thou not forget thine own sorrow long enough to leave me with a fair memory for my comfort?"

Llyonesse stared at him, thoroughly devastated. "Take me

with you!" she pleaded. "I would rather perish in Shiloh with you than die a thousand deaths waiting and wondering if you shall ever return!"

Joshua was silent long ere he answered her, his eyes closed, his forehead upon hers. Finally with a deep breath he opened them; they were twin pools of unfathomable anguish. "No," he said.

Llyonesse pushed away from him, cut to the quick. The matter had been long settled; that was evident. This day was to be all they would ever have together. He would depart for Shiloh and never return, leaving her with the agony of his kisses to haunt her for the remainder of her life. She wished she had never returned. Better to have fallen victim to Lucius in Shiloh knowing Joshua yet lived, than to bring them both to such a bitter parting. "It's getting late," she mumbled, refusing to look at him. "We should be heading back."

Their return to Ellioth was in silence and had her mare not thrown a shoe, Llyonesse would have ridden ahead in the hopes of finding a cliff or deep ditch to fall into to bring her misery to an abrupt end. As it turned out, she was compelled to share a ride on Paracletis within the circle of his arms while Buttercup walked behind. She did not try to hide the steady stream of tears which flowed down her cheeks, nor did Joshua give any indication that they were having any influence in changing his mind. In two days time they would be lost to one another again, probably forever. Llyonesse closed her eyes, fighting not to sob aloud.

When at last Joshua felt Llyonesse's head droop to his shoulder in exhaustion, he slumped in relief. Now, while she slept peacefully in his arms, he could rest his cheek against hers and kiss her to his heart's content. He slowed Paracletis down to a very slow walk, prolonging their last few moments together for as long as possible. She looked like an angel when asleep; her face perfectly smooth and serene. He snuggled her close, wanting to sear the sight, feel, and smell of her indelibly upon his memory. They arrived in the courtyard long after the sun had set to find that a search party was being organized to look for them. They were all immensely relieved when they saw him ride into the courtyard safe and sound.

"The mare is lame," Joshua informed the farrier who came to take charge of their horses. "I think there may be some swelling." He dismounted, still holding the sleeping Llyonesse in his arms.

"I'll see to it, my lord," whispered the farrier, leading the horses away. Joshua looked up at the darkened windows of the castle, noting that the one to Llyonesse's chamber was still brightly lit. Clotilde was evidently waiting up. He carried her through the silent hallways and up the winding stair to her chamber, pausing before the door to gaze upon her peaceful face one last time. At that moment, Clotilde yanked the door open. She was in her nightdress and shawl, holding a candle aloft. From the look on her face she had spent the evening worrying herself into a frightful state. Her look of anxiety quickly gave way to relief then anger the moment she got a good whiff of them. Joshua smiled despite himself. He could well imagine how it must have looked: they were hours late; they reeked of ale and mead and Llyonesse, for all intents and purposes, appeared as if she had passed out.

"Come inside, my lord," Clotilde said tight-lipped. She stepped back until she stood against the opposite wall where the smell was not quite so overpowering, watching in silence as Joshua gently laid Llyonesse upon the bed and smoothed some strands of hair away from her face. The tender gesture mollified her somewhat.

"You must be weary, mi'lord," she said kindly. "I'll take over from here. Go now to thy rest; you've much to do before you leave."

Joshua backed toward the door so he could look one last time at Llyonesse's beloved face. He smiled at Clotilde, indicating his clothes. "She squirted me with the wineskin," he explained, his voice cracking with emotion. "We never even tasted a drop."

Clotilde waited until the heavy oak door shut behind him, and stood in silence, not knowing whether to laugh or weep.

Joshua and Llyonesse saw very little of each other in the next two days. He was busy getting the ship prepared and Llyonesse paced like a restless cat in her chamber, growing more frantic by the hour. From her high window in the castle, she had a clear view down to the harbor. It was sheer torment to watch the barrels, crates, and trunks being loaded onto *The White Stag*. How could he expect her to sit idly by while he left her behind? They had had only one day together in ten years! *One day!* She could not sustain herself on such a fleeting memory! At least if she were to accompany him to Shiloh they might enjoy several weeks together.

Llyonesse stopped dead in her tracks. If she could not dissuade him from going then she would just have to find a way to go with him! He would no doubt probably become very, very angry with her, but it was a risk worth taking! Joshua could shout, scold, and even lock her in the hold as punishment, but none of these eventualities were as bad as being separated! Llyonesse lifted her skirts and raced through the castle, sweeping dust and rushes aside. She went first to the garden, then through several other chambers and halls until she finally found Clotilde in the solar with some other women at their needlework. Clotilde looked up in alarm when the door to the solar sailed open with a bang. Llyonesse stood before her, panting and sweating profusely, her eyes blazing with stubborn determination.

"*Milady* . . . !" Clotilde began to chide, then fell silent, already knowing it was no use; she knew that stubborn look well. Clotilde set down her needlepoint with a sigh of resignation. "What would you have of me?"

"Any luck, Penloth?" Joshua asked for what must have been the twelfth time that morning.

"Nay, mi'lord," Penloth answered, vexed at his failure to find Llyonesse. "We have searched every niche of the castle and grounds, but it seems thy lady is most determined not to be found."

Joseph Fitzbaton approached them, his face visibly anxious. "My lord," he whispered with concern, "the tide is going out, we can delay no longer."

Joshua cast a sorrowful glance at the high window that belonged to her chamber, hoping to see her face peering out. He turned imploringly to the king. "Father?"

"Speed thee on thy way, my son," said Eloth, putting his arm about his shoulders to comfort him. "I will see to Llyonesse myself immediately upon thy departure."

Joshua nodded silently, bitterly hurt that she had refused to come to bid him a last good-bye. "Cast off," he mumbled, turning away.

Stubborn girl! Penloth seethed to himself as he left Joshua's side. He had a good mind to turn Llyonesse over his knee and give her a good spanking! With a last solemn embrace, Joshua's father and friends disembarked and stood with the multitude on the dock that had gathered to wish him farewell, their hearts very heavy. Joshua stood in the bow, watching the distance slowly increase between stern and shore, still hoping to see some sign of Llyonesse. When he was finally too far to distinguish one face from another, he turned his back upon Ellioth and set his face eastward, toward distant Shiloh.

Chapter Thirteen

*L*lyonesse peered out into the inky blackness, holding her breath as the rusting hinges of the trunk uttered a whiny creak of protest. As usual, the noise went unnoticed, muffled by two levels of heavy planking above her head and the footfalls of those above. She pushed it open all the way, fighting the overwhelming urge to groan aloud with pleasure as she straightened then arched backwards to stretch out her aching spine and limbs. Had she known how exceedingly uncomfortable, cramped, and cold she was going to be inside the sea chest, she would have thought twice about sneaking aboard. As close as she could reckon, she had lain hidden within the hold for several days, coming out only in the dead of night to relieve herself, stretch her aching muscles, and get a brief taste of fresh air before returning below to eat her cold meal of dried meat and water. During the day, she tried to sleep, biting the inside of her cheeks to take her mind off her hunger pangs and worsening bowel problems. Her food and water were running out more swiftly than she had anticipated and she was sick unto death of loneliness, hard tack, and stale water. She had at least another week to wait before they were too far out to turn back to consider taking her home, but she didn't know how much longer she was going to be able to keep it up. She had lost all sense of time for she dwelt in constant darkness. She went to sleep in it, awakened in it, and spent hour after lonely hour in it. She was desperate for fresh air, hot food, and sunlight, but most of all, she longed for Joshua's company, the reason for which she had stowed away in the first place. She winced at the now familiar cramping in her bowels. She could wait no longer. She clambered out; little caring whether it was midnight or noon day. If she didn't take care of business this instant, the resulting smell would bring all above decks down to her anyway! After a brief (but thorough) stretch, she stuffed her hair into a sailor's cap and pulled her collar up. She was taking extraordinary precautions not to be noticed at first glance and even had strips of cloth wrapped about her bosom to flatten it under her boy's clothes. With any luck, nobody would pay her any mind. After several blind gropes, she finally caught the rope which lowered the ladder into the hold and pulled downwards. It lowered quietly and she crawled up rung by rung until she was high enough to lift the hatch and peek out. Luck was still with her; it was nighttime.

"Must be near midnight," she muttered to herself, looking overhead. The heavens were dark, but the deck was awash in the silvery light of a full moon. Save for the pilot, who was far astern, the deck appeared quite deserted and quiet except for the ever present creak of timbers, splash of waves, and gentle flapping of sails. She crept out and tasted deeply of the fresh air. Oh, if only she could remain out here and sleep lying flat under the stars! She tip-toed to the starboard railing reserved for private use and paused for a moment, struggling with the knot in the drawstring of her trousers.

"Couldn't sleep either, eh?" said a male voice, startling her.

Llyonesse's back stiffened with instant recognition. *Joshua!* Panic-stricken, she lowered her face into her collar, continuing to fumble with her breeches. "Too much ale," she said in her best male impersonation. Joshua did a double-take, his eyebrows climbing high into his hairline upon hearing a very feminine and familiar voice issue from the supposed "deck-hand" before him. He took a closer look and smirked with sudden comprehension. It was Llyonesse! So that was why she had not been on the docks to see him off … she had been stowed away all this time! His heart soared with joy, but then his lip curled with sudden mischief. *He would play at her little game and then some.*

"Ale?" he drawled, sliding his arm about her shoulders in a friendly manner. "Have thee any more? I was under the impression that only water and mead had been brought onboard. C'mon now, give us a taste!"

"Why. … uh, uh—" stammered Llyonesse, all pretense of trying to sound male was lost in her rising panic. "I only had a small flask. It's all gone now … "

"Gone?" echoed Joshua softly, unable to suppress the growing warmth in his voice. "Mayhap you can make up for the lack in some other manner."

To her complete horror and amazement, Joshua spun her round, yanked her against him by the collar and fastened his lips on hers, kissing her passionately.

She put both hands on his chest and stiff-armed him backwards. "*What do you think you're doing?*" she screeched.

"Kissing you, silly wench!" He replied then began to shake with laughter.

Llyonesse stared at him, first in astonishment, then amazement, and finally in relief. He wasn't angry with her! She had suffered all this time in the hold for nothing!

"What's this? What's this?" Joshua asked when she began to cry. He gathered her into his arms and held her close. "Ssshhhh," he soothed, rocking her gently. "It's all right now, sssshhh, quiet now, Llyonesse."

But Llyonesse continued to sob anyway, enjoying his attempts to comfort her. He removed the cap, smoothing the hair off her face and wiping her tears with his fingers. "Be comforted, I am not going to have thee keel-hauled or shackled, though I daresay it would teach you a good lesson for disobeying me! Where have you been hiding all this time? Have you had enough to eat? You are thinner now than when you first came to Ellioth!"

"I was in the hold, in a large sea chest," she replied, closing her eyes wearily. "I took a week's supply of food and water, but it is almost gone and I am glad, for I am sick to death of it!" She looked up. "I did not want to be parted from you again," she whispered. "And so I sneaked onboard the night before you left. Are you very angry with me?"

"I should be," Joshua replied, hugging her tighter. "But I might have done the same were I in thy place." He gave her nose an affectionate tweak. "Come, thou shalt abide in my cabin for the remainder of our voyage." He took her by the hand and led her down a short flight of stairs into the main cabin. "Make thyself at home," he said, indicating a chamber pot behind the door. "I'll be back shortly." He kissed her forehead then closed the door behind him to give her some privacy.

Llyonesse looked about the handsome cabin with happiness. No more cramped trunk, no more darkness, no more loneliness! The cabin was in the stern of the ship with a number of stained glass windows that looked out over the sea and which opened to let in the fresh sea air. They were making good time, judging from the frothy wake fanning outward in the sea behind them. Two glass lanterns swung to and fro from the low ceiling as the vessel rode the gentle swells, casting a golden glow about the room that was paneled in rich mahogany. Just under the windows was a large berth which harbored a very appealing-looking bed with snowy white blankets and pillows. Llyonesse brought a pillow up to her cheek and buried her face in its softness. It smelled of Joshua. At that precise moment, Joshua walked in on her. Llyonesse dropped the pillow instantly, her face crimson.

Joshua grinned as he set down a heavy pewter charger filled with very appetizing food. *So she liked the smell of him, eh?*

"Oohhhhh, hot food!" Llyonesse half-groaned, half-sang. She grabbed it away, plopped down cross-legged on the bed and set to, not even bothering to use the cutlery.

"I thought you might be hungry," Joshua said, sitting on a stool next to her. Llyonesse nodded vigorously in agreement, stuffing the herbed fish, glazed vegetables, bread, and compote into her cheeks until they were bulging like a squirrel's.

"Slow down!" he warned her, catching her wrist. "Small bites. See first whether thy stomach can tolerate such hardy fare."

Okay. Llyonesse nodded, her mouth too full to speak. She gulped it down, offering him a big grin. "No problems whatsoever!" Her stomach rumbled loudly as the first mouthful of food hit bottom then settled down. Evidently it was going to behave itself. They grinned at one another in amusement; however, Llyonesse ate more slowly from then on, chewing each bite thoroughly and drinking plenty of water.

"While you continue gorging thyself, I'll deal with thy hair," Joshua said, pulling his stool up behind her. He gathered it into his hands and gently began working the comb through the snarls. Despite her hunger, Llyonesse could not help but close her eyes in pleasure as he ran the comb through in long, smooth strokes. Soon she forgot all about eating entirely and gave herself up to his wonderful ministrations. Even Clotilde, who had performed the task for years, had never been this gentle nor made it feel so incredibly pleasurable. Joshua combed out her tangles as though he valued each strand of her hair above gold. For his part, Joshua was enjoying himself immensely. Combing a woman's hair was quite a novel experience and Llyonesse's was splendidly thick and soft, with red and golden highlights and natural curls that wound flirtatiously about his fingers. He took his time, smiling as she tried valiantly to concentrate on eating, aware of the effect his attentions were having upon her. She quickly abandoned her attempts at eating and sat with eyes closed, leaning against him, her face a study in rapture. When the last snarl had been worked free, he laid down the comb and braided her hair, tying it off with a white piece of fabric at the end.

"Come," he said, removing a half-eaten Johnnycake from her hand. "It's time you got a good night's sleep."

"Mmmmm?" murmured Llyonesse sleepily, eyes still shut with combined pleasure and drowsiness. She was in clean clothes, she was warm, she was fed, and she could want for nothing more. Docilely she stood and allowed him to tuck her into bed, swaying as he pulled back the covers then tucked her in, bending low to place a gentle kiss upon her brow.

"Sleep well, my love," he whispered softly then doused the

lanterns before leaving the cabin to join the crew below in their hammocks.

Llyonesse awoke the next morning feeling refreshed and restored but momentarily disoriented, forgetting the events of the night before. She blinked at the warm sunlight blazing across her coverlets then smiled when memory returned and stretched languorously. The fresh sea air was cool upon her cheek and a welcome change from the dank air of the hold. It was so good not to be hungry, cramped and cold anymore in that smelly hold! She sat up when the door to the cabin opened and Joshua came in bearing another tray of hot food. Llyonesse's stomach grumbled loudly.

"Hungry again?" he grinned, carrying the tray to her bed. The inviting smell of warm bread, eggs, and sausage seeped out from under the domed platter.

Llyonesse regarded him with awe. "You wait on me as though you were a manservant!" she chided.

"Tis a service of love," he replied, thrusting a fork into her hand. "When thou hast eaten and dressed, meet me up on deck…I shall be waiting for you." After placing a kiss on her cheek, he turned and left the cabin.

Not much later, Llyonesse met him upon the foc'sle. "Joshua!" She waved at him.

Joshua turned around and smiled at the fetching image she presented in men's sea scanties. He put his arm about her shoulder and drew her close. "Good morning," he murmured, kissing the corner of her mouth. "Didst thou sleep well?"

Llyonesse nodded. "Yes. I'm not sure how many night's sleep I've lost so far, but it felt like a month's worth at least. How long since we put out to sea?"

"Almost a fortnight," he replied.

"A fortnight!" A look of extreme annoyance crossed her features. "I planned only to remain hidden for a week!"

"Consider the extra day's punishment for disobeying me," he replied, his face growing serious. "Though I have shown thee great patience in this affair, disobedience is no small matter, Llyonesse, regardless of whether thou art in agreement with me or not! Stowing away carries the penalty of keel-hauling or forty lashes!"

Llyonesse hung her head in sincere shame. "Yes, mi'lord," she said meekly.

"I am still Joshua to thee, whatever thy transgressions," he said, lifting her chin. "Pray fret no more over it, for I forgive thee wholeheartedly. I shall find some other way to chastise thee, but for now, let us enjoy our last few weeks together; it may be all we shall ever have—"

Llyonesse looked at him in fear. "I will yet hope for years of joy together," she replied.

"It is the hope of that joy which shall sustain me in my darkest hour," he murmured, drawing her close.[32]

Another week passed, a week in which they grew closer and fell more deeply in love but despite their happiness, the dark specter of Shiloh hovered like an ever-present storm upon the horizon. Llyonesse feared greatly for him and her resentment for the rebels in Shiloh who would take him away from her grew stronger by the minute.

Why must he go there? That sword of his was not worth risking his life for, let alone his fickle subjects! Why must she trade his personal safety and their future together for hard-hearted rebels who cared for nothing but themselves? If it lay within her power to save him from throwing away his life for that realm of ingrates who would as soon spit on him then she would have to do something! Better to endure his anger than everlasting guilt for not having at least tried! Despite her promise not to interfere, she found herself thinking more and more on how she might talk him out of his quest.

Llyonesse stared woefully out through the windows of her cabin at the swirling wake of the ship, chewing her nails down to the quick in growing anxiety. She had been struggling for hours to find the right words to say to Joshua to turn him aside from this foolhardy quest. When the time came for her to join him out on deck as was now their daily custom, she found herself quaking with fear. She found him standing alone and staring out to sea, his handsome face pale and careworn; almost as if he already knew what she had planned to say. With trembling hands she reached out to touch him, then withdrew them. "Joshua?" she whispered, forcing herself to continue. "May I speak freely with you for a moment?"

Joshua nodded but did not turn around, his eyes closed as if he were in pain. Llyonesse swallowed, her throat suddenly gone dry. He wasn't going to make it easier on her; that was certain. If only he would put his arms about her, or at least *smile*.

"Please do not go," she suddenly blurted out. "Please, please let us return to Ellioth and be married as we always planned. Oh, Joshua! I love you so. Must you sacrifice our happiness to rescue people who hate you? Please, I beg of you! Forget Ephlal! Forget Shiloh! Return us to Ellioth! You risk your life and our happiness for nothing!"

To her immense shock, Joshua covered his face with his hands, a soft moan escaping from his lips as though he were weeping. The sound sent a knife through her heart. When he lifted his head to stare at her, his eyes were dark with anguish. "For shame, Llyonesse, *for shame!*" he rebuked her. "You speak as Lucius might in thy place!"[33]

His indictment stung her to the heart. Her eyes flooded with tears. "I'm ... I'm—it's only that. ... " all remaining words failed her. Llyonesse gathered her skirts, turned, and fled from his presence, weeping bitterly.

The land of Shiloh was sighted the very next hour and word quickly passed throughout the ship. But it was the first mate, not

Joshua, who came to her cabin to deliver the news. Llyonesse nodded in silent acknowledgment and closed the door upon his sympathetic face; her heart leaden with sorrow. Their time together was over and had ended on the very bitterest of notes.

Chapter Fourteen

Although they were many leagues up the coast, well out of sight from any spyglass and under cover of night, *The White Stag*'s lanterns were doused and sails furled several hundred yards out from shore. Lookouts were posted upon the bowsprit to guide the ship in as close as possible, finally dropping anchor a bare three furlongs away from the beach.

Llyonesse stood silently on deck, watching miserably as the crew carefully lifted Paracletis, Joshua's white stallion, out of the hold using a special pulley and harness designed for transferring animals. The stallion's legs dangled out through the holes in the heavy canvas which bore him, whinnying loudly in protest despite Joshua's efforts to calm him.

Llyonesse watched everything with swollen eyes, her heart aching. They had not spoken since earlier that day when he had rebuked her, and time was quickly running out. In a few moments he would be rowing to shore and she would never see him again. If only she could undo the events of earlier that day; if only there was not this breach between them! *If only he would change his mind!*

Paracletis was finally lowered into the water below and began swimming for shore. Joshua hefted a large haversack and water skin over his shoulder then paused to look at her one last time in farewell, his face etched with sorrow. Llyonesse returned his stare, her heart in her throat, eyes brimming with tears.

Joshua could stand it no longer and held out his arms for her. "Llyonesse!" he whispered. Llyonesse went to him, allowing him to sweep her into his arms. She clung to him, sobbing with mingled relief and renewed sorrow, the crew watching in silence as the lovers bid one another a last tender good-bye. Finally, Joshua gently pushed her away from him, staring longingly at her face. He wanted to remember the way she looked with the moonlight shining on her dark hair and glistening upon her tear bedewed lashes, her beautiful eyes full of love for him. Llyonesse stared back at him in numb silence, her heart in her throat as he lifted her hand to his lips for a last kiss. Then in the next instant, he disappeared over the side of the ship, descending the rope ladder into a small boat which bobbed along-side. He set his oars against the shipboards and pushed away, rowing until he reached the shore.

Llyonesse watched from the railing until the darkness swallowed him up, waving although she did not know if he could even see her, then turned away and went below decks where none could see or hear her weep.

Joshua dragged the boat out of the surf, and covered it up with long ropes of seaweed. When he straightened to look back across the water and see *The White Stag*, he could not find her. With her sails lowered and lanterns doused, she was as good as invisible. He gave a last blind wave, little realizing that Llyonesse was doing the very same, then turned to retrieve Paracletis. After fumbling blindly in his haversack, he found the curry comb and used his sense of touch to brush the excess water out of his mane and coat. When satisfied that he had gotten most of it out, he threw a blanket over him and mounted bareback, guiding the stallion with subtle movements of his body, confident Paracletis would avoid any pitfalls they might encounter. Shiloh laid approximately fifty leagues directly south. All he need do was stick to the coast and travel under cover of night to avoid the many patrols Lucius had roaming the wild. With any luck, he could cover at least half the distance before morning and the remainder the next night, arriving at the outskirts of Shiloh just before sunrise on the third day. It was a fair night for traveling; the sky was clear and the stars and three quarter moon provided sufficient light to steer by and so he set off. It was a bone-wearying journey, but he managed to cover at least twenty leagues before stopping prior to dawn to sleep. He made no fire and ate a cold meal of dried fruit and meat before rolling himself up in a blanket to sleep while Paracletis quietly stood watch over him.

He was awakened by a gentle nudge in his shoulder, the horse's low whinny bringing him to full wakefulness. Joshua cracked open one eye and peered up at the horse's face, bare inches from his own. Paracletis snorted in greeting then shook his mane. Joshua looked about. The sky was already growing dark; time to get up and cover the remaining distance to Shiloh. He would need to be even more cautious now than before, for the closer he drew the more likely he was to run into Lucius' patrols. He stood up and stretched, gazing with a frown toward his destination. For the first time since he arrived, he noticed a brown haze and faint acrid smell hanging upon the air. After another cheerless meal, he repacked his meager belongings and remounted, riding in melancholy silence throughout the night, the memory of Llyonesse occupying his thoughts. When Paracletis abruptly stopped, he was brought out of his private thoughts. They had arrived at the crest of a hill which overlooked the valley of Shiloh just as dawn was about to break. Joshua dismounted, tied Paracletis up to a thorn bush, and stood upon the cliff edge to behold his kingdom for the first time.

The smell and haze of smoke he had seen from twenty leagues out was evidently from the refuse fires which surrounded the walls as mountains of human garbage. Open sewage was flowing in the streets and byways and had there not been cottages and shops still standing, he would have thought a terrible battle or catastrophic pestilence had devastated the land. Beyond the village, where once had stood fertile farmland, stretched a bleak vista of blackened meadows, hacked-up orchards, and weeds. There was not a hint of green upon the land for as far as the eye could see. Every sense he possessed was assaulted with the sight, smell, and sound of ruination and decay. Joshua lifted his stinging eyes from the horror of the valley and looked upon Lucius' cruel citadel. Not the ivory palace that Ardon had envisioned with lush gardens and fountains, but a distorted monstrosity with cruel turrets and battlements which openly gloated upon the misery of his people in visible triumph. Joshua beheld the utter ruination that had become his kingdom and wept.[34]

He reached the city limits just before the noon hour, arriving on foot in the marketplace which was abuzz with activity despite its decrepit appearance. Numerous stalls were crammed together; vendors yelling aloud and holding high their assorted wares. A great amount of livestock were penned into a very small area, most ridden with disease, underfed, and peering dejectedly out from their muddy enclosures or cages. Crates of sickly looking rabbits and chickens were piled everywhere; cattle and oxen lowed plaintively in filthy stalls and swine rolled in fetid pens. What produce was available was either wilted or infested. Joshua passed among his own people completely unnoticed, his face concealed beneath the cowl of a tattered hood, observing their hopeless faces with an aching heart.

It needn't have been like this, he thought to himself. *Their lives needn't have come to this end: devoid of hope and empty; existing from one miserable day to the next. Had they been watchful, had they not succumbed to Lucius' lies, it could have been so different. They were living in a hell of their own choosing.*

The press of the crowd forced him to shoulder his way through, making it increasingly difficult to hang onto the money pouch dangling at his belt. Twice in the past ten minutes he had felt foreign hands groping for it, but when he whirled about to confront his assailants, the culprits had melted away anonymously into the jostling crowd. He scanned the perimeter of the square, his height enabling him to see over the heads of most around him, finally spying that which he sought. With quick strides he pushed his way forward until he reached a pen of odious smelling swine and interrupted the bartering session by tapping the swineherd on the shoulder and pointing. "How much for the entire herd?" he asked.

The swineherd turned and gaped at him; his beady eyes attempting to calculate the amount of money in Joshua's pouch. " 'ow much ye got?" came the response.

"How much per head?" countered Joshua, incensed at the man's outrageously dishonest method of bartering.

The swineherd frowned, obviously displeased at having to do business with a shrewder man than he. "Five shillings a head," he finally said, squinting to see within the cowl of Joshua's hood. It was a scandalously high price, but he was in no mood to barter further. The swineherd's eyes practically popped out of his head when Joshua emptied his money pouch without counteroffering with a lower bid and counted out enough silver to purchase the entire herd.

"Bloody hell," he swore under his breath in self-condemnation. He could have demanded ten times the amount and not even put a dent in the man's purse! He continued eyeing the pouch greedily as Joshua stuffed it back into his tunic. "Shall I 'ave them delivered to ye on the morrow, mi'lord?"

Joshua stared at him. *Did the man think him an idiot?* "No, I'll take them now and this as well ... " he said, plucking the stave out of the swineherd's astonished hand. He opened the door of the pen. "I don't think you'll be in any further need of it for awhile."

As the swineherd gawked after him, Joshua herded the pigs out of the pen and into the clogged street. It took every ounce of skill he possessed to negotiate the high-strung animals through the jostling streets while keeping a keen lookout for Lucius' henchmen (who still roamed about the city in the tattered raiment of Ellioth's long dead knights). Several times he almost bumped into people he recognized, seeing firsthand what years of Lucius' rule had done to them. Oh, how he longed to cast away his disguise and shout that their captivity was almost over! It took him half an hour to finally escape the smells and cacophony of the bustling market square but once in the clear he drove the herd up the hill toward the castle gates at a great pace. It was a long, hot climb and the dust kicked up by pig's hooves choked his nostrils and stung his eyes. The swine trotted on before him, oinking and squealing in protest at the pace he set, their large bellies swaying from side to side. He cast a cautious sideways glance at the knights who stood guard as he passed through the portcullis, but they showed no more interest in him than any other merchant. Evidently, there was nothing out of the ordinary for swineherds to barter their wares before the castle gates. Joshua peered ahead, heart pounding, his eyes finally catching sight of Ephlal's golden light shining from within the courtyard. It stood even as Dwayne had described, the blade embedded into the thickest part of the cornerstone. Upon either side stood a guard, each facing in the opposite direction from the other, their blades unsheathed as per orders. Joshua smiled grimly. One guard was wavering on his feet as if he dozed and the other just stared right through him as though he were invisible, bored from years of monotonous guard duty. Well, it would not be boring for much longer! He quickened his pace, urging the agitated swine on before him as he came closer. He broke into a run, goading the swine faster. "Pork!" he cried. "Pork for the master's table!"

The guards glanced at him, scowling with annoyance at having their peace and quiet broken by the squealing pigs. The first head of swine was almost upon them. With a loud cry, Joshua swung his stave and gave the lead pig a hard smack on the rump. It squealed loudly and charged forward.

"*Look out!*" he shouted, smacking another. The entire herd suddenly went berserk. Several hundred pounds of infuriated pork careened into the guards, knocking them over and then trampling them; their curses and shouts drowned out by the frenzied squeals. For a brief instant, the way to Ephlal stood clear. Joshua lunged forward, grasping the hilt with both hands to draw it forth.

"Draw the sword and Llyonesse dies!" shouted a voice directly above him.

The words stunned him like a blow to the head. Joshua stiffened as if struck by lightning and looked up to behold a sight that froze his blood. Lucius stood above him upon a balcony, his arms wrapped about the body of a young boy... *NO! Not a boy... his Lessie. .and he had a knife against her throat.* Lucius' lips curled in an ugly victorious smile of triumph when he saw Joshua's eyes widen in horrified recognition. The courtyard balconies above Joshua began to fill with dozens and dozens of armed men taking aim upon him with longbows and crossbows while more poured into the courtyard, surrounding him with a thicket of lances and swords. A loud *bang* behind him signaled the dropping of the portcullis, cutting off his only means of escape. *He had walked right into a trap!*

Joshua glared up at Lucius, still poised to withdraw the sword.

Lucius smiled at him, confident in his superiority. "Back away from the sword now or I'll gut her like a fish!" Joshua's eyes darted to Llyonesse who was staring back at him in naked terror. On her other side stood an aged man robed all in black, rubbing his withered hands together and muttering in apparent glee at the goings-on.

When Joshua did not respond, Lucius grabbed Llyonesse by a handful of hair and shoved her to the very edge, hanging her upper torso precariously out into midair and shouted again. "This is my final warning... step away from the sword!"

Joshua hesitated only a moment, his eyes riveted upon Llyonesse's face.

"Take the sword," she mouthed silently. Ephlal's golden hilt was pulsating with light in response to Joshua's grasp; he could feel its awesome power resonating through his flesh. His choice was clear. With eyes closed, he released his hold and backed away from the sword, raising his arms in surrender.

"*No!*" Llyonesse whimpered, wilting with despair. Encouraged by Joshua's docility, Lucius' knights immediately fell upon him while Lucius laughed with glee. They dealt brutal blows to his body and face with their boots, clubs, and swordhilts.[35] By the time they grew exhausted of their sport, Joshua was on his side, curled in a ball to protect his head; blood flowing from his ears, mouth, and nose.

Lucius shoved Llyonesse into Scheldrake's grasp. "Hold her!" he commanded, exiting the balcony.

"With pleasure," hissed Scheldrake, pressing the knife firmly against her neck to discourage any struggles.

Lucius hurried down the staircase with mounting excitement and arrived in the courtyard just as his men were finishing securing Joshua's arms behind his back. They roughly yanked him back up onto his feet to face their lord. Upon coming face to face with Joshua for the first time as an adult, Lucius was greatly taken aback. The Prince, who was less than half his age, towered over him, an imposing figure of a knight with powerful muscles and a stern majesty despite the awful beating he had just endured. Joshua slowly looked up through swollen eyes and focused his steely gaze upon Lucius' face, giving him such a wilting glare that the former baron found himself backing away intimidated. Sensing his fear, his knights dutifully dug their lances into the small of Joshua's back as a warning. Wearily, Joshua lowered his eyes.

With his men to protect him, a small measure of courage returned to Lucius. "Wast thou merely playing the fool to amuse me or have thine brains been curdled by the sun?" he demanded. "Did ye not, at any time, suspect that thy journey hither was far too easy?"

Joshua made no reply.[36]

"Well, no matter," Lucius continued after an embarrassingly long pause. "I have planned a long time for thy return. I'm certain thy people will be most interested to learn why their prince attempted to enter his realm secretly and in disguise. They have been chafing to air their grievances against your majesty for more years than I could count." Lucius nodded to his men in the tower to summon the villagers. "This way, your *highness*," he sneered, pushing Joshua before him through the castle doors while the bells rang out. The curious crowds left their stalls in the marketplace and began marching up the hill in response. Joshua was half-pushed and half-dragged through the castle by a leash that had been looped about his chest, his face already swelling and purpling from the beating he had received at the hands of Lucius' men. When he was finally dragged before Llyonesse and pushed onto the floor, his face was almost unrecognizable.[37]

"Oh, Joshua!" she cried out in anguish, falling to her knees and putting her arms about him. Joshua weakly lifted his head, barely able to see her face through his haze of agony. "Lucius was expecting us," she whispered, gently cradling his head in her hands. "His men boarded the ship only hours after you left and sailed it back to arrive before you could. We walked right into his trap."

"Where is the crew?" Joshua whispered through swollen and bleeding lips, raising himself painfully onto his knees.

"Dead of course!" Lucius interjected as though surprised at the question. "With Llyonesse as my hostage I had no further need of them!" He turned around and stepped out onto the balcony, watching as the crowd filled the courtyard below. He raised his hands for quiet and they silenced instantly as if by magic, gazing up at him with curious and attentive faces. Lucius smiled benevolently upon them.

"People of Shiloh, thy king has come to lay claim to his kingdom at last! Will you welcome him?"

Joshua looked down upon the milling crowd in silence, barely able to see out of his swollen eyes because of the beating he had suffered at the hands of Lucius' men.

"*Noooo!*" screamed the enraged crowd, raising their fists and shaking them at Joshua. "*Go back from whence thee came!*"

Llyonesse could not believe her ears!

So horrific grew their insults and revilings that she wanted to stuff her fists in her ears to drown it out. As word spread throughout the village, more and more people flooded into the courtyard, all of them giving vent to years of pent up rage.

Why doesn't he say something? Don't they know it is Lucius and themselves who are to blame? She screamed inwardly.

"What should I do with this stranger who claims to be thy king?" continued Lucius with a knowing leer. He had no doubt as to what the response would be.

Llyonesse held her breath, fearful of what would happen next.

"Take him away! Take him away!" screamed all the villagers. *We'll not have this man to rule over us!"*[38]

Joshua listened to their screams in stony silence, his heart leaden with anguish. Nothing he might have said in his own defense would have mattered. Lucius had done his job well; they were convinced that he and his father were to blame for their misery and they were out for revenge.

Lucius turned to gloat at him in triumph. "Well, my good prince, it seems quite apparent to me that thou art no longer wanted. The only question which now remains is: *what am I to do with thee?*" Lucius turned and looked upon the face of Llyonesse, scowling in jealously at the tears of love and pity streaming down her cheeks. This seemed to fill him with wrath. "She esteems thee greatly, does she not, oh prince?" he said in a dangerously soft voice. He turned murderous eyes upon Joshua. "Perhaps a demonstration of who is the superior man here? What say thee, whelp of Eloth? I have long desired to see if thou wouldst bleed blood or goats milk when pricked!"

Joshua's face colored at the insult, but he remained silent, infuriating Lucius all the more.

"I will take thy silence as consent," Lucius hissed in response, violently shoving Joshua out of his way. Dumbfounded, Llyonesse watched Lucius divest himself of his overcoat and doublet and pluck a saber from off the wall. Her heart leapt with momentary optimism.

"Fool! Joshua will cut you to ribbons!"

But Lucius' next words instantly froze her blood.

"Of course, I need not tell thee that the common rules of chivalry do not apply here!" he said, his black eyes deadly serious. "If you so much as rip the cloth of my vesture, Scheldrake shall visit cut for cut, slash for slash upon Llyonesse; I shall have her injured thrice for every wound you visit upon me!"

Joshua's face darkened with alarm, but he made no reply as Lucius cut his bonds and thrust a saber into his hand, giving him little choice but to defend himself as best he could. Immediately Lucius began circling about him like a stalking panther, goading him into making the first charge by describing in gory detail what he planned to do to her once Joshua lie dead. Joshua did not rise to the bait, despite how angry he became at Lucius' threats, knowing it would be his undoing. Without warning, Lucius suddenly lunged forward, thrusting his saber at Joshua's vitals. Joshua easily deflected it, knocking the blade to one side with a flick of his wrist, careful not to injure the baron. Joshua had no rival when it came to swordplay, but Lucius was no novice and he fought dirty. Every piece of furniture and object in the room not nailed down was hurled, flung, or shoved into Joshua. He grabbed a tall, metal candelabrum and pushed it over toward Joshua's left while slashing to his right. Joshua somersaulted away with a grunt of pain, narrowly missing both, rolling back onto his feet and silently blessing Sir Luther and Penloth for grilling him so unmercifully when he was a boy. With an angry growl, Lucius whirled about, swinging low with his blade to cut his legs out from under him. Joshua jumped high only to dive low again when the return swipe whipped around high enough to take off his head. His frustration and fury mounting, Lucius threw chairs, platters, urns and stools at Joshua, many of them finding their intended target as Joshua could barely see out of his swollen eyes. One vase caught him a glancing blow off his temple, stunning him momentarily. Lucius took advantage and shoved a large table into him, pinning him against the wall. Joshua struggled violently, ducking under the table seconds before Lucius' blade could penetrate his eye. Instead it bent in half upon the wall then splintered in two. Joshua was then forced to stand by helplessly and do nothing while Lucius lazily selected another weapon from the wall. The battle continued. Now Lucius was armed with the heavier, more deadly broadsword against Joshua's lightning fast saber. Around the chamber they battled, upending tables, tripping over debris, while Llyonesse watched the scene in mounting terror. Even her untrained eye could see that Joshua's reflexes were slowing and that he was parrying fewer and fewer sword thrusts. It was all too obvious that he was growing fatigued from the unending battle and beating he had taken earlier. Blood was running from dozens of ugly slash wounds that criss-crossed his body. His shirt was slashed and hanging in bloody ribbons and he was panting for breath. Lucius danced about him like a mad thing, slashing and hacking at will, exulting in each new wound he dealt him with a scream of crazed triumph.

Llyonesse struggled vainly against Scheldrake in horror. *This was all her fault! Had she not disobeyed Joshua and remained in Ellioth as he had bid her they would not now both be facing their imminent doom!*

Llyonesse suddenly stiffened in alarm and opened her mouth to warn Joshua whose vision had become blurred by blood and stinging sweat. He never saw Lucius' sword coming until it was too late. With a mighty swipe, Lucius laid Joshua's sword arm open to the bone. He fell onto his knees with a loud groan of agony, clutching his mutilated arm against him, his saber clattering onto the floor.

"Stop it! Stop it!" Llyonesse shrieked but neither of them paid her any heed. Blood lust was heavy upon Lucius now that victory was so close at hand. Joshua struggled weakly to his feet, barely avoiding another sword thrust, his broken ribs aching in protest. He cradled his useless right arm against his body, and grabbed the saber with his left, thankful he had been trained to fight with his left arm as well. Lucius was slightly dismayed but undaunted. He had felt Joshua's ribs gave way under the impact of his boots. *One more punch in the right spot and Eloth's son would crumple like a rag doll!* He feinted toward him as if to strike with his sword, but instead rammed him like a bull, catching Joshua squarely in his broken ribs. Together they hurtled backwards through the chamber until Joshua's back slammed against the iron railing of the balcony behind him. Joshua cried aloud upon impact, dropping his saber. Without so much as a moment's

hesitation, Lucius dropped his sword and grabbed Joshua about the throat with both hands while kicking him with his metal shod boots. Joshua slowly crumpled under Lucius' punishing blows, oblivious to Llyonesse's wails of horror.

Her eyes widened in sudden alarm as Lucius swiftly withdrew a hidden dagger from his boot…"*Noooooooooooooo!*" she screamed, but it was too late. With a victorious snarl of triumph, Lucius plunged the blade hilt-deep into Joshua's heart and watched with glee as Joshua's body stiffened momentarily then went slack, his eyes rolling back into his head. With a mighty shove of contempt, Lucius pushed his lifeless body backwards over the railing, watching with glee as it plummeted silently onto the courtyard fifty feet below, its fall broken by Ephlal's cornerstone. The villagers scattered like rodents in all directions.

"*Revenge!*" shrieked Lucius, dancing about in maniacal glee. "*Revenge! Revenge! Revenge at last!*"

Momentarily forgotten in their moment of triumph, Scheldrake released Llyonesse so he could get a better look at Joshua's body. Llyonesse also stumbled out onto the balcony and through swimming eyes beheld the lifeless body of her beloved Joshua, sprawled like a twisted and bloody rag doll, bare inches from the sword that would have saved them all. The crowd grew strangely silent, gathering in a ring about his broken body, watching his life's blood slowly pool about Ephlal's glowing blade.

It was over; Lucius had won! Llyonesse collapsed onto her knees, sobbing brokenly. *Joshua was dead. All hope was gone.*

Drunk with victory, Lucius lifted both arms in the air to crow in triumph, but in that instant, Joshua's blood reached Ephlal's blade. A ferocious stab of blinding light lanced outwards in all directions. The villagers screamed in fear as the ground began to quiver then shake violently beneath them. Black clouds gathered together and boiled overhead rumbling in harmony with the earth still shaking beneath them. Lucius and Scheldrake backed away from the balcony, flattening themselves against the far wall to escape from Ephlal's terrifying blaze. Its light penetrated the chamber searing them all with mind-numbing light. A mighty roar of thunder issued forth from the heavens above and earth beneath.

Llyonesse struggled to keep her feet, staring in dumbfounded shock as Lucius and Scheldrake fell onto the floor screaming and grappling like madmen with some unseen foe. A third quake, stronger than the previous two, finally sent her sprawling. Plaster and masonry rained down upon them and it seemed as though the castle would be rent asunder from the earth's violence.

"*Woe unto us!*" she heard a voice keen somewhere far below. "*Woe unto us! We have murdered our king!*"[39]

Then the world went black.

Chapter Fifteen

*L*lyonesse slowly opened her eyes. Save for the ringing in her ears; all was deathly still and silent. She sat up and looked around at the destruction which surrounded her.

How long had she lain unconscious? An hour? Several hours? Days? It seemed like an eternity had passed.

She rose unsteadily onto her feet, stepping over chunks of plaster, shards of glass, and shattered furniture until she finally stood again upon the balcony which was remarkably still intact. The sky was still dark but no longer black. It had become a sad, melancholy gray from which fell a steady rain as if in lamentation for her slain prince. Llyonesse closed her eyes and tilted her face upwards, allowing the cool raindrops to mingle with her hot tears. She did not wish to look below again and see his poor, disfigured body lying twisted and bloodless upon the pavement. She wanted to remember him as he was: tall and strong, his face alight with laughter.

Two hands suddenly caught hold of her and forcibly dragged her back from the railing. She was hurled round to find Lucius leering at her, seemingly no worse for the wear.

"Not so fast, my sweet. I still have unfinished business to attend to!" he growled, reaching for her sleeve.

"No!" Llyonesse screamed, comprehending what he was about to do. "*Let me go!*"

"*Silence!*" Lucius shouted, pushing her down onto the floor and pinning her flat with his full weight. He looked into her terror-filled face, his eyes smoldering with hatred and lust. A nasty leer spread over his mouth which was bare inches above hers. "This time there is no escape for thee!" he hissed.

Llyonesse glared at him with naked hatred, longing to rake his hideous face with her nails. With all the venom she could muster she gathered a mouthful of saliva and spat at him. Lucius growled at her with fury, then backhanded her, snapping her head to one side. Llyonesse gasped in pain, on the verge of blacking out. She struggled to stay conscious, determined to fight him off with her very last breath.

"*No! No! I won't let you!*" she screamed, struggling wildly beneath him. With a snarl of frustration Lucius let go of her arms and grasped her by the neck, choking off her screams and air supply. Llyonesse clawed at his hands but was unable to loosen the death grip about her throat. She felt herself grow faint … her vision blurring as she began to lose consciousness.

Suddenly a shadow fell across them. Lucius turned round to see what manner of fool had dared to interrupt him when a hand of iron suddenly grasped him about the collar and flung him across the room. Lucius crashed to a stop against the opposite wall and shook to clear his head. When he was finally able to look up, all blood suddenly drained from his face.

His eyes bulged with disbelief. "*Joshua!*"

Llyonesse looked up and beheld a sight that made her heart pound with disbelief and sudden hope. Standing protectively before her was none other than Joshua and in his upraised hand glowing white hot was Ephlal!

"*Behold thy doom, Lucius!*" Joshua's voice boomed, the walls vibrating with each syllable. Against his will Lucius felt himself forced to gaze upon Ephlal's blade, horrified at the sight of flames licking up and down its length but even more terrified by the fell light glittering in Joshua's blazing eyes.[40]

"*This isn't possible!*" he shrieked, trying to shield his eyes from the horror of Joshua's wrath. "*You were dead! I killed you!*"

Joshua advanced upon him, the chamber sizzling with the potency of his unbridled fury.

"*Thou hast earned the penalty of death many times over, Lucius!*" he thundered.

"But thine own people rejected thee!" Lucius squealed plaintively. "If I am to stand condemned then what of them? They are every bit as guilty of treason as I am!"

"*I came to Shiloh willing to lay down my life on their behalf, but yours is an entirely different matter,*" Joshua replied sternly. "*The requirements of my law have been satisfied! Those who now choose to honor me as their rightful king shall receive the mercy I bought for them. But You ... you, Lucius, didst seal thy doom when thou didst unlawfully spill my blood!"*[41] Joshua raised Ephlal high to smite him.

"No!" shrieked Lucius, cowering against the wall like a cornered animal. *"No! No! Noooo!"*

"This is for betraying my father!" cried Joshua. Down it came in a shower of blazing light; shearing off his right arm. Lucius fell against the wall with a scream; writhing as blood spurted from the stump.

"This is for my brother, Ardon, Zarabeth and Llyonesse!" Joshua cried again, every syllable causing the walls of the chamber to shudder with their power. Down came the holy blade again as Joshua sheared off Lucius' other arm.

His knees collapsed, bringing him hard upon the flagstones, yet he was still unrepentant. His face twisted into a mask of fear and loathing; and with monumental effort, Lucius spat upon the floor before Joshua's feet in utter contempt.

"I still will not bow my knee to you!" He screamed in impotent rage. Joshua's face was impassive but the look in his eyes filled Lucius' heart with a cold terror. Ephlal again came hurtling toward him and instantly sheared away both of his legs from his torso; effectively forcing his face onto the floor before his King in his own spittle and blood. Lucius lay prone and utterly defenseless knowing instinctively there was only one last part of him left for Joshua to remove.

Powerless now to do anything else, Lucius twisted his neck up and watched Joshua, the only Son of Eloth and rightful Lord of Shiloh, raise Ephlal for the last time in abject terror.

Joshua's face, if possible, blazed even brighter at his next words—the look in his eyes more terrifying than Ephlal's glittering blade.

"YOU ARE FINISHED!!"[42] Joshua shouted.

Ephlal came crashing down upon him in a shower of sparks as Lucius uttered a last blood curdling shriek. There was a blinding flash of light, a loud *boom*, then all went deathly silent.

Llyonesse waited and listened, trembling uncontrollably on the floor, her face hidden in her arms. Moments later, she felt Joshua's gentle hands encircle her and pull her against his breast. "Ssssh, fear not," he said gently, holding her close. "'Tis over, Lucius is no more."

Llyonesse wiped her sodden face with shaking hands then fearfully looked upon him. Gone was the terrible lord who had stood protectively over her with a sword of flame; he was Joshua once again, the gentle young man she had known and loved all her life.

Joshua entwined his fingers through hers. "Be comforted, my Llyonesse; I am no phantom," he whispered.

"Oh, Joshua!" she whimpered, tears flowing fresh down her cheeks. "I don't understand! I saw you slain with my own eyes! You were dead. *Dead! How can this possibly be?*"

Joshua drew her close to calm her, rocking her as if she were a frightened child. He felt warm and solid enough yet he appeared wholly unscathed.

"It was Ephlal," he whispered in response to her question. "*The holy blade suffers not the stain of innocent blood.*" He brushed the tears from her cheeks. "Come, Llyonesse, I must hide thee in a secure chamber and shut the door behind thee for a little moment, until my wrath has passed over the land. It is time for me to deal with my stiff-necked people!"[43]

Llyonesse stood shakily to her feet, hesitating at first, then placing her hand trustingly within his. Joshua led her down the hall even as cries and shouts began to rise from the village and the bells tolled, calling all to man the cannon on the cliffs. A warship had been sighted upon the horizon and its mainmast bore the Standard of Ellioth! Joshua's armies had come and the wrath of Eloth was about to fall upon Shiloh in full measure.

Moments after the alarm had gone up, those upon the ships heard cannon fire issuing from the castle battlements. The first volley fell short, plummeting harmlessly into the sea in an explosion of spray.⁴⁴ Those upon the incoming ship regarded the assault in grim disbelief.

"Captain!" shouted Sir Penloth. "Turn us to starboard and give them less of a target to aim for. Look lively there, men! Get those cannon prepared to fire upon my command!"

Eloth stood upon the forecastle, looking through the spyglass as he searched the battlements for any sign that might save Shiloh from utter destruction.

"Aim for the bluffs first, where the cannonfire came from," he called down to Penloth. "Fire not upon the city until I give the order!"

The Vengeance tacked and came about, returning fire, her cannon balls impacting just below the cliffs in mushrooms of smoke and flames, just missing their target. A second volley of cannon fire issued from the cliffs and some found their mark, exploding upon Eloth's ship and catapulting some of the crew into the sea in a shower of flame and splinters.

"How long are we to provide them with a floating target, my lord?" shouted Penloth, his face blackened with soot from the small fires raging uncontrolled upon the ship. "If one of those cannon balls hits the powder room we'll be blasted into toothpicks!"

Joshua heard the report of cannon fire and saw the flame and smoke rising from the distant cliffs. The ship was in mortal danger! He swiftly unsheathed Ephlal from its scabbard and pointed its tip toward the cannons in the distance.

"*Enough!*" he cried in a loud voice that reverberated outwards like a deafening clap of thunder. A spear of white hot light leapt from the shimmering blade, flying like a javelin directly for the cannon mounted on the cliffs. It impacted in silence, but the result was an ear-shattering roar as the entire battery of cannons erupted in a blast of fire that boiled upwards into the sky. All within Shiloh froze at the violence with which Lucius' cannons had been suddenly and mysteriously obliterated.

Thinking they had achieved a lucky hit, all aboard *The Vengeance* cheered loudly, encouraged with their sudden triumph, unaware that it had been the power of Ephlal that had saved them. *Now was their chance!* Penloth turned about and began barking orders. "Bring her in close, captain and make ready every cannon! We are going to blast Shiloh until not one stone is left upon another!"

Surmising that Shiloh's utter destruction was not long in coming, Joshua sprinted up a flight of nearby steps to the flag tower two at a time, clearing the last step just as another burst of cannon fire sounded. He leapt toward the flag staff and with one mighty yank, he brought Lucius' standard of a winged, scarlet dragon slithering down. Without a moment to lose, he attached a scarlet and gold banner that he had carried with him all this time and in several swift yanks, raised the Lion of Ellioth high. The wind picked it up and sent it streaming outwards in graceful billows. Joshua then turned and raised Ephlal high, sending shafts of blinding white light shooting off its blade in every direction as far as the eye could see.

"*Behold!*" Eloth shouted, seeing the light from his sword and his own standard flying high above the castle. "*Belay that order! Do not fire!*"

"*Cease fire!*" shouted Penloth to all on the ship. "Cease fire! Joshua has won the day!" Just in the nick of time, torches were immediately withdrawn from the cannon fuses.

Confident that his father's ship had seen him, Joshua secured Lucius' downed pennant to the base of the pole. He slid down its length to a balcony below just above the main courtyard.

People were running to and fro in frenzied panic, paying no heed to the shining figure above them until he set his fingers to his mouth and let forth an ear splitting whistle. They froze in place as if struck dumb, staring up at him in surprise.

Far in the distance, came the answering neigh of a mighty steed. The villagers shock turned to unanimous fear when all recognized the prince standing before them alive and well and filled with wrath they could not comprehend. Many paled and fell to their knees, others fled as they heard the approaching thunder of mighty hooves shake the very ground beneath them. Horses in the stables broke free from their head stalls and galloped off in terror at the approach of Paracletis. Down he thundered like a whirlwind upon the village, tossing his head and snorting in fury. Fear of him cleared the road as he passed through the gates and galloped into the courtyard, tossing his mane and neighing loudly in greeting. Joshua raised Ephlal high, flames running up and down the length of its blade.[45] A great cry of alarm went before him as he rode through the village like a storm cutting down all who dared to raise a weapon against him.

"Eloth's sword! The Sword of Judgment is come upon us! Hide from the wrath of him who sits upon the white horse!"

At that moment the first of the longboats from *The Vengeance* reached Shiloh's shores. Angry knights spilled out and swarmed toward the village, their swords drawn and faces grim. Adult and child alike fled back toward the castle seeking refuge within its mighty walls, but Joshua blocked their way, his face terrible to behold. Panic erupted as the inhabitants of Shiloh realized they were trapped between Eloth's knights and Joshua's sword. The multitude milled about in panic, their wails of fear rising on the wind.

Joshua stood in his stirrups, addressing all in a loud voice. "Behold!" he cried, raising Ephlal high. *"I have set thee free from Lucius' tyranny! I put to thee again the same choice Lucius offered thee not mere hours ago. Each one of you, consider carefully and choose this day if thou wilt serve me, thy rightful king!"*[46]

A long, indecisive pause ensued. *What manner of sorcery was this?* They wondered. *Had they not seen him die with their own eyes? Were they really to believe he had come back from the dead? Did he really expect them to bow their knee to him after all their years of slavery? What did they really owe him?*

To the amazement of those around them, a small number of penitent souls stepped forward and stood humbly before Joshua, their heads bowed in contrition, their choice made.[47] Joshua smiled upon each one in turn, waiting patiently for any others who would receive his mercy. When it became obvious there would be no others, he turned a stern eye upon them. Their faces were surly and spiteful; their hearts too filled with pride to beg his pardon.

"Get off with you!" shouted a woman who stood nearest the front. "How are we to know you simply aren't some magician with a clever bag of tricks? I saw the prince fall to his death. Why should we believe you are he?"

Joshua's face grew stern, his compassion exhausted. "Very well," he said grimly, dismounting. They had forfeited their last opportunity to receive mercy and were now without excuse. He had willingly spilt his blood, asking for only what was his due in return and still they defied him to his face! His eyes glittered with terrible anger. *"By thy own choice thou art condemned!"* he pronounced. *"If thou wilt have naught of me, neither shall ye have any part in my kingdom!"*

Upon saying these words, Joshua thrust Ephlal's blade into the flesh of the earth before their feet and rent it asunder as though it were made of fabric. An enormous fissure opened before them like an enormous mouth; the dark throat descending down into the very bowels of earth. Those who had chosen judgment over mercy found themselves plummeting to their doom before the face of their angry king. There was a loud *boom* and just as suddenly as it had opened, the earth resealed itself over them.[48]

Grimly Joshua sheathed his sword and turned to behold the precious few who had chosen him. They fell onto their knees in terror, fearful of what would happen next.

"Fear not," he said gently, looking at each one in turn. "My judgment is passed; you shall endure no more sorrow."

With instant relief they swarmed about him, eager for a consoling word or forgiving smile. Joshua greeted each one, saddened that so very few had chosen to receive his mercy.

"*Let us through, let us pass!*" shouted a familiar voice from the back of the crowd. Sir Penloth appeared moments later, followed by the seraphim and finally the king himself. Immediately a path was cleared for Eloth.

"*Father!*" Joshua exclaimed with joy, going down on one knee. A smile of infinite tenderness suffused Eloth's face as he looked upon his beloved son. He extended a trembling hand and caressed the crown of Joshua's head. Tears filled the king's eyes upon beholding his son for the first time since his departure, for Eloth saw Joshua as others could not—bloody, beaten, and severely disfigured, just as Lucius had left him; an eternal reminder of the price he had paid.[49]

He lifted Joshua up by his hands and embraced him.

"Well done my good and faithful son; let us now enter into the *joy* of thy kingdom!"[50]

Chapter Sixteen

enloth peered down into the inky darkness, wrinkling his nose in distaste. "Are you sure this is not another refuse dump?" he asked the old man who stood directly behind him. "I've no more patience for mucking about in the dark for prisoners that don't exist."

"I'm certain of it, my lord!" said the man, wringing his hands. "I escaped out of this dungeon myself three years ago; they *must* be down there!"

"Yes, but are they still alive?" Penloth countered softly.

Joshua stepped forward, torch in hand. "We shall soon see," he said, stepping onto the dank stair. Behind him followed seraphim, villagers, and even the king, every third man holding a torch to light the treacherous pathway. As they descended the darkened stairwell a horrible reek engulfed them which originated from somewhere far below. The deeper they descended, the more odious became their path. Vile insects crunched under their boots and scuttled across their hands as they grasped the slimy walls to steady themselves, and the granite stair grew increasingly slick from the accumulated moss and slime. The unhappy few who bore torches were finding it difficult to both pinch their nostrils shut and keep their balance at the same time, but Joshua and Eloth bore the darkness and stink in grim silence, hearkening with pounding hearts to the sound of distant wailing below them which grew louder with every step. After what seemed an eternity, they finally reached the bottom and rounded a corner.

"*Bloody hell*." choked Penloth, stumbling backwards. His torch fell onto the wet floor and guttered out. Sir Eric clapped a hand over his mouth, his throat filling with bile.

Dozens of poor souls were trapped in the most hideous torture devices they had ever seen: their arms and legs partially severed, rotting, or twisted at wrong angles as though they had been broken and forced to heal in ways physically unnatural. The stench of human refuse and vomit so permeated the air it caused their eyes to sting and water profusely. While most of the party tried to adjust to the horror of the pit, Joshua marched up to the nearest torture device and withdrew Ephlal from its scabbard. Pure, golden light filled the dim chamber causing prisoners to weakly lift their heads in beleaguered wonder and disbelief. With a cry of anger, Joshua sheared the metal rings asunder with one swipe, freeing the old man who had half-stood/half-hung in excruciating pain for as long as he could remember. Joshua caught him in his arms as he collapsed to the ground, gently laying his head upon his shoulder.

"Disperse!" he commanded in a hoarse voice, putting a waterskin to the old man's lips. "Rest not until every last one has been freed!"[51]

They went forth in pairs and thoroughly scoured every loathsome nook and cranny of Lucius' vast dungeon until all he had imprisoned were liberated. There were literally dozens crammed into cells meant for only a few, living with the remains of the long dead, their corpses left as another means of unending torture. All had to be physically carried out, weak from long suffering and lack of food, air, and light.

Joshua bore the old man out whom he had freed, speaking gently to him that all would be well. Eloth followed close behind, bearing a young woman in his arms. Next came Penloth, carrying two bawling children, one within the crook of each arm who had been born in captivity, hugging them close and murmuring soothingly to them. When the rescue party finally ascended out of the fetid stairwell, villagers rushed forward to relieve them of their precious burdens. Even with a multitude of knights and villagers it took five additional trips before the dungeons were completely empty of both the living and the dead. The wounded and maimed were tended by those who had skill in leechcraft and those who had not survived to see their redemption were buried with honor. When he had carried the last prisoner out, Joshua gave orders to clear the entire perimeter round the castle and for kindling to be gathered.

"Only fire can cleanse the misery and filth Lucius left as his legacy," he said as stacks of wood were piled about the walls and drenched with oil. When all was done, the assembled crowd watched as Joshua threw a flaming brand upon the wood, stepping back as the flames roared to life. Great tongues of flame rose heavenward, greedily devouring Lucius' fortress as if it too loathed it and hungered to destroy all his evil works. The mighty stones blackened quickly in the awesome heat, the mortar crumbling. When the blaze became too great to bear, they went down to the shore to watch the fiery spectacle from a safe distance. The inferno blazed on for many hours, with many a muffled roar and explosion emanating from deep within its bowels as new sources of fuel ignited. As the day waxed old, Eloth's knights distributed blankets, victuals, and tarpaulins which they had brought with them, erecting them in the barren fields far from the heat of Lucius' pyre.

Twilight was just beginning when Llyonesse straightened from her labors and felt Joshua's arm slip about her waist. She looked up to where he pointed. "Behold!" he said softly. A mighty rumble was issuing from the foundations of the castle; the walls first trembling then swaying drunkenly. The rumble grew in intensity, building to a loud roar. All upon the shore paused to watch the final death throes of Lucius' castle in grim silence; the towers and battlements falling inwards upon themselves. Llyonesse put her hands over her ears and backed away, staring in awe and fear as the hated fortress finally collapsed in upon itself with a mighty groan. The flames were instantly suffocated by a mighty column of dust and smoke which billowed high into the deepening twilight. The rumbling ceased then all became deathly quiet.

Llyonesse exhaled, feeling as though a great weight had been lifted from her shoulders. It was over. It was finally, blessedly over. There would be no more terror, no more pain, no more tears … no more sorrow. Lucius' reign of terror had come to an end at last. A new era had begun and it would be ushered in with their wedding back in Ellioth.[52]

In the weeks following their return to Ellioth, preparations had begun in earnest for Joshua and Llyonesse's wedding. Clotilde and many other seamstresses worked night and day to finish her bridal gown in time. They stitched and embroidered by candlelight until every last knot had been tied off. The embroidered train would drape a full five feet behind her and was crusted with pearls and beads of jasper. It had taken many hours of intense labor, but when it was done, it was a thing of beauty.

Llyonesse sat upon a stool within her tarpaulin, gazing into a large mirror as Clotilde combed out her long tresses. "Do you think he will be pleased, Nana?" she asked softly.

Clotilde plaited the last pearl into her lustrous hair. "How could he not be?" she replied, beholding how lovely Llyonesse looked with her face aglow and eyes sparkling. Llyonesse smiled in response, then hugged Clotilde close before lifting her feet to step into the bodice of her wedding gown.

Once it was on, she paused again to regard her image, frowning. She was fully gowned and her hair coiffed but she was still bothered with the feeling that something important was missing; something she couldn't put her finger on.

"There is still something amiss, Nana, don't you think?" she asked.

"Maybe this is it?" replied Clotilde, arranging a delicate veil of hand-woven tulle upon her curls. It floated down like a gossamer cloud, falling in graceful folds about Llyonesse's face and shoulders.

Llyonesse smiled momentarily then shook her head. "No, that is not it either! There is still something wanting." she replied, sorely vexed.

At that moment a young page appeared before the tent and cleared his throat for attention. Clotilde poked her head out then looked down, finding a young lad in velvet togs bearing a silver-domed tray as though he bore something very precious.

"A gift from the bridegroom," he explained, handing the tray up to Clotilde.

Clotilde smiled down at the young lad. "Milady thanks you," she said. "I shall convey it to her with all speed!" The page bowed then left as Clotilde pulled down the flap, carrying the tray back to Llyonesse.

"What is it?" asked Llyonesse curiously, turning about.

"Lift the dome and see!" smiled Clotilde, already guessing what lay inside.

Llyonesse lifted the silver dome. Her face became wreathed in smiles upon beholding Joshua's gift. Clotilde unfolded the note that came with it and read it aloud.

"*For the Bride,*" she murmured. She nodded in agreement. "You were right all along," she said, watching Llyonesse arrange the beautiful wreath of flowers upon her veil. "There *was* something missing."

for the Bride

Llyonesse lifted her skirts and stepped forward.

"*Now* I am ready," she smiled.

As the sun rose high in the clear blue sky, all of Ellioth and those who had returned from Shiloh gathered in the meadow where a pavilion had been constructed. It has been months since Lucius' fall and was almost Mid-Summer. Flowers were in full bloom, filling the air with the aroma of spring. Butterflies flitted about like leaves upon the wind, alighting upon the flower bedecked archway and altar where Joshua and Llyonesse were to be wed. The air was filled with the sights, sounds and aromas of rejoicing and laughter. Common folk took seats amongst the aristocracy, all attired in their finest gowns, tunics, jewels and doublets in honor of Joshua's coronation and wedding fete. The heralds set their trumpets to their lips and blew a magnificent fanfare, signaling the commencement of the dual ceremonies.

Eloth lifted his arms. *"Behold thy Victor and rightful King!"* he cried.

In one accord the crowd turned and paid homage as Joshua strode toward the dais, leading the ranks of seraphim in their silver mailcoats. One by one, his subjects bowed as he passed by them, exchanging smiles with those whose eyes met his, finally stopping before his father. Father and son looked upon one another for a quiet moment then exchanged a simple embrace. To many that beheld them, it seemed that they shone with a brilliance which surpassed even that of the sun. Then Joshua bowed his head, knelt upon a scarlet pillow and lifted his hands to receive his father's sword. Eloth lifted Ephlal from the altar, unsheathed it, and laid the naked blade upon the flat of his palms.

"There is none more worthy to bear Ephlal than thee, my son," he said. "Henceforth, bear it upon thy thigh to execute justice forevermore."

Joshua received the sword with a kiss, stood to his feet, and faced the assembly. Eloth next removed the silver chaplet from Joshua's head, replacing it with a golden crown of emeralds and diamonds. "Hereby do I bestow upon thee the Kingship of Shiloh to which thou wast born," he said, "Rule her in equity and justice, my son!"

"I will," replied Joshua solemnly.

Another great round of cheers went up. "Long live Joshua, King of Shiloh!" they cried. "Long may he reign!" The coronation ceremony thus concluded, Penloth stepped up to Joshua's side, nudged him in the side and pointed into the distance.

"A white horse approaches, my lord," he said with a grin. *"Thy bride cometh."*[53]

"At long last," Joshua smiled, watching with great anticipation. With a nod to his men, Penloth's knights split into two columns, forming a long corridor between them through which Llyonesse rode under their crossed swords. Eloth's bard, Gillian stood just before the dais and laid his fingers upon his wondrous harp, filling the air with enchanted music to herald the arrival of the bride. With a voice as pure and dulcet as an angel, he began his sonnet.

> *"All Thy garments are fragrant with myrrh and aloes and cassia; and out of ivory palaces stringed instruments have made Thee glad. King's daughters are among thy noble ladies. Listen, O daughter, give attention and incline thy ear; forget thy people and thy father's house; then the King will desire thy beauty; Because He is thy Lord, bow down to Him. The rich among the people will entreat thy favor.*

> *"The King's daughter is all glorious within; and her clothing is interwoven with gold. In the dawn of a new day she shall be led to the King in embroidered work; the virgins, her companions who follow her, will be brought to Thee. They will be led forth with songs of gladness and rejoicing; they will enter into the King's palace ... "* [54]

With these words floating up to her upon the wind, Llyonesse was delivered unto her bridegroom under a shower of falling rose petals, sitting side-saddle upon his white stallion whose silver headstall, mane, saddle and tail were bedecked with ribbons and flowers. Upon her veil sat the crown of pink rose-buds, ivy and lily-of-the-valley as a living crown. Llyonesse alighted from the saddle into Joshua's waiting arms, her gown of purest white linen and golden embroidery twinkling in the light of the noon-day sun. Joshua smiled upon her, his heart bursting with happiness. Llyonesse was exquisite in her wedding raiment and he was very pleased to see that she wore his gift. Llyonesse walked forward, her hand upon his, mounting the dais together as Gillian continued, now addressing his ballad to the Prince:

> *"Thou art fairer than the sons of men, and grace is poured upon Thy lips. Gird Thy sword on Thy thigh, O Mighty One, in Thy splendor and in thy majesty, ride on victoriously. For the cause of truth and meekness and righteousness; Let Thy right hand teach Thee awesome things! Thine arrows are sharp, the peoples fall under Thee; Thine arrows are sharp in the heart of the King's enemies.*

> *"Thy throne, O King, is forever and ever; A scepter of uprightness is the scepter of Thy kingdom for Thou hast loved righteousness and despised wickedness; Therefore God, Thy God, has anointed Thee with the oil of joy above Thy fellows ... "*

Behind the sheer, white gauze of her veil, Llyonesse smiled happily upon her bridegroom, admiring how very tall and proud he stood, crowned with gold and mantled in sunlight. With soft words of love, Joshua clasped her hands tightly within his, bestowing upon her the most brilliant of smiles as Gillian ended his song.

> *"I will cause Thy name to be remembered throughout all generations; therefore, thy people who art called by thy name shall give Thee thanks, forever and ever and ever!"*

The harp strings stilled and before the eyes of his people, Joshua took Llyonesse as his queen and bride, placing a golden ring upon her finger. With joyous hearts they sealed their vows with the wedding cup of sweet mead.

It was now time for the moment all had been waiting for. Eloth smiled and nodded to his son. Llyonesse's heart pounded as Joshua gently lifted away the veil from her face. She gasped in astonishment, her eyes wide with disbelief.

Joshua's face and eyes were ablaze with a light so brilliant it appeared as though the very sun itself stood before her in human form.[55] In the depths of his eyes she beheld a love deeper and stronger than life itself. No longer was he the boy-hero of days gone by but a mighty Lord; a King above Kings. Joshua drew Llyonesse close to him in a gentle embrace, placing a lingering kiss of infinite tenderness upon her lips to seal their troth. At last they were wed!

With a loud, exultant cheer, the wedding guests rose to their feet, showering the bride and groom with flower petals, rice, and shouts of joy.

The dovecotes opened and out issued a multitude of turtle-doves with a flutter of ivory feathers. They soared and dipped over the heads of the crowd, white ribbons fluttering and curling in their wake.

Joshua led his bride by the hand down the aisle and deftly lifted her onto Paracletis' waiting saddle then mounted behind her, drawing her close against him.[56]

"*I am my beloved's,*" Llyonesse sighed, laying her head upon Joshua's shoulder.

"*...and she is mine...*" he whispered softly into her ear.[57]

"*... Two princes wage the battle for eternity, but the Victor has been known from the start...*" Amy Grant, "*Fairytale*" *Father's Eyes Album* Myrrh Records (1979).

Endnotes

All verses are from the New American
Standard Version of the Bible

1	Ephlal is "judgment" in Hebrew
2	Hebrews 4:12
3	Isaiah 14:12–15
4	Isaiah 14:12
5	Malachi 3:1
6	Proverbs 16:12
7	Ephesians 1:4
8	Matthew 19:6
9	Genesis 1:28
10	Psalm 119:105
11	Matthew 20:26
12	Job 1:7
13	Genesis 3:17
14	Psalm 58:11
15	Matthew 1:1–35
16	Genesis 3:5
17	Genesis 3:24
18	2 Peter 3:4
19	Matthew 24:12
20	Psalm 45:3
21	2 Samuel 18:33